HOW TO WIPE YOUR ARSE IN THAILAND

BY

PETE WOOD

Copyright © Pete Wood 2016
This book is sold subject to the condition that it shall not, by way of trade or otherwise, be lent, resold, hired out, or otherwise circulated without the publisher's prior consent in any form of binding or cover other than that in which it is published and without a similar condition including this condition being imposed on the subsequent publisher.
The moral right of Pete Wood has been asserted.
ISBN-13: 978-1533495235
ISBN-10: 1533495238

For all travellers, especially those yet to travel.

CONTENTS

CHAPTER 1. *The Old Ford Shed* 1
CHAPTER 2. *Meat and the Lady-boy* 10
CHAPTER 3. *Sawat, Noppi, and the Great TAT Swindle* 19
CHAPTER 4. *Night Train Waiting Game* 49
CHAPTER 5. *In Chaweng on the Cabana Trail* 68
CHAPTER 6. *Further Round the Cabana Trail* 92
CHAPTER 7. *Off the Trail with Mr Lee* 111
CHAPTER 8. *Samran I* 132
CHAPTER 9. *Bags, Big Gun, Boats, and Buses* 138
CHAPTER 10. *The Man in the Pink Shirt* 148
CHAPTER 11. *Lucky Lime Green* 153
CHAPTER 12. *Mr Tong's Brother* 167
CHAPTER 13. *Colonic Irrigations* 175
CHAPTER 14. *The Pink Suitcase* 205
CHAPTER 15. *Washed Away Dry Remains* 214
CHAPTER 16. *Pink Shorts and the Girl Who Got Stung* 225
CHAPTER 17. *Red Bandana Man and the Fat, Naked Intruder* 238
CHAPTER 18. *Trang* 257
CHAPTER 19. *Empty Graves* 269
CHAPTER 20. *Samran II* 281
CHAPTER 21. *The Mouleng Boutique* 286
CHAPTER 22. *Samran III* 293
CHAPTER 23. *Back to Chao Ley* 298
CHAPTER 24. *So Long Sawat* 309
CHAPTER 25. *Trip's End* 313

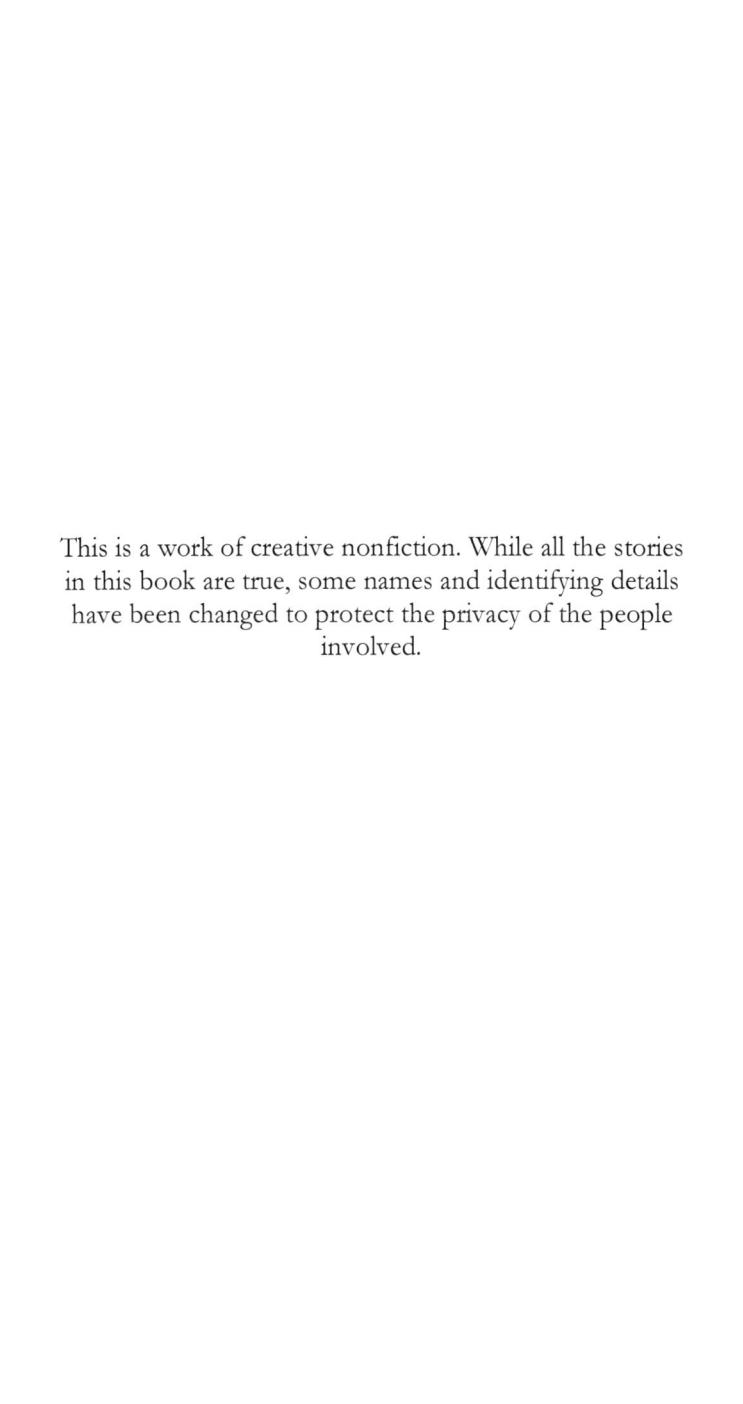

This is a work of creative nonfiction. While all the stories in this book are true, some names and identifying details have been changed to protect the privacy of the people involved.

CHAPTER 1
The Old Ford Shed

The idea of vanishing down the hippy trail into Southeast Asia and Australia started back in 1990, inspired possibly by the trippy Thai weed then being sold in our home town for £10 a bag. A bloke called Dave who I'd met one day walking down the street on LSD talked me into agreeing to go, an old mate now lost in times gone by, keen to do what was then called 'a continental'. But after our preparation for partying outspent our savings, plans were abandoned, and Dave disappeared like a microdot into the distance, fluttering away like a small piece of blotting paper blown by the wind. Fifteen years later I somehow managed to get it together enough to go.

Before Boxing Day 2004, most people knew what a tidal wave was, maybe like me from books at school, but hardly anyone had heard of a tsunami. That day changed history, and after the devastation, Thailand – as well as many other affected countries – suffered both with its own loss of lives and communities, and economically as a result of many tourists wishing to avoid the aftermath. It was said that recovery projects had enabled even the worst-hit areas to welcome back the tourists that brought in the wealth on which their livelihoods depended. However, that very much depended upon the tourists wanting to return. Not only was there now a fear of sudden huge waves, but much of the atmosphere of the once laid-back paradise had been swept away. Who then would wish to spend time in a place that used to be good when there are so many places in the world less scarred, still in full happy swing? On the other hand, atmosphere can largely be what people make it, and life goes on with time, regardless of the past.

So I saved up, quit my job, and bought a copy of the *Rough Guide*. The plan was to have the summer off, sort out the flat (which was rented anyway), get rid of my car (which was an old shed), and go. A good friend, Amanda, was to be my travelling companion. I'd known her for years, oddly enough someone I'd met around the time Dave and I were still figuring out how to manage the effects of perhaps a few too many liberty caps. One of her main reasons for going was for a health spa course – a week spent fasting and cleansing – to help sort out some health issues: this, she assured me, was best undertaken in Thailand. I just wanted to go somewhere hot for a while, a long way away, to relax, get some perspective.

I'd thought of South America, but Thailand fitted

in with Australia and Indonesia too, so that was the plan. Adding in South America pretty much doubled the price of the ticket, so that idea was left for another time. It was to be four months in Thailand, two months in Australia, a week in Bali, a couple of nights in Singapore, and then home. The guy in the travel agent thought four months in Thailand was a bit weird, and wondered what we'd do for that long: I didn't feel like explaining that for most of it I was hoping to be laying in a hammock under a deep blue sky in the sun listening to the sound of waves sweeping across exotic seashells on the shore, under the influence of just as exotic herbs; nor that it was due to a bit of a lack of funding, Thailand being so much cheaper than Australia to spend time.

I've noticed that when such people realise that you haven't actually got very much money then they kind of seem less willing to give free assistance. In this commission-driven world, that's just the way it is. And we were needing lots of assistance, not having really planned it at all. By the time we'd finished with Vic, the STA travel agent so helpful and happy to see us arrive, he looked glad we were leaving.

It was last-minute decisions all the way, and less than a week before we were due to leave, Amanda finally faced up to the fact that she wasn't ready to go. She hadn't even given notice on her flat and needed to get more money together. We'd changed the dates once with Vic already when we went to pay the balance after the deposit, which had meant lots of amendments. Again he'd looked very relieved when we'd completed things. Now we were back with more changes, and the shop was busy, dark outside, claustrophobic in the central heating amongst the buzzing static of the computer screens and the whirring fans.

Getting closer towards Christmas and the cold winter, many people were heading off abroad; flights were becoming expensive and dates limited. Further rearranging wasn't easy, being a cheap multi-stop deal that was now discontinued, and even then Amanda was unsure of a date; out of necessity Vic made her pick one, becoming more flustered and agitated as time passed in draining indecision. She picked a date in early January, just after New Year; the plan was for me to spend five weeks out there alone before we met up at Bangkok Airport.

The day before leaving we met up in town. It was cold and grey, a late November afternoon. She had a cold so was feeling ill, made worse as the reality of being left behind was almost upon us and beginning to sink in. I'd not only given notice on the flat but had already eaten into some of the savings by delaying the trip. My gran had been ill in hospital since early September and I'd visited her almost every day. Suffering a second bout of double pneumonia in three years, instead of either recovering or dying she clung on for months, stuck on the ward, too weak to look after herself yet desperate to stay alive. In the end it was a case of go now or cancel the trip until the following winter.

I had a list of things to do, things that could only be done on the very last day. Most stuff I owned was old and cheap so I either gave it away or chucked it, but I had a few boxes to store for when I returned. The schedule was tight, but so long as all went smoothly it would be ok. I needed the mattress to sleep on; I then needed to hire a carpet cleaner to clean the carpet and avoid the cleaning fee being deducted from the deposit, which I would need when I got back, but I could only clean the carpet once the mattress had gone and I wouldn't be sleeping on the damp floor. I needed the car to get rid of the mattress and collect and return the carpet cleaner on the same day I was leaving. A scrap dealer was to collect the car the next day, and post the twenty quid to Amanda, the car slowly dying anyway and worth only the price of the metal.

It was a bright and sunny morning, though very cold and frosty. All seemed ok, I was up early and had until four o'clock to get things done. First trip was to the dump, a few miles up the road, before taking the mattress over to a friend's, the boxes to my dad's, saying cheerio to him, and collecting the carpet cleaner en route.

I knew the battery was going, struggling more to start as the week had gone on, so I'd delayed trying to start the car until the very last moment, even then building the faith just prior to turning the key. Fully loaded, the groan of the engine revealed it was flat. I let it be for a while, not wanting to drain it completely, for it had a habit of suddenly firing even when it sounded dead. I decided to let it warm up a bit and pushed it out into the sun, returning indoors looking for something to do; all was ordered out of necessity, and I needed the car to start before I could do much else. Twangs of panic began to gnaw at the nerves holding them in check as I saw the day's plans collapse into a series of phone calls and left mess.

Then I found that they'd cut the phone off one day early anyway, so couldn't even use that. So in a typically English way, I sat down and had a cup of tea and a smoke.

I was not the only person who had car trouble in the street that morning. As I finished the tea I saw a breakdown van arrive to help someone. I wondered how generous van man would be if I asked him for a jump start. With nothing to lose I went outside and got in my car. He was getting ready to leave so I thought, if nothing else, he'll hear my failed attempt which might help pave the way for an approach. The engine slowly turned, coughed and started. Wow, I was truly amazed, for it had been a real cold night. When everything was sorted, and the farewells had been said, I left the keys on the table and shut the door of the flat I'd lived in for the past six years.

Heathrow was dark and freezing cold. My thin travel trousers clung to my legs as I strode across the car park, the pockets laden with tickets, passport, money, cheques, tobacco, and other needed items. The rucksack felt heavy, packed with essentials, many of which would have been cheaper purchased in Thailand, some not even needed. These are things that you only really learn on a trip; this was my first, and one of the motivations for travelling is to learn through experience. With the benefit of hindsight it is clear that this is why experience is so valuable, for it teaches better than anything.

At the check-in desk, I asked the girl if it was a window seat. She said she'd check, as if she wasn't sure. With truly positive optimism she told me that I was one seat away from the window, as if that was a good thing. Further, she'd put me down for a possible upgrade. I wasn't sure what that was, or whether I'd have to pay more for it, so just went on to find the boarding area, wandering around feeling like an intrepid explorer one minute, then nervous the next, as the reality of being alone not only flitted back into my mind, but became exposed. You can walk down a road on your own and people watching may think you're going to meet somebody; but when you walk back up, still alone, people know that you are on your own. It's the same when you stay in the same place for a while: people know that you are not waiting for someone, no friend nor chance of support is about to show. I moved around a bit, browsing and smoking alternately.

After the last roll-up before the long journey had been smoked, I joined the queue and boarded the plane. The boarding girl never mentioned the possible upgrade, so neither did I. My one seat away from the window spoken of so positively turned out to be the middle seat of three. I guess it wasn't in the middle of the middle section, but then it was neither a window seat nor an aisle seat. I've learnt subsequently that the aisle seat is preferable, for not only have you got space to stretch your legs, but you can get up when you like, and have at least one guaranteed armrest. Never mind, I was hoping to sleep anyway.

The lady in the window seat was from Scotland, visiting Australia for a family funeral. The same plane was heading all the way to Sydney, merely stopping at Bangkok for a refuel. She'd arrived at Heathrow in the morning due to Edinburgh connections, and had been ready to check in at gate opening time. Being both friendly and having suffered bereavement, I thought perhaps she deserved to have the window seat after all. The guy who had the aisle seat looked from the Middle-East, but he said nothing for the entire duration of the trip, so I don't know how he got his. Maybe the plane had enough people like me on board who'd bought the 'next to the window seat is good' story, and not bothered trying to change it at check-in.

We took off, a strange feeling after not having been on a plane for sixteen years, though I noticed nobody else seemed to be laughing, most didn't even seem to find it that weird; some even carried on reading, fiddling around with things. I stretched my neck to look past Scottish Lady, to see the lights of London fade below. We levelled out, and she reclined back and rested her head on the window, not looking out of it but blocking the view, closing her eyes. I was slightly irked, and hoped that she'd at least put it to proper use at sunrise. We were fortunately on the side of the plane that would see it, and I tried to calculate where we'd be, how long it would be before we got there. It was just about then that an announcement came out to shut all window flaps, since this was a night flight and people would be sleeping. Even though most of it would actually be in daylight, because we took off late at night this was the rule. I felt a bit disappointed; Asian man to my right was evidently unaffected by the announcement – he'd not only reclined but was under his blanket, fast asleep.

No such chance for me; try as I did, I could not sleep. I watched the map and listened to the radio which I realised after a while was actually a recording on a loop. Eventually my ears started heating up so I took the phones off, and drifted mentally into a detached world of possibilities and circumstances, contemplating events to date, what it would be like, would Amanda ever actually make it? All sorts of things had chance to enter the imagination. Eventually the guy's snoring got the better of me and I woke him up and went for a wander round. Scottish Lady took the opportunity too, just another drawback of the window seat that you're not allowed to look out of, it seems. At night, mid-flight, if you need a pee and you have to wake up two people to get out, you can find yourself spending half the time in discomfort, just waiting for one of them to wake up or for the right moment to wake both of them. No such dilemma in the aisle seat, where you can just get up and go for a walk round when you feel like it. Not that guy was making full use of his, laid there fast asleep, snoring.

The night slowly passed, and the cabin reminded me of a hospital ward, full of people who are really just strangers, all arranged together in close proximity, vulnerable: laid back amidst dim light with heads fallen to one side, mouths open, some with headphones still on, some with eye masks, snoring, breathing heavily, loudly, the hissing sound of the air-conditioning pumping away like some kind of respiratory apparatus for the infirm. I went back to my seat, surprised at how cold it was, and spent the night trying to get warm.

CHAPTER 2

Meat and the Lady-boy

In the 'morning', so to speak, the flaps were all opened and bright sunshine filled the cabin, warming things up, though with that sort of clammy feeling that happens after sleeping in your clothes. Breakfast was served and as the caffeine activated the digestive systems that had been so unnaturally dormant for the last eleven hours, the inevitable queues for the toilets began and lasted like some strange extended rush hour, as several hundred people waited to take a dump, shuffling from side to side, no doubt squeezing out silent wind whilst clutching their toothbrush and travel-sized tube of toothpaste. The aisle seats near the toilets were not quite so advantageous now, being at nose level with a slow parade of arseholes jammed, contents well baked.

We began to descend and all strapped ourselves

back in, seats upright. Slightly nervous as the dropping in altitude sent odd sensations through my stomach, the apprehension increased when the guy next to me got out his Quran and started praying. I realise it is a very stereotypical reaction, and I blame it largely on the media, but I hoped he wasn't a suicide bomber, giving out one final prayer before taking us all down. It wasn't so, of course, but with no sleep and all that, it just felt weird for a minute.

Then came some instructions for those of us leaving the aircraft at Bangkok. We were given a small immigration card which required completion before landing. It looked merely like an unimportant administration formality but I thought I ought to fill it out. I borrowed a pen, mine being stored safely away in the overhead locker with the food I'd brought but had been unable to reach. It turns out that this small form is actually very important, and is in two parts: one part for entering the country, and one part for departing. I was still filling it out when the air hostess started to tell us about what could and what could not be brought into Thailand. Apparently there were very strict rules. I thought she was just talking about drugs, guns, and other such obvious things, and if you could buy it in a British shop then it would probably be no problem. Not the case at all: it seemed that one of the things that was forbidden entry was any type of meat product. In my bag, buried safely away, beyond the guy saying his prayers, was a six snack-pack bag of pork scratchings. Were they a meat product, I wondered? They were pork, which was meat. There was also a small picture of a pig on the packet, which kind of gave the game away, even if the person looking spoke no English. But was that the sort of meat product they meant? I mean perhaps it was fresh meat only, as if anyone would consider doing that. But then, was it the sort of risk I really wanted to be taking as soon as I arrived into the country? What if I was arrested, taken away and charged? Anything could happen out here, I'd heard. The air hostess had said about a fine and possible imprisonment for anyone caught breaching this law. I imagined going to a Thai jail for bringing in pork scratchings, and how crazy it would be. I thought perhaps I would ask her next time she came by, just to confirm.

When she passed, I returned the borrowed pen and was just about to speak when she turned round to talk with someone else. She went on and before long we were rapidly descending into the smog that shrouds Bangkok. Too late, I decided just to dump them after we landed.

The heat hit me as I walked through the tunnel before reaching the air-conditioned area of the airport. It was bright too, making me squint to see; too hot and too bright for the proper time of day, though right for the real time and place. Strange to be walking on solid ground again, tired yet wired, stiff. I headed for the toilet, needing to pee anyway. Alone for a minute, I noticed there was a small bin lined with a polythene bag, virtually empty. I looked around, trying not to appear shifty, but thought maybe it would be even more suspicious dumping it in there, one item left by the one person in the vicinity. I imagined cameras in the toilets spotting me, then following me round the airport until being arrested by the Thai bomb and terrorist police. No, best be up front, I'd simply ask at customs, realising that the inevitable was now delayed until the very last possible opportunity for giving up the stash; I hoped they wouldn't classify it as being brought into the country already, the crime of smuggling by then – perhaps even now – firmly committed, the man guilty.

As I walked along I heard a little *toot-toot*, and stepped aside as an airport porter's truck drove by. The driver was a small Thai, and looked like a young feminine man; I guessed it was a 'lady-boy' but had to look several times to see if it was a lady dressed like a man or if it was a young man that looked a bit like a girl. I figured it was most likely the latter, one perhaps who dreamed of the bright lights of the stage whilst driving his airport truck. He caught me looking and said something in Thai English. It took me some time to develop the ear for their way of speaking English, and I can only imagine that my attempts during my time there to speak their language were probably at least as difficult for them to understand. He seemed to be asking me where I was going but since I wasn't sure, I couldn't really say. His voice was very high pitched but I was still thinking it was a he and not a she, just practising the voice maybe. He kept saying something about a visa and asked to see my passport; I hoped that he wouldn't raise some alarm and have me arrested, as if he knew perhaps that I was trying to smuggle meat in. I probably looked a bit confused.

Amanda and I had already obtained sixty-day visas from the Thai embassy in London, mine now firmly stuck inside my passport. He pointed to the visa and then pointed right up the walkway where I'd been heading. I took the opportunity and showed him the pork scratchings. He sort of took a small gasp in a slightly effeminate way, like when naughty children show each other what they've stolen from the sweet shop, so I offered them to him. He virtually snatched them from my hand and put them in a compartment in the front of his truck. He wanted to see more of what was in the bag; still hoping no alarm would be raised, I willingly complied. He saw the bar of nougat and his eyes lit up. I gave it to him. Same with the liquorice allsorts, though he looked as if he wasn't quite sure what would be inside the packet. I showed him the cashew nuts and he pushed them back towards me, turning up his nose, shaking his head. These were the untouched snacks I'd brought for the flight that had been out of reach all night. Still, he looked more than pleased with himself and beckoned me to jump on his luggage truck with him.

On I got and he tooted his way all along towards the far end of the walkway, calling out impatiently as if we were on some kind of important mission, past the crowded queues passing through immigration. Stopping further on, he pointed to a small queue of about six people. This turned out to be the queue for people who already had visas; the previous very much larger queues were for people who were applying for the free visitor's visa obtainable on entry to the country. Safely offloaded, I was glad I'd seen lady-boy, for otherwise I would have joined the first queue, and things may well have become difficult.

As it was, I was through in a few minutes; I retrieved my bag, slightly surprised again at how heavy it was, and headed for the exit. Before I knew it I'd reached the crowds of people waiting behind the barriers to greet arrivals as arranged, holding signs, calling out to people. For no reason I looked to see if there was a sign for me; of course there wasn't, nobody was arranged to meet me, though nobody there would have known that. So here I was, the public side of customs, in Bangkok for real, the loud bustle of foreign sounds filling everywhere in a complete contrast to the night before. It was quite overwhelming, and I headed towards the outside doors, not really knowing quite where I was going, somewhat swept along with the flow of the crowd.

'Sir, sir, you want taxi, sir?' I heard the voice and caught the look from a pretty Thai girl. Well, I did need a taxi and didn't feel too much like quibbling over a few baht so went along with her to her ticket booth. I told her the name of the hotel where I wanted to go. She hadn't heard of it, and looked it up in a directory to find it on the map.

'It will cost seven hundred bahts,' she said, which kind of surprised me, having read in the guide book that for three to four hundred baht you could go all the way into Bangkok. Though I wasn't exactly sure where my hotel was, I wondered if I was being ripped off. She noticed my reaction and pointed to the map with concern; it was right on the far edge, quite a way out, she said. I got out my map of Bangkok in the book and asked her to show me where it was on that. She looked at it, slightly frowning, and said it was off the edge. A bit concerned at where Vic might have booked me in, I was too tired to argue any further, especially being totally lost in the unknown. I paid her the money and she took me outside to an airport taxi.

Though the airport had been warm, I hadn't realised quite how air-conditioned it was until we stepped outside and I felt the hair-dryer warm air. Years ago Dave and I had sat in my old Mini on a really hot day with the windows wound up for as long as we could, just to see what it was like, as a bit of practice and preparation for the trip that didn't happen. It got stuffy and very hot, though I guess the difference was that in the Mini we could wind the window down or always get out. Here, ironically, with air-con in most Thai vehicles, it was cold getting into the taxi. The driver looked at his instructions and after a brief conversation with the girl, we drove off. It was only later that I realised what had happened here.

As we headed along the highway towards the city, the sun was setting and it was beginning to get dark. It felt strange; dark so soon after getting up and having breakfast. The sky was clear, turning shades of pastel around a golden sun as we drove along the road busy with traffic perhaps from the airport, or maybe just part of the working day rush hour, people returning from their everyday business or work, to homes and families, looking tired, heading somewhere as people do all over the world; except here people looked very different to people back home. The road signs reinforced the unfamiliar, not only unknown names but an indecipherable language. Skyscrapers with neon-lit giant advertising boards flashed global household names, however, announcing that Bangkok was part of the modern technological world long before we reached the city.

The driver spoke about as much English as I did Thai, so conversation was kept to a minimum, though he was playing a Thai radio station that played English songs. As Kate Bush and Peter Gabriel warbled away in the background, I wondered if he had it tuned in for his benefit or for his passengers', perhaps to make them feel a bit more at ease, a small piece of home in a foreign land. We approached some kind of motorway toll and he turned around and said something. I didn't get it but he persisted. Eventually I realised that he was asking me for twenty baht. I thought he was just hassling for a tip before we'd even got there, so I said I'd give him forty baht when he got me to the hotel, if he was quick enough. I'd clearly misunderstood: it seemed that the seven hundred baht did not cover the toll charge. I gave him the money, wondering what else might not be covered. I'd read horror tales of people getting kidnapped in unmarked taxis, sold as sex slaves or robbed of their internal organs. *Surely*, I thought, *not me, not here now.*

The music on the radio was interrupted by a few brief news headlines followed by the weather. I'd not really been paying attention until I heard the dreaded words 'humid with a likely chance of rain showers towards the weekend'. Rain showers? In hot and sunny Thailand? I knew the rainy seasons varied across parts of this tropical country, and was planning to try and avoid the tail end of any monsoon weather that may be lingering. I hadn't anticipated rain in Bangkok though, so soon after leaving cold, wet England. I consoled myself thinking at least it would be warm here.

The driver turned off the main highway and the roads became smaller. He took a few sharp turns into some side streets and we seemed to be in the midst of some backstreet shanty town. People sat outside on small wooden chairs, watching any passing traffic with the scrutiny allowed by such close proximity. Some just stood around, chatting, smoking; motorcycles lined each side, small mopeds, mostly quite old and dirty, dust everywhere, some dilapidated and appearing abandoned. Shaky-looking shacks of corrugated iron and rough timber frames crammed together filling every possible space, giving shelter to the inhabitants who had made it their home.

Occasionally a shack front had been converted into a garage workshop, appearing to offer motorcycle repair services; often food was being served and eaten. As we passed through similar scenes along the way, I noticed that everybody looked Thai. I realise I was in Thailand, and should have expected it to be that way, except I'd half expected to see at least a few Western travellers, tie-dyed or dreadlocked, walking around. I hoped that the driver really wasn't part of some elaborate airport scam, collecting lone travellers in a taxi who were either never to be seen again or found lost and bewildered several weeks later, never quite the same afterwards. The dusky streets looked very much like the sort that my hotel wouldn't be on, and very much like the sort of back alley that might do illegal organ transplants behind a few old motorbikes.

We swung back out onto a busy main road and the driver said something in Thai. Puzzled, I looked at him. 'Siam Beverly Hotel', he said, pointing. Phew, relief, safe arrival. The building appeared to be quite plush, with its bright lights and tall stone pillars, and I thought what a good move it had been to get this hotel. I tipped him, got my bags, and walked up the well-lit concrete steps to the reception.

CHAPTER 3

Sawat, Noppi, and the Great TAT Swindle

Checking in, I headed for the lift to my room on the ninth floor, figuring out that the slide key had to be slid in and out in one quick movement for it to work; this I discovered just before I'd headed back to reception declaring that there was a problem with it, fortunately avoiding the embarrassment. Entering, I saw the double bed, relieved that it wasn't two singles. A quick look round showed all was clean and neat, just right for three nights to settle in and adjust, perhaps see some of the city. I pulled the curtain across the double window, shutting out the dark and hiding my lit silhouette safely from any sniper that might be lurking in the bushes below. Nine floors up, this was even less likely than the unlikely fact that anyone might want to snipe me, but you never know; walking around a lit room when it's dark outside always makes me feel exposed.

I unpacked a few things and noticed that my glasses case wouldn't open. Having lost the screw I'd superglued the lens back into the rim of my sunglasses to hold it all in place, and had put the tube with both pairs of glasses into the case for safekeeping during the flight. I had intended leaving the glue sealed until after the flight but it had been so sunny on the day I left that I'd needed them. I had, however, taken the precaution of carrying them in my hand luggage for extra protection. This turned out to be an error, a complete miscalculation, for the pressurised cabin had caused the glue to leak. Never mind; though I'm short sighted, I can just about get away with not wearing glasses. I figured I'd get the case open when I had some spare time. I sat down, smoked a roll-up and gathered my thoughts, hoping that the glasses situation was not the beginning of a trail of misfortune. Needless to say, all felt very strange, a long way away, both in time as well as distance.

With the heat I wasn't that hungry, besides breakfast felt like it had been just a few hours earlier, but I knew that if I didn't eat then I'd wake up hungry in the night, far away from any known late-night shop or takeaway. Since Lady-boy had taken most of my snacks, I went downstairs to find the hotel restaurant which was on the third floor. The Thai lady welcoming guests explained that it was a buffet for a fixed price of 190 baht. All I really fancied was some chicken fried rice but it seemed cheap enough; she called a waiter over who showed me to a table. He very carefully laid out the cutlery, not rushing in the slightest, as if slowness added to the quality of the service, and took the drink order which he noted with deliberate precision in his notebook, along with both my table and room numbers.

The tables were set out in a square grid, with the small tables for two in a line running alongside the windows. On the opposite side, a large Thai chef with a white floppy hat stir-fried the flaming contents of a pan over a lit stove, smoke rising out from the sizzling smells which emanated. In between were larger tables, some evidently catering for large groups eating together. Already Christmas decorations hung around, though in hindsight there are so many festivals held throughout the year in Thailand that these decorations may well have been for something else. Out of the window I could see the lights of the busy street below and the front of the hotel where the taxi had dropped me. My room must have been at the back for the ground below was less lit up and there was no view of the road. *That's good,* I thought. *No traffic to wake me up in the morning.*

The waiter came over with some cutlery and waved his arms towards the food suggesting it was self-service so I should go and serve myself. He stepped a few paces away and watched, present yet unobtrusive, as if learnt from a waiter's handbook. It was clear from his interactions with the other staff that he was new, though he was making a meticulous effort to appear as an experienced professional in his work, at ease. I tried to appear just as experienced in restaurant attendance when I approached the chef stir-frying. The truth was that I rarely ate out, occasionally in a pub, very rarely in a restaurant. If in doubt, copy someone else, is sometimes the easiest method. The trouble was that the last person had just been served and I'd missed the expected etiquette of how to request what.

The chef pointed to the pile of plates, as if that was what was holding me up. I thanked him, as if that was what was holding me up too, helped myself to a plate and stood there, hoping he would take my order, hoping even more so that he would take my order in English. He spoke to his assistant chef, something I didn't understand, and they both burst out laughing. *If in doubt, just smile,* I thought, and made my best effort to say hello in Thai. They both laughed even more, but he said hello back.

'You choose,' he said, pointing to the array of green leaves and vegetables in front of him. Someone else came up and started loading up their own plate with greenery before passing it to him to stir fry. I did the same. 'No meat?' he said, surprised.

'Err, you have chicken?' I asked, wondering how on earth I'd ever learn to say that in Thai. He pointed to the raw meats in front of him; it seemed that even this was help yourself. I'd expected the Beefeater Sunday carvery type of approach where the vegetables were help yourself but the meat was very carefully rationed by the carver who dished it out; no such restriction here, though he was a big guy and had a large knife beside his wok of flames, and the meat was close to him.

I'd been away from my table for a while by the time I'd figured the procedure, and I walked back towards it at the same time as the waiter brought out the freshly squeezed fruit juice I'd ordered. I looked for where my place setting had been but couldn't see it. Without my glasses I needed to get to the tables to be able to check the numbers. The waiter and I both saw the couple who had parked themselves where I'd been sitting at the same time. He looked flustered, wondering if he should ask them to move. I simply sat at the next table along, still with the same view out of the window, and sort of mimed an eating gesture hopefully indicating my need for some more cutlery. The waiter went and brought a new place setting over before fetching back the neat drinks order; he made a show of scribbling out the old table number, noting down the new one with much less care than had originally been taken, now that the page had been ruined by the black scribble, soiled. He tutted, slightly shaking his head, as if this was the sort of thing that waiters like him had to deal with every single day, as if perhaps a less experienced waiter would not have known quite how to handle the situation. It was amusing, I've done jobs myself where I've had to pretend to know what I was doing, at least make it look so even when I hadn't hardly a clue, and recognised it.

The stir-fry tasted superb, though the pile of vegetables had shrunk quite a bit during cooking so that there wasn't that much there. He'd asked if I wanted it hot; I'd said yes, even though he and his colleague laughed just slightly more than was entirely reassuring. It was indeed hot and made me feel even hotter than I was already feeling. The juice was good too, possibly one of the tastiest I'd ever had, so sweet and fruity.

I wondered if I should go back for more, or what the etiquette was now. Was someone watching to see how much I ate, in case I breached the reasonable allowance for the price? I couldn't see too clearly but there appeared to be a lot of food laid out down the far end away from the chef, and I could see people sat at tables beyond the aisle of food. This, I thought, must be a private party going on. Our end of the restaurant was fairly quiet and the chef wandered past my table. I said that the food was delicious, which pleased him. He looked at my empty plate and, possibly figuring that I hadn't a clue about how things worked in this buffet set up, asked if I wanted some more chicken. His English was tricky to understand, but was better than my Thai. He walked up the private buffet aisle and came back a few minutes later with a plate full of chicken satay sticks, some peanut sauce and some pickled chillies. This too, was delicious. When he saw I'd finished he came back again with a bowl of ice cream. I guessed it was made from coconut milk, and it had small candy-like balls inside; it was truly amazing. I finished up, paid, tipped, smiled gratefully, and went outside for a smoke.

The heat of the street hit me as soon as the porter opened the door. He was friendly, a young guy with jet-black hair dressed in black trousers and shoes with a crimson jacket, and wore a small black hat with a badge on the forehead. I walked out and went and sat on the car park wall, rolling a cigarette. The porter came over and I offered him one, which he took. He said his name was Gaga, like the famous footballer, he explained, when I couldn't understand his pronunciation. I knew very little about football but nodded as if that had explained it, saving further awkward repetition. He asked how long I was in Thailand for, where I was going, what I was doing. I said I was thinking of going down to Koh Samui. Aah yes, he said, I should go to Koh Samui, and to full moon party on Koh Pha Ngan.

I asked if it was expensive down on the islands. He said the cheapest way was to book through a TAT agent; this, he explained, was because TAT agencies were sponsored by the government to encourage tourism. I asked where I might find such an agency. Then, as if summoned by magic, a car pulled up and out got somebody that Gaga clearly knew very well.

'Sawat – this is Pete,' he said to the driver, who was certainly Thai but looked different to Gaga. He was an older man, not very tall, with short dark hair combed back, and wore a permanent smile. He was very pleased to be introduced. Gaga brought him up to speed with our conversation about Koh Samui and TAT agencies; I could tell because every now and then between the Thai words he would bring me back in. Sawat, he explained, was a taxi driver who would be able to take me to such a place. Some TAT agencies were better than others, but of course Sawat knew the best place to go. In fact, he said, Sawat knew all the best places to go around Bangkok, and would be my own personal guide and driver.

I felt a little overwhelmed, suddenly having had a chauffeur booked for me so quickly, and had visions of all my savings being blown on a luxurious city break that I hadn't planned or wanted. Sawat was straight on the case, fetching brochures of Bangkok nightlife for tourists from his car for me to browse through whilst we stood there. I smoked another roll-up; Gaga reappeared with three small bottles of drink and gave me one. I noticed that he unscrewed the lid before he gave it to me and thought it a bit weird. I hoped that it hadn't already been opened. Actually, what I hoped was that it hadn't already been opened and spiked with ya baa, the crazy drug I'd heard about that can be found in Thailand. Apparently it sends you a bit mad after keeping you awake for five days solid. Who knows, often such horror stories are exaggerated in the press. I drank it anyway, not wanting to appear impolite, I mean, it was 26°C so I could hardly say I wasn't thirsty. It was actually quite tasty, like a strong flavoured lemonade drink. Gaga assured me it would give me energy after such a long flight. Energy? Did he mean like ya baa energy? I hoped not.

Though Sawat did his best I told him that tonight I was tired and needed to get some sleep. It had, after all, been some time since I'd slept properly. He promised that tomorrow he would show me the city, so I thanked them both and went up to my room. Losing an entire night's sleep, I thought I'd simply go straight off, wake up in the morning for breakfast, and pretty much miss the whole jet-lag fuss that people went on about. Laying there it was more difficult getting to sleep than I thought it would be. It would have been late afternoon UK time, and I'd been up since early morning the day before. The more I lay there the more awake I felt. I wondered if Gaga had ya baa'd me, though could see no advantage in it for him, unless he'd thought that I'd go off on a city tour with Sawat and get a cut of whatever I happened to blow on Bangkok night-time entertainment. Maybe I was just being paranoid.

I must have dozed off for a while for I woke up startled by a strange animal sound from the bushes below. I couldn't decide if it was a monkey or a screeching bird. Now it had started, it wasn't going to shut up; perhaps it was nocturnal, rising every night to make an impression that during the day would have been drowned by the noise of the traffic and gone by unnoticed. Not so at night: it had my full attention. The room was very hot and stuffy, difficult to breathe. I eventually relented and put the air-con on for ten minutes. I'd switched it off as I dislike the idea of coming to a hot country and trying to cool it down. I always think if visitors don't like heat, go somewhere cold. Everyone knows what Bangkok is like, how hot it gets. Ten minutes wasn't enough and hadn't made much difference, so I left it on for a bit longer. I wondered what time it was but hadn't brought a watch with me, thinking I was trying to get away from serving the clock and wouldn't need it.

Time passed by as I read bits of the *Rough Guide*, trying to figure out where to go, where would be hot, and where would be a cheap place to spend the next five weeks. I thought of beach huts and hammocks, smoking some Thai weed around a small bonfire on the beach with a bunch of hippies. I tried to find where the hotel was on the Bangkok map I'd found in the hotel room but couldn't correlate it to mine in the guide book. Tomorrow, I decided, I would locate where I was, get my bearings.

The monkey bird kept on and on. It seemed to know when I put the book down and turned the light out for it would shriek even more. At times it was as if it was stuck in a cage whilst somebody tormented it through the bars with the specific intention of making it squawk. It seemed like hours later when the cockerel joined in, and I figured dawn must be approaching. I wondered what time it got light here at this time of year. The cockerel and monkey bird started to compete for air time, and the night dragged on, and on. At regular intervals a mosquito came and buzzed in my ear, occasionally causing me to punch my own head in my failed but quite irritating attempts to finish it off. Eventually it began to get light, and I began to get really tired, and fell asleep.

When I awoke I could hear busy traffic. It seemed there was a minor road round the back of the hotel which people used as a shortcut or diversion to get to the main road out the front. High up as I was, all I could really make out were the brake lights coming on and off as the traffic moved slowly along. I decided to get up, not wanting to miss breakfast, though hardly refreshed from the good night's sleep I'd hoped for.

Breakfast too was a buffet affair. Mornings were evidently busier than evenings, no doubt something to do with the fact that breakfast was included in the room rate. With lots more people here to gauge etiquette, this was much more straightforward than the night before. Besides, they'd catered for virtually everything found in a cooked English breakfast and more, as well as Thai food for native guests. The food was excellent though both the bacon and the sausages tasted quite unlike our versions of the same; the fresh fruit was as delicious as it gets, though I took care to avoid going near any durian, not that I knew what it looked like or even if there was any. Out of the window I watched the busy street below as a constant stream of slow moving cars edged their way forward. Odd to see the different colours of Bangkok traffic; bright yellows, oranges, and even many pink cars, colours rarely seen in England.

I decided to explore the hotel and went up to the roof for a cigarette. The pool that had appeared so large in the carefully angled photograph was in reality not that big. You could dip in and cool off but swimming would be a bit tricky since you'd be at the other end just after kicking off. I sat there for a while, feeling rather done in, and decided it wasn't even really a place to sit in the sun; the fumes from the streets below and the hotel generators seeming to linger in the close, hot atmosphere. There was hardly a breeze moving anything, and there sure was no sign of that rain the weather man had mentioned as the bright sun pierced through the smog that slightly paled the blue of the entire sky. I went back to my room and promptly fell soundly asleep.

I nearly jumped off the bed when the phone rang. It was Gaga calling from reception downstairs. Half asleep, blinded by the bright sunshine, thirsty and somewhat disorientated, I managed to work out that apparently Sawat was downstairs waiting for me, as arranged. I asked him what the time was but couldn't understand what he said. I told him I'd been sleeping, to apologise to Sawat for me, and that I'd be down later. By the time I surfaced Sawat had gone and Gaga was off duty. A different porter called me over and said there was a message left for me. It was from Sawat: he'd had to go off somewhere but would be back very soon.

I went for a walk down the road, just to explore. I

wanted to find a shop to buy a pair of cheap sunglasses to replace mine that had been ruined by the leaking glue. Maybe get a cheap watch too so I'd know what time it was as I lay there in the dark trying not to fall asleep and miss breakfast.

The road was so big and so busy that the only way to cross it was by one of the large footbridges that were placed every quarter mile or so. I walked past the first, opting to cross over at the next one down, the pavement on this side giving a better view of the canal just down the road. It turned out to be quite murky-looking, overgrown, and rather un-picturesque. No pleasant footpath ran alongside this stretch of water, like a stream in England may well have had. It was actually a bit smelly, and I quickly walked on, finding the smell difficult to leave behind. What I found out much later is that this wasn't actually a canal but an open air sewer, as is often found in Bangkok. The road fumes were bad too, and I noticed the traffic policeman directing the flow at one of the busy junctions was wearing a mask. I moved on, looking forward to hitting the beach.

The area wasn't as I'd imagined it would be; I'd had visions that Bangkok would be full of streets like the infamous Khao San Road as seen on TV; thankfully it's not like that, which is, I guess, why Khao San Road is famous for being what it is. As fortune would have it though, I came to a street stall selling both watches and sunglasses. They weren't prescriptions but the fake designer glasses would at least keep out the glare. It had hazed over so I tried them quickly and took them off. Later on I noticed that they had a strange focus going on so I couldn't see too well out of them, nor could I wear them for long without getting a headache; the watch was ok though, and kept good time.

Walking back, I passed several street beggars; young girls with children frequent the road bridges hoping to find sympathy in passers-by; some just sitting with head bowed down to the pavement, perhaps with a small sign saying 'please help'. One poor old chap looked like he might be blind, and had no feet, just stumps. It was so pitiful, I couldn't help but wonder how life had got so difficult for him. His dirty clothes were torn, ragged, and his hands and stumps calloused, tough from abrasion from the hard concrete that gave him little comfort. In a way I wished I hadn't seen him; actually what I really wished was that he hadn't reached such a poor state or hadn't existed even. On the other hand, if he existed, like he did, then perhaps it is better to see such things, to know that they exist, to gain a true reflection of the world in our minds instead of living in the fantastic world of illusions, sex, parties, celebrity, and intoxication, whatever is our chosen method for distancing ourselves from harsh reality.

Later that evening, as I stepped out for a smoke before heading in for another bash at the hotel buffet, this time a little wiser than before, Sawat pounced on me. 'Aah. Teep,' he said, with one of the biggest smiles I'd ever seen. He could never quite get the P and T in the right order for my name, but as I keep saying, his English was far superior to my Thai. I only really got his name since it's the same for the Thai word for hello; who knows, maybe I was getting his name wrong all the time and he was just having a laugh back, with me unaware.

Dinner went much smoother; it turned out that all the food down the aisle that I thought was for the private party was actually part of the buffet. No wonder chef had thought me weird, having paid for the buffet but not eaten anything. The irony is that it could have been seen as insulting; odd that in trying to be polite, and avoid an accusation of encroaching on – of all things – someone else's food, and the ensuing embarrassing scene, one can actually appear to be quite rude. Anyway, I got stuck in tonight, sampling some wonderful curries and all sorts of Thai dishes, as well as the array of fresh fruit, perfectly ripe, juicy, and recently picked as opposed to ripening in a cold ship's hull sat on the ocean for days on end only to be stored in a warehouse until previous stocks have run dry. I could see Sawat outside through the window, parked in his usual place, polishing parts of his car as he chatted with one of the porters.

Gaga had introduced Sawat as the hotel taxi driver, as if he worked for the hotel. He drove an old unmarked dark blue Mercedes, the type that was once seen on UK roads but now is more or less obsolete, perhaps a few collectors' models around, you hardly ever see them. Though aged, apart from a few small areas fighting off the rust, the body work looked immaculate, Sawat clearly giving it much attention during times of waiting. Maybe the heat causes metal to rust slower than in the cold; or maybe there's just not enough oxygen in Bangkok for rust to rust things.

When I stepped out after dinner he was polishing the chrome, and rushed over and greeted me with a smile. Though I may have missed the day tour –

Grand Palace, sleeping Buddha, laying down Buddha, big Buddha, little Buddha, many other different Buddhas, floating markets and so on – he was more than keen to show me the nightlife. He reeled off a list of different types of show we could see, most involving girls having sex, then mentioned the different types of massage I could have, most involving or ending with girls having sex. 'Two girls for you, one for me,' he kept saying, showing me photographs. In a way I thought I should do something, I mean you can't come to Bangkok and stay in your hotel room for the evening; I just wasn't used to going out much, having been staying in and saving for ages.

Sawat welcomed me into his vehicle, hurrying around to open the door for me, still very much smiling. His seats were so well polished that I nearly slid off; he certainly kept a tidy car. I found it a bit odd that for a hotel taxi he had no taxi badge, no hotel uniform (unlike the porters who all wore the same formal dress), only a photographic licence hanging from his rear view mirror, along with the almost obligatory bunch of shells, flowers, and incense that hang inside almost every Thai car. Often sold by street walkers who approach cars stuck in traffic, these decorations are meant to bring some kind of good luck and protection to the vehicle. In Thailand there is a belief in the spirit world far more evident than in our western culture. Most taxis have a number as well, for identification purposes, and virtually all of them have the photographic licence on display somewhere inside; not that the photo always bears much resemblance to the driver, a bit like a passport photo with the forced lacked of expression, and perhaps a different haircut rendering an un-aged image that now bears very little relation to reality.

Out came the brochures again, this time somewhat more explicit and graphic. I tried to explain that I hadn't come to Bangkok to have sex in some sleazy back street with girls, boys, or girls that actually were or once were boys. However, I'd had a bad back from work and a knee injury which had put an end to my martial arts, so was interested in a proper Thai massage. Though in England I'd had treatment that, whilst was pleasant and relaxing, hadn't really addressed the issues, I thought that perhaps in the Thai heat, with a masseur experienced and proficient in what has been a tried and tested method throughout their cultural history, treatment would be more effective, and cheaper. Sawat said he knew just the place. In fact, he went on to tell me how he too had had a knee injury, so bad that it had prevented him from working. He'd seen 'the doctor' who had cured him completely. He demonstrated how he could easily bend his knee now. Before, he said, it would not move. Now, back to normal. He showed me again, bending it with ease, smiling. It seemed a coincidence too good to be true, that he'd had the exact same problem. Every symptom I cited he nodded with enthusiastically in agreement, pointed to his own leg and tapped the brochure on a random page saying, 'Doctor will cure.' It was even the same leg, the left one; important, he said, for changing gear.

As we drove into town I tried to remember the roads and turns which would enable me to head off tomorrow on my own if I felt like it. I didn't feel too much like undertaking a trip around crowded monuments placed for the purpose of tourism as much as for culture, and I didn't need to buy loads of fresh fruit and vegetables so the floating market had little appeal. However, it became clear as we travelled on that I was staying quite some distance away from wherever we were heading. I lost the way after about the fourth turn; the busy streets all looked the same, and it was dark so I couldn't really make out any landmarks, not that I knew any anyway. Sawat pulled over to take me to one of the very few money exchanges still open this time of the evening to change a few cheques. He even confused himself as he tried to park and I began to question my confidence levels in his aptitude as a city guide. But he seemed like a decent guy, friendly, and whenever he answered his mobile phone, as he said, "Allo,' in his rising tone, he smiled wide as if the person he was speaking to was right in front of him.

He had a Chinese look about him, dark-skinned, and not very tall; I guessed he was around fifty years of age, and combed his dark but thinning hair regularly, no doubt partly out of habit. He was from the northern part of the country, where his family still lived, whom he went back to visit every three months, taking back his Bangkok earnings to support them. He told me he had a son who was a footballer, played for the national team and was due to have trials with Manchester United. He said to look out for him, for he was still young but would one day be a star. He said his name, as if I may have heard of it, but since I don't follow football, I had no idea if it was all made up or true. Thais seem to love football, especially European teams, often having a strange ability to recite the entire team's names, results of matches, who scored and when: these facts, I found out later, are memorised largely due to the amount of gambling that takes place, where history becomes the guiding form, especially bets on final scores.

The night market through which we walked to reach the money exchange sold virtually everything: cooked food, raw food, clothes, silks, household goods, all sorts of things, every type of market in one. It looked quite something, a vast array of colours amidst a myriad of stalls, lit up and crowded with night shoppers as if this was a normal time to do your shopping. Sawat led the way through to the money booth, keen to get on now he was on a mission to get me to 'the doctor' for a massage.

When we pulled up outside the massage place it looked as if we had come around the back way. Though completely lost I had seen several signs for foreign embassies nearby and made a note to check later exactly where I was. We walked across the dusty ground of the dark and quiet car park and went through an unmarked door, where we were greeted by a group of Thais. They seemed to know Sawat who appeared to be explaining my medical needs. He told me that fortunately, it was good news, the doctor was here tonight and would see me, we'd just have to wait a little while. He kept smiling as if that reassured me; I always remember that bit in the Godfather where he says something about being careful with expressions, for your own hitman will no doubt approach with a smile before shooting. On the other hand, at least if someone smiles when they do you over it kind of takes the edge off of it a bit, something like if Ainsley was to oversee a funeral, counting down the minutes to cremation with that winning grin in a breakaway series of Ready, Steady, Cooked.

We sat in one of the rooms along a corridor and waited for the doctor. The side walls were a thin sort of ply board, a visual shield more than a solid partition, and there was quite a gap between the top and the ceiling; the back wall was the outside of the building, the front was a pair of curtains, similar to those used in a hospital ward. A young Thai girl brought us in some scalding hot Thai tea to drink whilst we waited. The same girl then brought in a bowl of steaming water and washed Sawat's feet. When she pointed at mine I waved her away, saying thanks but it was ok. She gave me a determined and insistent look, and Sawat pointed at my feet too, nodding as if it was kind of compulsory.

I found out afterwards that Thais are quite particular about feet, like removing shoes before entering many buildings, never pointing at someone with your feet, always walking around someone's feet – not their head – but not stepping over their feet: culturally feet have their own significances and correct treatment, etiquette. So she washed my feet as I squirmed and wriggled, me having feet so ticklish to be verging on the ridiculous; at first she found it amusing, soon annoying, as her attempts to relax me with soothing actions had quite the reverse affect. Sawat laughed as he drank his tea, and though I was thirsty, mine was still too scalding to risk sipping whilst prone to convulsions, and before the girl had finished the doctor came in through the curtains and told the girl to leave. As she packed away her cloths and bowl she quietly hissed, 'Tip for me, tip for me.'

I began to rummage around with some change and, seeing the coins, she shook her head and hissed, 'Fifty baht, fifty baht.' Before I'd given her anything another doctor came in and gently shoved her out.

This, it seemed, was 'the doctor', the infamous cure-any-leg doctor of Bangkok. She was dressed in a small white gown very much like a proper doctor might have worn; I was relieved at least that she hadn't come in wearing some sexy strip outfit, Sawat thinking he was doing me a favour by arranging it on the sly. She spoke to him for a few minutes, though with all the natural changes in tone of the language it was hard to tell what they could have been talking about... how to put me to sleep and steal a few organs, and did anyone know I was here, perhaps? Not that I was too worried, after all I was kind of committed to finding out now. The tea was still too hot to drink and the doctor gave a little clap of hands as if to indicate it was time to get moving.

The massage was a proper Thai massage, most of it consisting of her standing on me and pulling me around. At one point she stood on my leg with both feet, and whilst steadying herself by holding the top of the partition, kind of pulled my leg in two directions; her feet curled around and gripped with surprising strength. For such a small lady I was amazed at how much pain she could inflict with her technique. I did not keep this fact to myself, in fact most of the building soon became aware that this kind of hurt a bit; a lot, even. Sawat was busy having a massage of his own, though comparably silently; I could tell that he and his masseur were finding it hilarious. Every now and then he called across and said, 'Teep, you ok yes?'

'Yeah, yeah, I'm ok,' I replied each time, trying to finish the sentence without a yell or a grimace, played by the doctor like a musical instrument, as if she knew exactly when to stretch things just that little bit further. When she'd finished she said something to Sawat, presumably to interpret for me since she seemed to speak very little English.

The girl came back with my sandals seeking her tip. I got out a twenty baht note and looked at Sawat; he nodded and I gave it to the girl who eyed it with scorn, evidently disappointed that her suggestion of fifty had been ignored. The trouble was that this was already costing me more than expected, and tipping everyone fifty baht would soon exhaust the funds, so she huffed off.

When I stepped out through the curtain a small crowd of Thais had gathered to see what the person who had made so much fuss and noise looked like. Somebody wounded maybe, or a badly beaten up Muay Thai boxer. They nudged each other, giggling when they saw it was just a farang. Then came the time to pay. One of the Thai guys I'd seen at the start came over so I got out 900 baht from my wallet. He took it, looking dissatisfied. I said '900 bahts right?'

He shook his head and said, '900 bahts for one.'

'That's 900 bahts there,' I pointed out.

'Yes but 900 bahts is for one,' he said, now looking at Sawat.

It slowly dawned on me that I was expected to pay for Sawat's massage too, like this had been part of the deal all along. My surprise must have been evident, and for a few seconds I wasn't quite sure what to do or how this was going to go. I looked at Sawat who fortunately began to talk to the guy, though I had no idea what was being said, and it didn't seem to be altogether straightforward. They deliberated for a short while before Sawat got out his own wallet and paid over a bunch of notes. I had no idea how much he paid – almost certainly less than me – and I felt a bit bad thinking that I'd deprived his family of no doubt much needed money; on the other hand, I would very quickly run out of cash at this rate if I wasn't careful. He then leant over towards me and whispered that I should tip the doctor 100 baht. She was standing next to me, smiling, waiting. I gave her the note as she smiled, gratefully but expectantly, and wondered how the 900 baht was split if she relied on tips, being the doctor.

When we were back in the car driving away, I felt more at ease. Sawat explained that the doctor said I might ache a bit as a result of the treatment: he wasn't kidding, my body felt like it had had a good kicking. But, he continued, my leg was very sick and would take a couple more treatments for it to be fully cured. It needed more massage but next time with a balm. It was a special type of balm that luckily he knew where to get and was happy to take me there tomorrow. Tonight, he said, the night was still very young and now I'd had leg treatment we should go and find some girls for a different type of massage. He showed me the books again, the girl brochures, smiling, saying two for me and one for him. I saw how with a guide you could see much of Bangkok, spending lots of cash in the process. It wasn't what my trip was about so we headed back to the hotel. As we drove back he chatted quite happily about our plans for the following day; I wasn't so sure about it all and wondered how much this night taxi tour was going to cost. Sawat didn't want paying that night, preferring to run a tab for me now he was my driver for the next few days. I didn't want to be committed so I insisted on settling up, agreeing to see him in the morning to arrange something.

On the way in I passed Gaga the porter who asked me if I'd booked up yet. TAT was the place, he reminded me, Sawat knew and would take me. I went up to my room, still aching, and a bit stiff, hoping to use it as a way to get off to sleep and slip into the change in hours. No sooner had I turned out the light when, like a jolt of remembrance of something important just in time but nearly forgotten, I suddenly felt wide awake. Just like the night before, try as I did, laying there in the dark, humid heat, I could not sleep. Eventually I turned on the light and read the guide book for a while, still wondering where to go: Koh Samui, where it seemed quite safe, though a bit commercialised? Or little Koh Chang, the small island off of the west coast where, the book said, it was still unspoilt, even such that there was no electricity for much of the time? Beach huts were supposedly cheap and simple, and this was exactly what I was looking for. But there had been the tsunami – the book had been printed prior to this, and it had been difficult finding any reliable information about remote islands such as these, even in England.

I suppose I may have had some romantic idea that I'd wander around the streets of Bangkok and perchance meet some fellow travellers who would tell me of such and such a place, and off I would go, safe in the knowledge that circumstance had guided me. I'd met no such people in reality, and from the day's exploring it seemed that it was unlikely I would do so on my current track. Sleeping most of the day hadn't helped, and I knew I only had two nights left to arrange something. I decided that the next day I would get up early and venture into the city, to see what chance may bring.

The night dragged on and the monkey bird did his stuff again, helping to prevent any sleep from settling. Eventually the cockerel joined in but tonight I was armed with my watch. I fumbled for the light switch, blurry-eyed and tired even though awake, and checked the time. My surprise at just how fast the night had passed was explained when I saw that it was only 2am. Why would a cockerel crow at two in the morning? And not just once, it was like dawn was always just about to break, for the next four or five hours, continually; it proved to me that even the birds are crazy in Bangkok, just like everything else.

Dawn came and I fell asleep for a couple of hours. I woke and went for breakfast, fortunately not missing out on such a good meal and sat by the window again in what had become my 'usual' vicinity of the restaurant. The food was real good as always, and this time I even managed to get the chef to fry me an egg just how I like it – broken and cooked both sides. As I sat watching the traffic below, people going about their daily business, I could see Sawat was already there, waiting in the car park. After the price of the previous night I was hoping to avoid any more expensive tourist tours, and hoped he'd go away. I went up to the roof and had a cigarette by the pool, looking over the edge to see if I could see Sawat from up there. It was too high and he was parked too close to the building. Stuffy from the rising traffic fumes and noisy from the generators and air-con units up on the roof, it wasn't exactly the relaxing poolside experience one might have imagined from a photograph. Besides, it's always the same with photographs, and the Thais seem to have an innate expertise in the art, that the angle and lens used always make the pool look like you could dive in and swim a few lengths, maybe hold a gala.

I went back to the room for some water, thirsty from the heat and the cooked breakfast, laid on the bed for a minute and fell straight asleep. When I woke up, still thirsty and hot, bright sunlight poured in through the window. I went to the shop just down the street to get some more water, noticing that Sawat had gone off somewhere; on a tour of the city with another newcomer, I kind of hoped, not feeling like another round of him persuading me to go and see all the Buddhas, temples, and markets that Bangkok had to offer. In fact I didn't feel like doing much; the heat and humidity were extreme. I felt tired, still a bit achy from the massage, but most of all felt that as a westerner I really stood out. Everyone around me – even most people in the hotel – looked Thai or Chinese, and I was very conscious of that. I couldn't speak, read, or understand any of the language apart from the only two words I knew; even the chef had started to make fun of me, walking around repeating, 'Hello, thank you, hello, thank you,' whenever he saw me. The trouble was that even those two words had taken me loads of practice, and I still probably hadn't got them quite right. At least he found it amusing, and was friendly about it.

Up the road in the other direction there was a Skytrain station. I had a quick look round and decided I would go back to the room, get my guidebook and maps so I knew exactly where I was going and where I had to get back to, and head off into the city somewhere. I was a short while getting my things together, like passport and traveller's cheques to change some more money (sooner than I'd expected). When I emerged again into the hot, bright sunlight I could see Sawat's car was back, though no sign of him. If I'm honest here I would say that secretly I was pleased he wasn't around, and turned to head off towards the Skytrain. A couple of Thais were tinkering with a car when one of them caught sight of me. He stood up, turned, and whistled to a grew of men who appeared to be playing cards just up the street, and I saw Sawat jump up and come quickly running over, much like my cat does when she knows it's time for tea, tail up, happy and excited.

'Aah Teep, Teep!' he called out, evidently pleased to see me, wearing his big smile, combing his hair as he ran.

Many thoughts went through my mind as I resisted Sawat's attempted persuasions to find the balm, have another massage before the usual city highlights of Buddhas and temples. The old city ruins sounded interesting but now, with less than twenty-four hours until checking out of the safety of the hotel and into the realms of the who knows what, I mentioned the TAT place to him. 'Aah yes, the TAT, we can go there now.' He smiled warmly. I felt for him for he was only trying to make a living, so I agreed to go, after all, going off on my own would only have meant the added need to find somewhere, and even then I'd just be another farang in off the street.

As we drove, this time in daylight, I quickly lost track of where we were and how we'd got there. So many of the streets are simply blocks of very tall buildings, crammed with traffic, with traffic lights at every junction. It's an open admittance of a simple display of ignorance, but to me it all looked similar, with no memorable landmarks to indicate where I was. Unlike my home city, Bangkok, I found out later, has no real centre, but several districts each with its own central area.

The TAT place was a travel agency, and was situated on a busy main road. Sawat came in, said something to one of the Thais inside, and went straight outside again, as if ordered out. A guy came over and offered me a seat. When I mentioned Koh Samui, another guy came over and introduced himself as Noppi. Evidently Noppi was the Koh Samui guy. He was very confident in his manner and seemed to represent something of a new and modern era, a young man of the city with a slick haircut and neatly cut suit. Long gone are the rice fields and fishing boats for this generation grown up with tiny mobile phones and computers that are a window into a bright and cosy world, looked into so often to create a pair of permanent spectacles through which the viewer sees even the real world distorted; into the world of trendy bars with flashing neon lights, where men really have become women so that the elephant with the ball is not really much of an interesting attraction any more.

Noppi was a gifted salesman: he'd shown me the glossy pictures of beautiful Koh Samui, the blue skies, deep blue seas, beaches, and lush tropical scenery, always sunny. I asked him if he'd been there and he confirmed, with a nostalgic smile, that he'd grown up living there. It looked good, just what I was looking for.

Eventually, after much arguing, we agreed on a price for pretty much all the bookings I'd need for the next month. The final figure happened to be just around that which I'd said at the beginning was my maximum; though he'd gone for a much higher number to start with, shaking his head, saying how busy it was at this time of year, how my guide book was out of date and so on. All my arguing had got back to my maximum, no less for sure. He took a deposit from me and said he'd put all the paperwork together ready for me the next day. 'The night train for Koh Samui leaves at 6:45pm tomorrow. You can stay in your hotel until midday, then Sawat can bring you here, you can pay, and then leave your bag here whilst you maybe explore until about 5:30; then we can arrange a tuk-tuk to take you to the station.' He said it like it was a set of instructions for a mission, almost as if it wouldn't be safe to divert from this plan. But he smiled widely as he finished speaking, and held out his hand to shake and seal the deal.

On the way back to the hotel Sawat asked me how much it had all cost. When I told him, he appeared to be working something out in his head. I asked him if he thought I'd spent too much. No, no, he assured me, I had got a really cheap deal for what I had booked; I wasn't altogether convinced, for it had cost a lot more than I'd anticipated, and could see funds rapidly disappearing.

That night I read the guide book again, now aware of my destinations. One thing the book had warned against was dodgy travel agencies that appeared and disappeared virtually overnight, taking all the payments for non-existent hotels and fake tickets with them, never to be seen again. I'd read this in England, so just to be sure I thought I'd book a morning call (avoiding the risk of missing breakfast before such a long day and night ahead) and politely check with the receptionist that Sawat was who he claimed to be. When I got down there Gaga was stood by the door. I booked the call and went back upstairs without asking her about Sawat, not wanting to be overheard enquiring and suspicious, mistrusting.

The longer the night went on and the more I thought about things, I wondered if I was being had, like some kind of set up from The Sting. I found the deposit slip and checked the agency's details; though the receipt had TAT marked in big black capitals, even then I knew that in Thailand you can find fake versions of everything, all marked as if genuine. I looked through the agency listings in the guide book, but couldn't find it. I searched the directory in the hotel room, the Bangkok version of Yellow Pages, but couldn't find them anywhere. Every so often I'd think of another category to look under, but the agency was never listed. Monkey bird screeched on, mocking and fuelling my worrying, as if he was part of it all. I killed a mozzie, squishing it on the bed, and a small patch of bright red blood appeared on the white sheet. I wondered if it was my blood for it looked as if it had had a good feed very recently.

By the morning I'd decided that all I could do was go along with it and just take a chance, after all, you always risk being ripped off somehow or another. It's odd that the less you try to spend, the greater the chance of being stung. Even the hotel internet, with its foreign keyboard was seemingly designed to delay the typing as the fifty baht for fifteen minutes clock ticked quickly by; the first keyboard had keys that didn't work, and even when I changed computers it had taken me over five minutes to find the '@' key required for the email. In Thailand this key is towards the top left of the board and marked with a different icon; it all felt a bit like the computer was sucking away at my wallet as I watched on. I tried to ask the receptionist about Sawat again, but in my attempt to be discreet, and as if it didn't matter, like it was just out of interest, she didn't really get what I was asking, especially with the language differences. The awkward conversation merely just about confirmed that Sawat was a taxi driver, not much else.

I checked out around noon and waited for Sawat, who typically had been briefly called away on another job. Just like life to make me want for my own adversary to take me to my own demise, I wondered, still trying not to worry. Think about things long enough and they tend to happen, especially if it's something you don't want to happen; I focussed on the sunny beaches and blue skies, and some much-needed sleep in a comfy hammock as the sea lapped gently at the shore.

CHAPTER 4

Night Train Waiting Game

Sawat pulled up outside the TAT office and for a moment I thought it had disappeared. The shop was empty and the windows were whitewashed over, but this was actually the shop next door. We went in and Noppi appeared, smiling as always. He said something to Sawat who went outside, and we sat down to sort out the paperwork. To be fair he'd put it all together quite neatly, each resort booking in a separate envelope, marked with its name and the island. The travel tickets were with the relevant envelopes, and pretty much every journey was booked. All I had to do, he explained, was to get a couple of buses on Koh Samui, which should only cost about 50 baht each; he wrote it down on one of the maps. There was even a day's hire of a 4x4 to drive around Koh Samui thrown in, he pointed out. I looked shocked, and said I had no intention of driving in Thailand, pointing to the crazy traffic outside. He just smiled wider and said that driving on the island would be nothing like driving in Bangkok, everything would be ok. Being somewhat relieved that the place still existed after the previous night's thoughts, and also because I'd already paid over the balance, I argued no further about the driving and took the tickets. Noppi called someone over to put my bag around the back, we shook hands, him still smiling very widely, and I headed off until later.

Outside, Sawat was tucking into some noodles as he stood chatting to the street vendor. I asked him how much he wanted for the taxi fare here, conscious that I hadn't paid him for today. At first he tried to wave me away, saying that it was ok, I'd given him enough over the last few days; I insisted and paid him anyway, politely declining his offer to buy me lunch from the vendor. He asked me what time my train went, and what I intended to do until then. I said perhaps just have a wander round, look at a few things. He pointed up the street and told me not to go that way, but to go the other way where I would be safe. Then he warned me that if any strange men, especially if all smartly dressed in a suit, approached me and tried to lead me off, then I was definitely not to go with them.

'Just be polite and say no and keep walking,' he advised, really quite seriously. 'If you are polite and do this you will be ok.' He smiled, and we said bye-bye. Though it had only been a few days, it had been all my time in Thailand so far, and now everything that had only just about become familiar, the hotel and

Sawat, was gone. Now all I really knew and was reliant upon were Noppi, the TAT office, and my bunch of tickets. The link to plans felt fragile.

I took Sawat's advice and headed down the road. Up the road, it seemed, was Patpong, where the strange men lurked trying to lure unsuspecting people to who knows where for the dread to think of. Maybe there are a lot of made-up horror stories though, for sure there is some truth to some of them, fire behind the smoke; and if Sawat was saying it too then I'd been fair warned. As interesting as it may be for some people to watch girls who were once boys pop ping pong balls out of private orifices, this didn't appeal to me; even though it is apparently culturally acceptable for Thai men to frequent brothels and have sex with prostitutes, the whole paying for sex and the trapped enslavement side of what is nothing more than an oppressive industry puts me off and just isn't for me, so I avoided it.

The street was very busy with cars, and was another one of those that could only be crossed by footbridges. The turnings into side streets were just as busy; sometimes traffic lights made it easier, sometimes more complicated, as filter lanes could bring a sudden stream into the middle of the road, as if from nowhere. I tended to wait until other people were crossing rather than take my chances trying to figure out where cars might come from next. It's amazing how local people managed to know the sequences, and when it was safe. One thing about Thailand traffic lights is though there is no amber light in between red and green, there is a countdown timer telling people when it's due to change. Bikes and scooters rev up and edge their way out when the timer gets below ten seconds, roaring off as soon as it looks safe. Though I only saw a couple of accidents during all the time in Bangkok, given the number of cars and the apparent craziness, it's amazing that I didn't see more.

In this part of the city I still felt exposed as a westerner, a farang, out of place amongst so many Thais. I tried not to look around at things too much, and tried not to look lost. I'd not strayed from the one long straight road so all I needed to do was turn around and I would be able to find my way back at the designated time. I saw a sign indicating that the train station was just further on, so headed that way where I thought I could at least confirm that the train ticket was authentic, if nothing else. Out of all that Noppi had given me, the train ticket was actually about the only thing that looked authentic; even the flight back to Bangkok was just an e-ticket, a computer paper printout.

I'd booked eleven nights in Chaweng, Koh Samui; then over to Koh Phan Ngan for twelve nights, Christmas and the Full Moon Party. This was sold by Noppi as one of the must-see highlights, itself indicating how the celebration of free beauty that this once was became nothing more than a tourist attraction designed to extract cash from farang. Then back to Koh Samui for seven nights and New Year, returning to Bangkok the night before Amanda was scheduled to arrive. The last week in Koh Samui was in a place called Bophut; I'd had to argue a while with Noppi about costs, pointing to prices in the book, before he'd suggested this place. I'd asked why couldn't I stay there for the first eleven nights too but he had insisted that Chaweng would be the best place to meet some people. He had seemed very reluctant to budge on this one so I'd gone along with it thinking perhaps he knew best.

I reached a huge kind of double roundabout that I needed to cross to reach the station. I tried to memorise the way for the return journey, making a note of Thanon Rama IV. Here there were many foreigners and I immediately felt a little less exposed. A stranger approached me and asked if I wanted to buy a train ticket. I said I already had one. He wanted to see it, at which point I became somewhat suspicious, wondering if he wanted to snatch it off me. I made out it was tucked away somewhere too much of an effort to reach and walked on to find an official-looking desk. I checked with the lady who pointed towards the relevant platform before pointing to the time on the ticket, then to a clock on the wall, shaking her head to confirm that it would be some time yet before departure. I'd just wanted to make sure the ticket wasn't fake, and as I walked off, for the first time in a while I felt a bit more relaxed.

Outside people sat around on the steps smoking, some just stood around, people with bags, suitcases, and rucksacks. It was a bustling atmosphere, most people moving slowly due to the heat but with an air of excitement, heading for new destinations. A few more people tried selling me tickets or just asked where I was going, and I learned not to catch the eye of passers-by which, near the station, was evidently an invitation to be approached.

The humidity was increasing as the day went on,

and though the sky had been a polluted pale colour even when it seemed sunny, it was now turning greyer, and that rain the weather man had threatened looked like it could be on its way. I wasn't too bothered, heading as I was down to the sunny islands further south. A Dutch guy came past and we chatted briefly. He gave a slightly concerned look when I said I was heading down to Koh Samui, and said he'd heard it had been raining. *Oh well*, I thought, *maybe cool it down a bit*. Besides, I'd heard that monsoon rain was real heavy but might only last for less than an hour. He said he'd been living in Bangkok now for several months, and quickly went on his way, evidently seeing little interest in one so soon arrived. I wondered what he did with his time in this city.

A large area under cover around the platforms catered for every traveller's needs and reminded me more of an airport than a train station, with all its bars, restaurants, shops, and seating areas. There was even a large open section decked out with chairs in preparation for some kind of performance, almost certainly relating to the King's birthday which was less than a week away.

After a couple of hours shuffling around and trying to look inconspicuous, I went up the stairs to the row of bars that overlooked the open area below. Most seats were taken but I caught the eye of a westerner sat on his own. I nodded as I passed, and when he nodded back I asked him if he spoke English. 'That obvious, is it?' he smiled. We chatted for a minute and he offered a seat. Glad to relax, I sat down, declining the offer of a beer as the waiter brought him over another, with a fresh glass of ice that he duly mixed in as he drank. I didn't drink much at home and had decided to save both the cost and the dehydration by avoiding it over here, especially now with the budget blown.

His name was Daryl and he looked a bit like a young Dave Gilmour, as a lot of blokes do, but was actually more of a Led Zeppelin fan. He was heading up to Chiang Rai by train via Chiang Mai, to stay with Thai friends he knew who owned a bar right up near the Laos border. He pointed out his T-shirt which showed the bar's name, then showed me a copy of an old *Angling Times* with him on the front cover, wearing the same T-shirt. He explained how he was wearing it when he caught a large dogfish in the Thames and had made the front cover by chance; he was taking the newspaper to show his friends the free advertising they had unknowingly received. He'd been to Thailand a few times before and it was very useful chatting with him. Though he had a small bag with him, he explained that once he'd come out here with nothing but his passport, some money, and the clothes in which he was dressed. It was a commercial trick to sell you everything before you leave: he asked how I thought the Thais lived in Thailand.

I showed him my travel and accommodation tickets, confiding my slight concern that they may be fake, that I may have been ripped off. He mentioned a time when he'd bought a flight ticket from a dodgy-looking vendor down Khao San Road once who was selling flights from a foldaway wooden desk, and it had been fine; it was surprising that actually most of the time these tickets are accepted without question, like the whole system really relied on trust, and that the Thais had their own ways of making sure things remained stable, ways that we westerners wouldn't really understand.

When we went outside for a smoke he warned me of the 2,000 baht fine for dropping a cigarette end in the street; though you may see Thais do this right in front of policemen, if you – as a farang – try to do the same they will pounce on you. Another thing was marijuana: he said that even on the islands it was best avoided unless you had stayed somewhere for a while and really knew who you were buying from. In Bangkok it was a complete no-no. I hadn't felt the urge to be stoned amongst so much craziness, thinking nothing would be worse than perhaps losing my bag and missing my train because of some excessively relaxed lack of focus; it may have helped with the getting to sleep though.

He told me about some guy who'd got to know someone who set him up first deal: for him it had only cost him a few thousand baht; for others it can cost many more thousands, for out there money can persuade many people in lots of ways. He said he thought I'd be ok in Thailand; both me and them not being very big, the Thais wouldn't find me intimidating and wouldn't expect me to be any trouble. Though this was reassuring to know, I felt a little twang of awareness that I was only 5' 7½" and just about ten stone. Besides, he went on, the Thais were very rarely violent, and were friendly even when ripping you off, preferring to take money from farang with a smile rather than a threat, through trickery rather than force, preying on tourists themselves hoping to get much for next to nothing. When we went to the shop to get some more drinks, he gave me one last tip as he watched me struggle to understand the Thai lady serving me: 'Learn your Thai numbers, if nothing else.'

The right time came to move on and I headed back to the TAT place to get my bag. I realised I could have brought it with me but it was quite a walk and had not only saved lugging it around but had prevented me from losing it. By the time Noppi flagged down a tuk-tuk driver it was dark. He spoke sternly to the driver, and then told me how the tuk-tuk would take me to the station for 40 baht. I got in and had my first experience of riding in what can only be described as a metal frame welded onto a sawn-off motorbike, very noisy, fumy, and feeling quite unstable. I hung on, making no further attempt at conversation with the driver who had simply given me a bit of a stare. I guessed he was pretty fed up with seeing people like me come over with money and bright bags whilst he ferried them around for peanuts. He dropped me off a bit of a walk away and I couldn't help but wonder if it was his method for small revenge when I saw him again ride on by a couple of minutes later as I reached the station.

The train was long and the carriages stretched out of sight around the bend, full of bustling people finding seats and storing luggage, mostly Thais, the odd couple of western travellers. It's an odd thing that considering westerners are mostly travelling for fun, like an extended holiday, they always appeared to be more stressed out than the locals going about their business, even if it was just doing their routine work. My ticket indicated the designated seat which I found and sat in, made of moulded plastic, similar to a fairground ride.

Soon after departure a young waiter came around with a laminated menu card. Daryl had mentioned that he was looking forward to sampling the various foods as his train headed north; apparently, locals boarded at various stations to sell to passengers. I asked the waiter if we'd be stopping on our journey, wondering if I should wait for the food sellers to board before ordering. He looked at my ticket and said quite firmly that there were no stops before Surat Thani. I thought perhaps then the train food would be a reflection of the foods Daryl would be sampling, so placed my order. When it came, the waiter whisked out a board from nowhere and created a table by slotting it into the side panel. I paid him two hundred baht for the one hundred and fifty baht meal (not exactly cheap but I figured I was on a train) and he went through a little charade of searching his pockets before saying he had no change; he would go and get some, he promised, hoping no doubt I would say don't worry, keep it. And I would have done if the food had not be so cold and tasted so awful. I know I wasn't exactly on the *Orient Express* – though he had actually offered me a wine list too – but though I was hungry I had trouble finishing it, just because it was so unappetising. Even the fruit, so fresh and juicy-looking beneath the cellophane, was tough and tasteless. When I grew up everybody used to make jokes about British Rail food; this was on a par, maybe worse. He took the plates away and I mentioned the change: of course, he replied, he was still trying to get it and hadn't forgotten.

The waiter went by several times, scurrying past, intent on not catching my eye, looking like he was concentrating on something important. I heard banging and much commotion begin as the train steward came round and began making up the beds, ingeniously converting the seats into an upper and lower bunk with nothing more than a couple of boards and some curtains; a pillow and blanket were also provided. I'd been allocated the lower bunk, and I thought the upper bunk would remain empty until later when the train stopped and more people got on. Weird, I thought the waiter had said we wouldn't be stopping. I'd taken the precaution of locking my bag to the luggage frame as I didn't want to spend the night behind the curtain constantly checking to see if it was still there. It was actually surprisingly comfortable laid stretched out, looking out of the window, admittedly only into blackness. Pretty much everyone had their curtains closed, some evidently with couples chattering quietly behind. I closed in too, though it was still relatively early, and lay back and relaxed. Having had so little sleep until now, this was my chance to catch up and overcome the time difference.

From behind the curtain I hadn't seen the guy who'd got into the bunk above. I know he had a lot of luggage for I'd heard him tying it all to his bunk frame. What amazed me the most, however, was the speed and ease with which he fell asleep. Not for me: I just lay there staring out of the window into the dimness that seemed slightly less dark now all the lights on the train were out. I was surprisingly cold too, and in the darkness got through all the bag locks and searched through to find some extra clothes. It's amazing how much time can be spent arranging the contents of the rucksack only for it all be to completely jumbled up so quickly with one good rummage. I settled back down to staring out of the window, huddled in close under the blanket, not expecting to feel so cold considering I was in a tropical country. The train clattered on, making very slow headway, though very loudly as the echo of the clanging metal of wheels on tracks seemed so close below me. It reminded me of the sort of train seen in old war films, chugging along.

Out of the window, in the moonlight, I could make out what looked like large lakes alongside the track. As we continued, and as the rain began to fall, it was clear that these weren't lakes but flooded fields. The night moved slowly on, like the train. I knew the guy above had fallen asleep so quickly because he'd started snoring straightaway; his snoring continued throughout the night, resonating with the clatter from below; added to this was the noise made by his luggage as it bumped into my curtain with each sway of the train. Every bend, it lurched out and rustled back. After a while I looked out to see what it was: he'd bought what appeared to be some kind of bright red decorations, hanging balls made of a type of crepe paper that rustled when they moved around. When the whole snoring/rustling thing got too annoying I reached out and tied his luggage tighter, fixing it in place, stopping the rustle even if not the nasal vibrations.

The train toilet was unusual, being just a round hole about six inches in diameter drilled into a metal plate. There was an area each side of the hole with a raised metal pattern to stop correctly positioned feet from slipping should one feel the need to squat. Not sure I could have dumped even if I'd wanted to, so precariously positioned over the hole which I'm sure when I looked into it I could see the moving tracks beneath. Having a pee was tricky enough, and though there was a bar to hold for stability, it seemed the train swayed even more just as I got going. In an odd sort of way I found it a strange pleasure which I can only put down to the fact that it was so different and primitive that it reminded me of just how far from home I was.

Dawn revealed the dim images from the previous night more clearly. Hedge tops showed where fields began and ended in the expanse of water; occasionally a flooded road could be seen; the rail track too was flooded in places. The train stopped at a couple of stations and from behind the curtain I heard the guy above me get his things together and leave. In the morning when I pulled back the curtain I noticed he'd simply cut the strings that had tied his luggage in place: whether this was due to my zealous tightening or simply his preferred method of removal I guess I'll never know.

The waiter came round with the breakfast menu; after the previous night's experience I passed on the scrambled eggs on offer, but took the opportunity to remind him about the fifty baht change. Again he went through the charade of searching his pockets, promising to return later. We'd been delayed by several hours but I knew Surat Thani couldn't be too far away; I also knew the train went on down to Trang, so if he could avoid me for a while then he'd get to keep the change; it had already become a game. Maybe it was low of me but when the steward came round to put away the beds, recreating the seats by a swift reversal of the previous night's bed-making process, and the waiter happened to walk by, I pulled him about the change again. The steward saw me ask and spoke quickly to the waiter; after a few exchanges the steward gave him a quick slap around the head with his glove and the waiter reluctantly handed over the change: the scenario suggested that this was a frequent trick of the waiter that the steward at least appeared not to tolerate. But then who knows how much is for show, and exactly where the charade starts and ends?

When we reached Surat Thani it was grey and drizzling with rain. Though we were late for our onward connection, an array of coaches were lined up ready to head off in various directions. My concern about missing the connection was soon put at ease, for in Thailand the transport links are unlike in England; the Thais seem rather to operate in response to events rather than to a timetable. A guy dressed in jeans and a T-shirt pointed to an area to one side, indicating to wait there for Koh Samui. When a battered old coach pulled round it all seemed so vague and disorganised that I felt a little uneasy about putting my bag into the hold, out of sight, and hoped I'd see it again when I got off.

On board I sat next to a Canadian called Jessie, a young guy who'd been in Thailand for about a month. He had a ginger beard which looked about a month old too. He'd been trekking before also booking about a month around the islands with a TAT office in Bangkok, though a different agent to mine. As we drove towards the port we discussed the weather, the grey skies and rain, hoping it would soon blow over. Jessie mentioned that he might try and get in touch with the TAT office in Bangkok when he reached his resort, to try and amend his booking. His guy had told him that it was all flexible when he'd voiced concerns at the commitments for the month. According to one of the several Thais on board who were selling minibus tickets from the port on Koh Samui to resort destinations, apparently the forecast was the same for a few days, then possibly clearing. I asked him how much to Chaweng, he said one hundred baht. I said that Noppi had said it would cost about fifty baht; the seller said that that would be on the public bus which stopped all the way along the route, whereas the minibus went straight to the resort, much quicker. I thought about it for a while, wondering if I was being ripped off, and he moved on.

As we drove towards the port I could tell from conversations around me that Koh Samui had been hit by bad weather, which I guessed one of the Thais must have found out by phone. When he passed by again I said I'd buy a ticket after all. He got out a map, looked concerned, and pointed to several areas on the island where the roads were flooded and impassable. A feeling of dread filled me at the thought of landing on the island only to be stranded in the floods, all for quite an expensive price. He said that a minibus could reach my resort but it would have to go the long way round instead, so would cost one hundred and fifty baht. Was he pulling a fast one? I couldn't help but wonder. I paid the price anyway before it went up any further, and before he could find out that the long way was blocked too; by then I was feeling so tired I thought it was only an extra pound after all.

Jessie began to get dripped on when the rain got heavier and the coach roof leaked. He started talking about going straight to the airport and flying directly back to Bangkok to get a full refund. I had my doubts about how successful he would be but must confess that I thought it might be a good idea, kind of start again and go somewhere really cheap and hot. I thought about little Koh Chang with its candlelit nights and hammocks; but then, maybe the weather would improve and all would be ok.

We reached the port to see a large ferry just leaving. I say 'port', it was really just a very large slipway that happened to have a shop on one side and a toilet building on the other. Outside the shop was a seating area with a few tables under the cover of a bamboo roof; inside it sold drinks, crisps, biscuits, and anything that you might find in a packet, nothing fresh. The packets were obviously all covered with Thai writing; sometimes it was possible to tell what it was from the picture, sometimes not. I bought some plain crisps and a drink, feeling the need for something, combined with that weird physical state of having missed that morning cup of tea, after a night of no sleep; possibly not the best foundation for a pending boat trip.

Like on the train, the port toilets were quite an eye-opener; at first sight it looked like a row of shower cubicles, or like those changing cubicles that were once found in public swimming baths, where the door has a large gap beneath it and the floor, and finishes below head height. I went into one and was a bit surprised to see nothing in there; no curved porcelain furniture on which to sit, hence no seat, and no toilet roll holder nor roll: just a hole in the middle of the floor between two evident foot position points. A strange, small bendy chrome pipe with a trigger on the end hung from the back wall, presumably for washing down the pan afterwards, squirting away leftovers. I took a pee and left, not feeling a need for anything more; in fact I hadn't felt much of a need since the plane journey but now was not the time, and the set-up didn't encourage it. People milled around aimlessly for a couple of hours as the sky turned a strange brighter grey; it is a different sort of grey to an English sky, somehow more golden, and certainly warm at least. I thought of the freezing cold back home, glad anyway to be here rather than there.

The coach drove onto the ferry when it arrived, taking our bags with it, and we all boarded. Jessie and I found some seats on the top deck until we got moving and the spray combined with the drizzle made it too wet. The side walkways provided more cover but still gave a view of the sea and the horizon, giving the chance to see the islands appear in the distance as we approached. I was surprised at just how dark and murky the sea appeared to be; no clear blue turquoise like the pictures I'd seen had suggested. Dark brown coconuts, sodden, bobbed about in the water, appearing as a swimmer's head, along with driftwood and the odd plastic bottle. The water looked more suited to sharks than tropical fish, and did not appear inviting at all.

By now I was feeling so tired that it was difficult finishing sentences, though trying helped me stay awake: now was not the time to be falling asleep, I thought. We passed many small islands, dark silhouettes that appeared, of strange shapes jutting upwards, some with remote-looking beaches accessible it seemed only by boat, not that any boats appeared to have landed on them. On we went until eventually we headed directly towards a rather larger-looking island that appeared as a few mountains bunched together and stuck in the sea. On a warmer, sunny day I'm sure the arrival into the port of Nathon would have been much more scenic, and if I'd been less tired I may have appreciated it more. As it was, the water was just as murky as off the coast of the mainland, perhaps a little more of a golden tinge from the sand; and there was floating debris everywhere, not just coconuts but trees, bits of timber, and loads of floating rubbish, like a mass of weed.

It was a long walk along the pier to the mainland, to the area where we were supposed to wait for the coach that was due to drive off with our bags and unload. I kept my eye out for it, hoping that it would actually drive off the boat (I had visions of the boat pulling in its ropes and leaving, coach and bag never to be see again) and that it would stop when it did (and not disappear into the mountains, bags and all). The area was full of vehicles, some waiting to collect people, some waiting to board the boat and leave. It was an odd mix of new 4x4 type people carriers and Thai songthaews: these are the local buses which are basically made by welding a frame onto the back of an old pickup truck that has two benches for seats along each side, and covering it with a tarpaulin. Nearly always they are a burgundy colour with roof panels decorated with red, yellow, and blue floral-type patterns. A sun-strip in the windscreen names the destinations, many of them simply circling the island in one direction or another.

The coach eventually drove down to offload, though not before we'd all walked back up the pier towards the boat only to be turned around again by the ticket seller, perhaps as a form of entertainment for the Thais. Jessie went on his way and I found my minibus. The driver threw my bag on the roof and I got in, hoping the small roof bars would be sufficient to keep the bags from falling off, even if they weren't kept dry. When the bus was full, we drove on, through Nathon and away from the port.

CHAPTER 5
In Chaweng on the Cabana Trail

We were heading anti-clockwise around the island, the coast to our right and jungle to our left. Forests of coconut and palm trees led up into the mountains, and aside from the flooded roads, the number of fallen trees showed just how bad the weather had been, some falling into each other so propping one another up, like a few matchsticks would if you dropped enough of them. Puddles of varying depth showed how uneven the surface of the road was; water ran through channels that had been cut by rivers evidently flowing where normally the ground is dry. We all looked on, quite silently, occasionally somebody muttering a gasp or a comment at something particularly damaged, flooded. It was all I could do to stay awake; occasionally a strange wave would wash through my brain, sending me swimming through a dreamlike world of unfamiliar images, sounds distant in the background, fading, before I'd jolt myself awake again and catch some of the conversation going on in the front. The guy sat next to the driver had been here before and was explaining to someone just how easy it was to get a visa extension here on the island. I listened in, not that I was thinking about still being here in sixty days' time, but thought maybe I'd pick up something useful.

We got to the first drop-off, a resort called Amy's, and three guys got out, not looking too happy; the sea was higher than the steps on several of the huts, and even where it wasn't there were people trying to sweep the water out from inside. A Thai lady came out waving her arms as if the place was closed. The driver had a conversation with her, and she pointed up the beach; apparently there was another resort called Amy's the next bay along. This seemed weird, that there would be two different places with the same name so close to each other, and I thought there must be confusion like this nearly every day. Yet they hadn't changed the names? The three guys threw their bags back up and got on again, looking glad it had been the wrong place.

When everyone except the guy in the front and myself were left I realised that the minibus was probably slower than the bus, if I'd known exactly where I was supposed to get off. At least this way I'd get dropped off without having to find the place and getting lost. We turned off into what I found out later was Lamai Beach and headed down the street which was lined with accommodation, rooms to let, travel agents, restaurants, and bars: lots of bars. The driver pointed to the road up ahead, indicating that it was flooded as he pulled to a stop outside one of the bars. Three bar girls looked out, laughing loudly, and the guy in the front told the driver that this would do him as he grabbed his bag and headed into the bar with the girls who seemed more than pleased to see him, seemingly free of all worry, giggling at his approach.

The driver turned to me and pointed to the flooded road, like he couldn't get through it. I saw images of me wading through the river with my bags, soaked to the waist before embarking on the miles onward to Chaweng in a not very funny game of find the resort in the rain, tired; it was too much, so I just got out my ticket, pointing to it as I said, 'Go round, go round,' trying not to sound too agitated but really slightly panicking. I'd read somewhere in the paperwork that failure to turn up on the first night could jeopardise the entire booking; what I didn't need was to get so close and miss it now.

By no surprise it was an easy diversion for the minibus; even the scooters which buzzed around everywhere made it through; and they were everywhere, riders weaving in and out, some wearing brightly coloured ponchos, some just shorts, T-shirts, and flip-flops, accepting the fact that they would get wet; hardly any of them wore a crash helmet. One young Thai girl had been right beside us since Lamai. She was a pretty girl, wearing tight jeans that most western girls would love to fit into, a small T-shirt, and flip-flops, with long dark hair under a baseball cap. She tooted every time she went by, sometimes scooting up the inside, sometimes going round, losing ground when the road straightened and the minibus could accelerate, but coming back past whenever the traffic slowed at all, always tooting. I wondered if she was having a bit of a run-in with the driver, for in England people generally toot before giving some kind of insulting hand gesture or comment; not so on Koh Samui, where everyone toots as they overtake simply as an indication of what they're doing.

We drove into the mountains as part of the detour and I saw some of the most spectacular rocks and waterfalls amongst the trees. There were two enormous boulders sat beside the roadside on a slope which gave the impression they could roll forward any moment. The growth around them showed at least that they hadn't rolled for a while so were probably safely settled, but who can tell when something like that is going to move next? The roads on the diversion were wet and flooded too, and it was fortunate that the rain falling on the sinking island was light; even still, water flowed from the mountains across the roads like rivers in places that clearly it normally did not.

Back on the main road all activity seemed centred around either getting through flooded roads or clearing up flood damage. Everywhere were sandbags, boards, furniture stacked up at a height that was hoped to be above and beyond possible water levels, people sweeping mud and water out of shops; the evidence of a much worse flooding that had now receded somewhat was shocking. The minibus pulled into a gravel car-park indicating we had reached the resort. 'Chaweng Cabana?' I checked.

He pointed to a sign above. 'Chaweng Cabana,' he repeated back to me. I didn't want to be grumpy at the fact he'd made out the diversion that actually wasn't that difficult had been blocked, and really wanted to jump out all enthusiastic like the guy before in Lamai, like I'd been here before and knew exactly what I was doing, and whatever I didn't know was all just part of the fun of the ride. To tell the truth though, I was just glad to have got there and felt like sleeping for a few days.

I went up to the reception area, a small thatched shelter open on three sides with a desk and private area behind, inadvertently stepping mud through on the way. Clearly the mud was a problem here for they had laid down towels on the floor, though I couldn't see that they would have made much of a doormat to wipe the mud off your shoes. The guy said hello and waved away my apology at soiling the floor as if it didn't matter. He took my passport and TAT booking voucher before producing a small envelope from a drawer. In it were eleven small yellow coupons which, he explained, would be my breakfast vouchers. Each coupon had my room number and the applicable date neatly written on. He took a two thousand baht deposit and gave me my room key, explaining where I'd find the restaurant, pool, and beach etc. It didn't go in – and he must have seen my zombie-like state – so when I asked him where to go for breakfast he simply smiled and said come back in the morning and someone will show you. Just to make polite conversation, when he said that he had always lived in Koh Samui I asked him if he knew Noppi; yes, he confirmed, he knew Noppi, his brother and sister both worked at the resort. He called over a porter who hoisted my bag up onto his shoulder and led on. I would have been quite happy to have carried it up myself but he was most insistent. I tiptoed back over the muddy footprints I'd left and followed him up to the room.

He unlocked the door, stepped out of his flip-flops, and we went in. I was starting to see why the booking had cost so much. The building was rendered a sandy colour, and the marble-type stone stairs made it seem almost Roman in appearance, like a villa. He drew open the curtains and opened the large patio door that led out onto the balcony; there was even a fridge/mini bar in the room, he pointed out, waiting patiently. I remembered and tipped him, relieved to feel I was somewhere I could safely relax again.

Alone, I had chance to reflect: the images of flooding seemed overwhelming as I realised that there'd be little chance of swinging in a hammock in the sun here. The room was luxurious admittedly, but along with the weather it was not what I'd hoped for. I suppose it was a lot of mixed emotions being stirred up; feeling rather powerless from my realisation on the minibus that I was dependent on a chauffeur to find the place that I'd got someone else to book, somewhere I would not have even chosen, yet feeling relieved that though I'd spent more than I'd intended, I hadn't actually been completely stung. For the first time in a while I thought about home and realised that I probably wouldn't see my gran again; I'd rushed out here to the rain instead, which made it feel a bit worse. Then there was Amanda who should have been here too; all of it was not as planned and I couldn't help but feel quite low, depressed, and fell asleep.

I slept all through until the morning and woke up feeling much better to the sound of running water, like a hose pipe. Stepping out onto the balcony I could see the rain pouring down, not ordinary rain but real monsoon rain, like a sheet of water falling continually, as if there's hardly any space even for air. I saw many Thai girls scurrying around under umbrellas letting out excited shrieks as they ran back and forth. I headed down to find breakfast, strangely pleased to get to use the poncho so soon, even if a little self-conscious about wearing it. I passed by the room where the girls – who turned out to be the chamber maids – had gathered. As I passed they all called out, 'Sawa di ka,' in their chirpy songlike manner. My Thai was very limited so I simply said it back to them, trying to copy the accent, at which they all roared with hysterical laughter, which I took to seem friendly at least. Years ago I worked on a building site and someone told me beforehand that if they all take the piss then, strangely enough, it's because they think you're ok; if they don't like you, they'll just ignore you. I took it to be a similar thing and smiled as I walked on by, hidden partly by the poncho.

I found the restaurant situated right on the beachfront, more by chance than anything simply by exploring the maze of small pathways between the trees and various other huts. A waitress in a beautifully coloured Thai dress greeted me, showing me to a table. Breakfast was a buffet again, fried 'English' along with an array of fruits, juices, and cereals. After a couple of days I began to get chatting to the waitress, who taught me a few Thai phrases, and that most importantly, men and women speak differently, and I was getting it wrong. No surprise at the roars of laughter from the Thai women then; though there's no simple cultural equivalent, at home

I suppose it would be something like a man wearing women's pants.

When it rained they pulled down plastic flaps and tied them in place to protect diners from the weather; a terrace with outside tables remained unused, chairs tilted inwards to drain off the water as it fell. A small cat jumped up on the table and slowly edged towards my fried bacon, making me a little uneasy; it looked like a kitten but may have just been a small ginger Thai cat, and it was clearly used to defending itself from being shooed away, swatting back with its paw. I'd heard the scare stories about rabies and though I'd been (probably excessively) worried enough to have had the necessary jabs, I didn't fancy rushing off for further treatment right now. One of the waitresses saw our battle and came over and clapped him away. I could see him eyeing me from the cover of nearby shrubs, as if to let me know that left to fight it out alone he would have won.

Back at the room I sat out on the balcony and watched the rain. Just a low wall about waist height separated mine from next door's; an Aussie guy came out and we chatted for a while, surprised at how difficult it was for me to understand his Aussie drawl, realising that not everyone there speaks like they do on Neighbours. Whilst I'd been struggling to reach the resort, battling through as if on a desperate mission hindered such that it seemed only vital journeys should have been undertaken, he'd hired a motorbike to go exploring the island's flooded roads and waterfalls. He told me about how he'd attempted the big mountain but had turned back when the bike began to slide out from beneath him. He showed me a wound where he'd fallen off, a round patch where the skin had been scraped off sliding along the road, proudly referring to it as his 'Samui tattoo'. He was only staying in Thailand for a week on his way over to Europe, and told me about his night out at the Green Mango. I should go, just jump on a motorbike taxi and ask for the night-life, he advised. I was going to be watching what I spent so politely said maybe, and took the chance to find out about the likelihood of getting work in Australia without a permit. He said he knew it was pretty strict now but most likely would find something in Sydney no worries; just go anyway and see what happens. I'm sure too that this is what he would have done himself, but since he'd just told me how he'd slept with a sixteen-year-old girl from England on holiday with her parents after telling her he was eighteen and not twenty-eight, I could see his approach to life was different to mine.

The first morning, after breakfast, the phone in the room rang, surprising me. It was the guy from reception telling me that my hired vehicle was outside waiting for me. I tried to explain that I didn't want it, eventually deciding that it would be best to have this conversation face to face to ease communications. He pointed to the vehicle, offering me the keys. I tried to explain that I'd not really wanted it to start with, and that there was no way I would risk driving it around the flooded island, especially being unable to see properly. I must admit that I kind of hoped if I didn't use it then I might get a refund somehow, and left it there, parked in front of another almost identical vehicle. Each time I walked out of the resort that day I saw it parked there; each time I pretended it was nothing to do with me.

HOW TO WIPE YOUR ARSE IN THAILAND

I spent the first few days exploring the area. A few long walks along the beach revealed the extent of the damage: beach huts had been lifted off the ground and dumped, smashed up, and abandoned to the waves that still pounded; entire coconut and palm trees lay washed up like large, dark skeletons, with no sign of green life, just soaked bare boughs. Coconuts, also dark and sodden, lay on the beach amongst plastic bottles, disposable lighters, and all sorts of other rubbish and debris. As much again washed backwards and forwards in the crashing waves that swept right to where the beach turned to trees. The hotel itself was undergoing a major maintenance operation; all the paths that before had been merely bricks laid on sand, now washed away, were being replaced with concrete walkways. For the duration of the stay Thai builders mixed their concrete, pushed their wheelbarrows and laid their paths, also rebuilding the smashed steps that led down to the beach as if stepping into a Roman spa. I noticed even builders wore flip-flops in Thailand, and when the day was over, about thirty of them piled into the back of an open truck to get home.

The street was busy, though apparently this was the quiet end of Chaweng. Motorbike taxi drivers with numbered vests hawked the streets, asking me if I wanted a lift every time I stepped out. I always politely declined but they always made a point of asking. Occasionally they would almost encourage going somewhere I hadn't planned; sometimes they'd ask if I didn't want a lift anywhere, where was I going? I think they enjoyed just asking, knowing I'd say no, like it was some kind of joke amongst themselves. But truthfully I never felt intimidated or threatened, even at night. The suit sellers are similar, always asking, hoping to generate interest. Usually the conversation began with them asking where I was from before quickly moving on to football. It seems they are either all football crazy or think that we westerners are; since I don't follow it, they were always quite surprised. A guy from Burma working outside of a silk tailor's told me a few stories about why he had left his own country and preferred to live illegally in near poverty in Thailand.

It is easy to forget whilst in England, or be unaware of, just how harsh life can be simply as a result of circumstances for some around the world. He went on to describe the severity of the recent flooding which had damaged so many of the shops and their goods: no wonder, since the water had been running four foot deep through the middle of the main street. Some of the stores were on a raised level, and these had been damaged less, though none had escaped. Those where the kerb was more or less at street level had been washed right out, and left with the muddy slurry that the water dumps. Sewage had flooded out of the drains and had ran through the streets with the water. It smelt bad for weeks afterwards and things were still very much in the immediate aftermath when I'd arrived. Signs outside every shop reminded farang to remove shoes before entering; in Thailand the locals pretty much always remove their outside footwear when going inside. I realised that those towels on the floor of the resort reception when I'd arrived were not for wiping muddy shoes on after all, but were to stop the rain from washing in the mud so your bare feet didn't get dirty when walking through.

A travel agent over the road sold not only tours, travel tickets, and accommodation, but you could use the internet, make an international phone call, change traveller's cheques, buy postcards and stamps (they even acted as a post box), and get your laundry done too. They charged 30 baht a kilo for washing; when I got my bag back the first time there were small woollen threads still left in each item, presumably from where they were threaded onto a line to dry. For years after returning, I had clothes with a Thai laundry thread still in them, pink, orange, or purple strands of wool – a small but pleasant reminder.

I spent a bit of time just sat on the balcony, outside in the air but sheltered as I watched the rain fall into the tropical trees, listening to vans drive slowly by advertising Muay Thai over loud speakers, reading the books I'd brought in a couple of days. I took a screw out of the useless Bangkok sunglasses and was able to repair my own prescriptions. I kind of wished I'd waited until landing before opening the glue and fixing them, for they were completely smeared by dried super-glue, as were my normal glasses. However, improvisation is key, and I found that the mosquito deet (a petroleum-based liquid repellent) worked fairly well as a solvent, removing nearly all of it from the sunglasses. With the new screw tightened in they were fine. The spectacles weren't as easy, the glue having settled into a puddle in one of the lenses before solidifying; though I soaked the lens many times with the deet I could never get them clear enough to see through. Never mind, hopefully most of the time it would be sunny soon.

Whenever the rain stopped beautiful butterflies

appeared. At first I thought they were birds because they were so big; amazing colours, yellows and blues, and shapes to marvel with their finely cut wings with jagged edges. They flew around in the tropical trees of the garden above the builders repairing the paths, along with the chirping birds who stayed just out of arm's reach but were otherwise quite unafraid, scurrying around on their tiny legs with the big tail low down, swinging round widely like a rudder whenever they turned. Pretty birds that regularly scoured the restaurant floor for food.

I met a British couple who were staying downstairs, on their way back to Bangkok to change their flight dates. I confessed that I had spent more money than I'd hoped, perhaps had been ripped off, and that Thailand was more expensive than I had expected; they said the same, and admitted they were changing flight dates because of this fact. They had booked through TAT too. They gave me the address of the Qantas office in Bangkok in case I needed it too at a later date.

Two Scottish girls, Rebecca and Claire, shared the room to the left of me; though a stairwell separated the balconies we could easily chat over the gap. They too were heading on to Australia after Thailand. Their plan was travel all around the coast, perhaps visiting Uluru and Kakadoo as well. This they planned to do in just a couple of months. I thought my route plan had been a bit optimistic but they were hoping to travel more than twice the distance in the same time. They'd even obtained a work permit to help with funds, though I couldn't see how they'd have time to stop with that itinerary. I showed them the distances in the Australia guide book that had added to the weight of my bag. They'd also spent a lot more funds in Thailand than they had thought they would; they'd also booked through TAT, in Bangkok. I asked out of interest if it was Noppi, more of a joke to myself than anything. They confirmed that yes, it was Noppi they had booked through, and that it had been their 4x4 vehicle parked outside with 'mine' that day. They'd been brave enough to take it out for an hour or so, but had only really driven around the main island road in a big circle. I asked them if they'd wanted it and they confessed that it had been Noppi's idea. In fact, they confirmed, it was one of Noppi's sideline businesses on the island. Aah, the plot thickens, so to speak. I said it was a bit underhand, especially when people hadn't even asked for it but they'd thought it was only another thousand baht after all: I kept quiet but felt slightly irked at this amount. Noppi had clearly charmed them, and they warmly defended him, admitting they'd even given him a thousand baht tip on top after he had claimed he made nothing from the booking itself, an assertion I found really quite doubtful.

After a few more days of rain they called over one day and invited me out with them that evening, when they'd planned to meet up with a couple of Irish girls from downstairs. Being so wet outside, nearly everyone was staying indoors so meeting people was limited. We all met up in a bar down the road with Laura and Susan, two girls from Dublin. They'd booked through TAT also but were happy to treat the first month of a six-month round-the-world trip as a holiday, knowing they'd have to live on much less as their trip went on. We all got drunk on Chang beer, drinking so much that every so often the waitress would get out a box of promotional items; I collected a key ring and a large beer bar towel which I found in the morning to remind me. Chang beer is one of those Thai beers where the alcohol content can be so variable that they don't bother putting the amount on the label. I had a bad hangover the next day and decided not to drink again. The blue beer towel that advertised both the beer and Everton Football Club had its uses though, as I found out later.

Everywhere was wet and things weren't drying out properly. I saw some mould growing on my leather wallet that was in my bag, just from the damp atmosphere. More worrying was a strange rash that had appeared on my fingers, mostly on the skin in between where the fingers rubbed together. It was like patches of tiny blisters and I wondered what sort of tropical disease it might be. After eating a worried breakfast, hiding my hands in case anyone noticed and announced I needed to be quarantined, I went to the chemist down the road to find out: these shops seem to be run either by doctors or by people who have some medical knowledge; they were always pleased at least to have a look at something before going to see a proper doctor. I showed her the rash. She asked, did it hurt or itch? It was a bit itchy but not too bad; she confirmed it was most likely an allergy and offered me some anti-histamines or some cream. I took the cream, not really seeing how eating pills could cure a rash on the finger; it seemed to make the skin dry and peel off. The rash came and went after that whenever it felt like it; it wasn't a major problem.

During the night on the beer we'd all agreed to go

over to Koh Pha Ngan for the Half Moon Party. Rebecca and Claire were heading off to the west coast and wouldn't be around for the infamous Full Moon Party. Though Laura and Susan, like me, would be staying on Koh Pha Ngan then anyway, we'd agreed to all go over together. This was partly inspired by a successful drunken mission by Susan to obtain a large packet of slimming pills from the chemist over the road, similar to amphetamines. It was amusing watching her as we sat in the bar: apparently the chemist had been totally paranoid and unhelpful until the shop was empty of all other customers; then she quickly and surreptitiously passed her the pills she'd found from a drawer under the counter, urgently whispering, 'Five hundred bahts.'

By the time the day came I didn't feel too keen, and neither did Laura and Susan. However, Rebecca was insistent and eventually we all agreed. There was a travel agent next door where, she said, we could book the transport. She came out pleased, saying she'd managed to barter him down to just three hundred baht each, which included a taxi to and from the hotel, and the return boat trip. That evening our booked taxi turned out to be a ticket for the local bus which happened to pass by right outside, stopping at every possible stop on the way to cram as many people on board as was possible, even to the point of turning back at one point to collect even more. There must have been about twenty people all crammed into the back, some simply stood on the tailgate hanging on the bars.

I always imagined tropical seas to be tranquil and warm; admittedly the weather had been bad, but the sea was real choppy and a strong breeze kept things cool. As the ferry chugged out into the open seas it rolled backwards and forwards, pounding into waves as it moved sending spray right over us. Though Koh Pha Ngan is clearly visible from Koh Samui, it took longer than I thought to reach, and by the time we did I felt a bit sick and glad to get off. I was surprised at just how few people seemed to be heading over for the party but thought not much more about it as we walked through the streets towards Hat Rin. There was an altogether different atmosphere here than in Koh Samui, far fewer vehicles, hardly a motorbike taxi in sight, and no-one trying to get you into a particular bar or restaurant: laid back, as if the attitude was more, 'If you feel like it you're welcome,' rather than, 'Come in, come in, you must come in!'

After some food and a few bars, down at the beach the party looked as if it was just starting, and was mostly centred in and around one of the bars pumping out loud techno music, The Cactus Club. This was handy for just up the road, only minutes beforehand, we'd been given vouchers for a free drink. Small paraffin lanterns lined part of the beach outside the bar; a few twirlers spun fire sticks as people gathered around, dancing and drinking their 'buckets' of spirits through straws. I could see that if the entire beach had been full of such activity then it would have been quite an experience; as it was, it turned out that the bad weather had wrecked most of the bars, the sea was dangerously rough, and the party had been cancelled. When we tried to get our free drinks with the vouchers the barman just about managed to explain through the deafening music that we were too late and had missed the promotion hour.

I bought a drink anyway, a vodka and Red Bull, served in what is best described as a child's sandcastle bucket; it was extremely strong though both the alcohol and the mixer were of dubious quality, the whole thing more like a strange narcotic syrup than a drink. We were stuck there then until the morning: I hoped it didn't rain, and that the bar would at least stay open all night, which it did.

Sunrise came like a welcome relief. It was the first sunny morning since leaving Bangkok and everyone hoped that this was the start of the good weather. A walk along the beach showed the damage done; most bars and resorts were closed up, some smashed up from the storms with timbers hanging precariously, balconies half collapsed into the sand, foundations washed bare of stable ground. Bottles from the night before littered the beach area outside of the bar, along with a few crashed out bodies. Eventually the music stopped and a guy from the bar went upstairs and started spraying the crowd with a water pistol. I thought it was going to get out of hand when a farang threw a few handfuls of sand back up at him and tempers began to fray; quickly it all calmed down, which I thought was fortunate because the Thais had started to gather. The sand thrower was from London, off his head on ya baa, I think, and to be fair, he apologised, not intending to upset anyone. I kind of wanted to steer clear of him after the sand incident, hoping that people didn't think we were affiliated in any way, but he saw four girls and decided to hang around until our boat came. It would have been ok except he talked non-stop nonsense, I mean absolutely made no sense, and I was too tired to bother listening. He was staying on Koh Pha Ngan so when he boarded the boat as well – simply by waving a screwed up piece of paper at the boat man – I thought he'd never leave, and had visions of him constantly knocking my door for a crazy chat, stood there every time I opened it, waiting, each time continuing the nonsense where he'd left off. I guess if I'd been in a better mood and not been so tired I could have seen the funny side a bit more.

When we landed back on Koh Samui, there was no vehicle waiting to collect us. All those that turned up – as many do whenever a boat lands, just to tout for business – looked at our tickets and shook their heads. It turned out that if we waited by the road then a bus would come by and may have accepted them; the six of us each paid a driver fifty baht on top of the ticket instead. Rebecca was furious with the travel agent and suggested we all went in there and demanded our money back. Nobody said anything, most likely thinking the same as me: that there was no point in getting worked up over fifty baht, and that the 'principle', if there even was one, did not matter, was not worth an argument. We drove back through the middle of the island and I noticed that the roads had been smashed up everywhere, some partly collapsed, some with big cracks and ravines. It was a beautiful drive, as the sun shone through the palm and coconut trees, as if life was again rising up after the storm, lifted by the light. Here and there were huts and small dwellings, simple and somewhat isolated yet far from the busy hustle of the beach resorts, shops, bars, and money exchanges. When we reached the resort everyone just wandered off to bed and the whole ticket thing was forgotten. That was the last I saw of Rebecca and Claire, who left early the following day.

HOW TO WIPE YOUR ARSE IN THAILAND

The good weather was short-lived and the rain returned. I read both of my books again, even some of the Australian guide, occasionally wondering if it might have been better to have gone there first. Susan loaned me a book about a guy set up for murder who spent seven years in a Thai jail (Colin Martin's *Welcome to Hell*); I read it in a couple of days and felt extremely paranoid afterwards, worried at the level of corruption everywhere. There's corruption in England, no doubt, but it just seems that in countries where money is scarce, corruption tends to extend throughout more easily. I chatted a few times with the pool cleaner whose name was Saaw. He'd lived on the mainland as a monk for five years before coming to Koh Samui for work. Most young Thai men live as a Buddhist monk for a while in their lives, as part of their culture. His English was not very good but he always wanted to practice it by speaking with the guests. When I asked him why it was so important for him to learn it, he told me that in order to become a bell-boy you had to be able to talk to the guests when they arrived; bell-boys got tips, ten or sometimes twenty baht, whereas pool cleaners got no tips. To westerners the amounts are tiny: to poor people in countries such as Thailand, where poor really does mean poor, the amounts are significant. No surprise then that corruption is tempting for them, after all they see such wealth coming into their country yet have so little opportunity to earn the same. It's a strange twist though that we westerners pay so much to reach that which life provides for free, whilst those that live there desire the very means we need to get there.

Which makes it difficult as a farang to really trust anyone out there. Maybe that is the point of going, to learn to rely only on your own thoughts and feelings, the gut instinct, instead of what someone else says you should think, how you should interpret things, what you should do. Listen to advice, consider all things yet rush into nothing, perhaps.

I certainly took Daryl's advice though about marijuana. I'd heard how a dealer sells you some in view of a hidden policeman who appears as soon as the deal is done, accepting payment of a fine in what is really nothing more than a bribe, secretly returning the gear to the dealer who has made total profit on a sale for nothing. The only loser is the buyer. The first time I walked up the beach I was approached by about six or seven different sellers at different points. Each walked up carrying a catalogue of tattoo designs; when I looked over they'd show a bag of weed hidden between the pages, always towards the sea so that it was out of sight of any spying eyes. As much as I would have liked a smoke, and a good look too, out of interest, I always waved them away, making a point in broad daylight that I did not want to buy any marijuana on the beach. Maybe they were ok, maybe they weren't: I was in no mood for taking a chance, and thought what a pity it was that throughout the world such a big deal is made of a plant that grows. As Bill Hicks put it, to make marijuana, a naturally occurring plant, illegal... is like saying that God got it wrong.

On the way back, not far from the resort, another seller approached me. By now I was used to them, and preferring to sound friendly at least when I declined, I said to him that I was ok. 'You ok?' he asked, which I confirmed, waving and walking on. This may seem paranoid but that night I went for a walk back along the beach towards some restaurants I'd seen earlier. It was quite a walk, but as always, at night the sea would retreat, revealing a wide strip of fine sand. It was the same every night, as if the tide always went out the same time each night instead of being subject to the lunar month; oddly enough, each night the tide took the clouds away with it too, revealing a beautiful starry sky. Each night I hoped it was the last of the rain, and that it was the beginning of clear blue skies that would continue throughout the days.

The restaurant was right on the beach now that there was more sand, an area of reclined sunbeds with candlelit tables. Very young Thai children attempted to sell farang garlands of beautiful pink and white orchids; considering how pretty these looked I saw very few people buy them, partly I think because I found out later that parents send these children out as sellers and snatch the money from them immediately if they make a sale. It is one of the ways that people make a living out there which seems alien to us farang.

I sat there smoking roll-ups while I ate and drank, and noticed three Thai policeman hanging around. One walked close by, eyeing my tobacco, probably smelling the rising smoke. When I left the restaurant, they left too, and I wondered if perhaps somehow word had got round after my chat with the Burmese guy in the street. Maybe they were just bored, the tourism having been hit hard by the weather so that they probably didn't have much to do.

Back near the resort I saw a figure flick a cigarette into the sand; he said hello and I returned the greeting. As I walked by I saw that it was a policeman and, inadvertently walked straight past the resort, missing it in the dark. I doubled back when I realised I'd gone too far, and noticed that the policeman must have been stood right by the steps of my resort. Was that weird? I walked through the winding path that led through the trees, avoiding the areas recently concreted by the builders, and went up to my room. I went straight in and opened the curtains to see a silhouette run across my balcony, over to next door and out of sight. I unlocked the door and looked out but all was quiet. Questions fired in my mind: was that the policeman from the beach? Had they been watching me down at the restaurant? Had one of them followed me along the beach? Had he been waiting outside, perhaps waiting for me to skin up? Had that beach seller thought that, 'I'm ok,' meant, 'I'm ok, I've already scored, I've got some marijuana'? Ok, paranoid maybe, but who knows?

The evening after Koh Pha Ngan I began to feel ill. I wondered if it was something to do with the sanitation method of the bar we were sat outside. The chairs had kept sinking in the sand, and the morning had revealed that this had been due to the flow coming from the toilets, too much for the beach to absorb; in essence we may have been sat around a pool of sandy piss. Either that or it was dengue fever. The illness came on quick once it began. It was like the first few stages of flu in a matter of hours, sore throat, aching, freezing cold (though over 25°C?) and hard to breathe. I just wrapped up in bed and tried to sleep. Sometime in the night I woke up, completely soaked in sweat, feverish and delirious. I couldn't tell where I was, as if the familiarity acquired in the previous week or so was forgotten, and the room seemed strange, unknown, nothing recognised. It was a bad night and in the morning I felt battered, like the island after the storm.

I was still ill when I checked out a couple of days later. I handed back the keys and the reception guy phoned through to someone (presumably one of the maids) to check the room. The all-clear came back – I evidently hadn't stolen anything – and he said cheerio. I reminded him of the two thousand baht deposit, having already wondered if there would be any problem in getting this back. He gave a surprised look, tapped his forehead in a display of having forgotten, and retrieved the deposit from a cash box behind the counter: had he forgotten or had he hoped I'd forgotten, who can tell? I know I must have looked and seemed half asleep, still being foggy from the illness and the few days confined to the bed; appearing in such a state, an opportunist may have thought it worth a try, but as I say, who can tell if this was the case?

Per the itinerary I was off to Koh Pha Ngan, somewhere on the north-east coast. By what I guessed now was more than coincidence, I was heading for a place called Pha Ngan Cabana. It was an early start and the night before I'd hoped I'd be well enough to travel. I managed to grab some breakfast as they were laying things out ready, and one of the waitresses made me some tea, even though they weren't really open. I was still drinking it when the pick-up that Noppi had booked arrived, putting an end to my wondering if it would really turn up, and I left the Chaweng Cabana in the same drizzling rain as when I'd arrived.

CHAPTER 6
Further Round the Cabana Trail

The minibus drove up towards the north coast, loading up with farang at various stops along the way, before doubling back and cutting through the centre of the island. I'd expected to go from the same port as before, but we headed off in a completely different direction. When we arrived, the port was really just an area set back from the road behind a large car-park where vehicles lined up waiting for passengers, fenced off, with a small shelter made of bamboo. There were a few small tables where the ticket sellers/checkers sat, and before which the travellers queued. Apart from the walkway jetty in the water the whole set-up looked as if it could be taken down in minutes, removed without trace. Upon checking the ticket (just another one of Noppi's vouchers for me) the lady gave me a small sticker to wear, like one might find on an apple these days. My yellow sticker showed I was destined for Koh Pha Ngan; those heading on to Koh Tao wore green, and those taking the trip all the way to Bangkok had red: all simplified for the farang who is so easily confused.

The jetty was a wooden pier that looked rickety but seemed to hold up under the weight of the people boarding. I couldn't even see an outside area so found a seat inside. This trip was on the Seatran, a high-speed catamaran; so much newer and quicker than the previous boats, it reflected a change in culture that wealth brings, along with its time pressures and sense of urgency. It reminded me of the bridge in Star Trek, with its open-plan layout and things all high-tech. An announcement came out over the tannoy letting us all know that the weather was fairly bad, the sea was rough out beyond the shelter of the islands, and the journey may be a little rocky. Stewards began handing out small travel sickness pills to everyone; I took one, thinking that it might relieve the flu symptoms if nothing else. I don't normally get travel sick, and my head hadn't ever really landed after the first boat trip from Surat Thani, still swimming each time I closed my eyes; no doubt this would just add to and compound the feeling.

The trip actually wasn't that bad other than a few moments of crashing into a big wave full on so that it smashed right over the top, making everyone go, 'Whooo!' When we arrived at Thong Sala, the rain had pretty much stopped, and it felt warm. I found my next voucher and the relevant vehicle to take me to my accommodation. It may have been the main port of the island but there wasn't too much there, just a couple of streets with a few shops, nothing like Koh Samui, and not even like Hat Rin. We were quickly out of the other side, heading north along the coast, through scenery much more rural than the coastal roads of Koh Samui, winding alongside the mountains, through the trees, the road twisting round tight corners and hairpin bends. Small settlements occasionally appeared, along with the odd sign indicating that something could be found down a track, though everywhere seemed to be quiet. Gradually the minibus emptied as we went on, some at booked venues, others merely getting off if the place look alright; I realised after a while I'd be staying a fair distance away from Hat Rin and the Full Moon Party.

There was still drizzle in the air when we arrived at the Pha Ngan Cabana. It was a pretty-looking place, like a small village with quite a few small huts and bungalows set amongst the gardens. The restaurant was on the beach front, an open-plan rectangular area of tables under a bamboo roof; since my hut wasn't ready, I sat there and waited. It appeared that breakfast had not long finished, and many people were sat around in this communal area whilst the weather was as it was. I noticed a large screen and a board listing the films that would be shown throughout the day. Being away from any main tourist area, the only entertainment and bars were those attached to resorts such as this, though there were several roadside diners nearby for cheap Thai food and drink. There was a swimming pool with a terrace for sunbathing, just as in the flyer that Noppi had attached to the voucher, though somewhat smaller in size than the angle and projection in the photograph suggested.

The hut was a twin room with fan. It seemed that most places didn't cater for the single traveller, and there were two single beds: most budget travellers would have shared the cost, though I suppose that at least it gave me a choice of which side of the hut to sleep on. I'd managed to persuade Noppi that I really didn't want or need an air-conditioned luxury hut with hot water when we'd argued about the cost, hence the fan, which was hardly needed in the rain anyway. There was a western-style toilet and a small shower, though no hot water: the small steps away from western comforts continued, and my first cold shower felt surprisingly refreshing. Outside was a small garden area, a couple of seats and a table behind a low bordering bush. It all seemed ok, and even though a check of direction showed that I wouldn't actually be able to see the sunset from the hut, it was only a minute's walk to the beach where, as the flyer had indicated, the sun would set into the sea in its golden glowing tropical glory; given the right weather, of course.

It's a strange feeling checking in to a new place, having a wander round, exploring, wondering who you may meet. I found a shop over the road for water, though noticed it was more expensive than in Chaweng, most likely due to the cost of transport needed to reach such a remote area. It's easy for us to forget in the west just how much bulk and weight is involved in transporting drinking water; plastic bottles litter the sea and beaches, a major negative consequence of the disposal problems too, just because we cannot stomach even tap water from the local area. It is a constant underscore that we are farang, just visitors playing for a while.

The beach there too had been battered; even much of the sand had been washed away, evident from the now common sight of exposed roots of trees and bungalow foundations. There was a coral reef below the surface of the water, visible by the apparent change in colour of the sea; further along, towards the end of the bay, rocks from the crumbling hillside had fallen to create a headland which the sea was happy to smash. Under the grey sky the rocks looked black, battered by the dark sea with its rough waves pounding, and it seemed a long way from the picture on the flyer.

In the hut opposite me were two girls, one with long dark hair, the other blonde, both very beautiful. At least that was some consolation to staying in out of the rain. Next door I heard a guy strumming a guitar as a few people sat around. He knocked out a couple of Jack Johnson songs: I'd heard of 'Jack Johnson' back home before I came out, but had not heard much; out here though he was everywhere, very popular, presumably music more fitting for the warmer climate. It all seemed quite laid back, though the resort was charged with a buzz and the place was fully booked with farang heading for the Full Moon Party at Hat Rin the following night. Then a commotion began in the hut on the other side to the strumming.

Someone had seen a very large spider and wanted it removed from the hut; apparently it had looked bigger than a bird but I didn't actually get to see it before it was chased off. The panic caused was amusing to say the least, and as much as we want the sun, sea, beaches, and climate it's easy to forget there is unfamiliar natural wildlife that lives alongside such beauty. Some say it ran up a tree and for a while I looked in vain with a few others before conceding that it had got away. Was it really a bird-eating spider? One of the men from the resort who had come to resolve the situation, armed with a broom and a bucket, had just laughed at this, saying it was only a harmless spider, though he was hardly going to say otherwise, even if it had been the case.

I had dinner in the restaurant about six o'clock, just as it was getting dark, when I found out that my lights didn't work. The food was good, and not too expensive; I could have a drink, a meal and some ice cream for under a hundred and fifty baht. Since I was trying to get by on three hundred baht a day, after buying drinking water and cigarettes it didn't leave too much for partying. Having spent so much to date beyond the original budget though, I knew I'd run out of money if I wasn't careful. At least I could spend this month finding cheaper ways of doings things for when Amanda arrived, when we'd be sharing accommodation costs anyway.

Back at my hut I passed a couple of Aussie guys sat over the way on their balcony. I saw their light was on and thought perhaps the electricity must be turned on now. I'd figured maybe it had been turned off until a certain hour to save power, as the book said happens sometimes on the islands; I tried again and it still didn't come on, so went over to ask them how they'd got theirs working. One of them thought I wanted a light for a cigarette, and produced a flame. I explained it was the hut light I meant, and he came over to have a look.

In their bungalow, they had a key fob which slid inside a holder which turned on the power; these bungalows had air-con, so this prevented people from going out for the day and leaving it running, so as to be cool when they got back, unless they wanted to go out and leave their key inside with the door unlocked, when the maid would just turn it off anyway. Eventually, in my hut, it turned out to be a combination of switches that got both the light and the fan going. A third Aussie appeared with an armful of beers, and they invited me over to their balcony. Two were called Matt, and one was called Adam, who was one of the Matts' cousins. They were well friendly and went into great detail about places they'd been to in the north of the country, giving me a list of places to stay in that were cheap but good.

As we were chatting the two girls opposite my hut came out onto their balcony. They called out, and asked if it was ok to come over. Talk about unreal, only in dreams surely do two such girls come out and ask for an invite over. It turned out they were Aussies too, and they had all already met briefly getting off the boat from Surat Thani. Adam had apparently offered to help by loading off one of their bags, which had been so much heavier than he'd expected it had nearly pulled him over into the sea. Their names were Jane and Keren and they'd also been up north, trekking with elephants, and doing maybe too much shopping. They pulled out a bottle of vodka and some orange juice. One of the Matts headed off to the reception to find a CD player, and – to my amazement – was successful. He put on a Neil Young CD which he'd paid one hundred baht for in Thong Sala, and it was a pleasant evening.

I was still flued out a bit, as well as being on the

tight budget, so declined the offers of alcohol. It turned out that all of them were just on their summer holidays – in Australia, their summer time is over Christmas and New Year, of course, and with Thailand being sort of their side of the world, they were 'on holiday', so to speak, and eager to party. All were hoping to get to the Full Moon Party, and quickly the subject turned to drugs. It seemed everyone was happy to partake, given the right opportunity, though we discussed all the potential dangers in Thailand. Apparently back home, for them, things were pretty laid back and marijuana at least was easy to come by. Australia, with its virtually guaranteed good weather, English language, and such friendly people, was seeming more attractive by the moment.

The guys had hired motorbikes for the week; at one hundred and fifty baht per day it was too expensive for me, and I had to explain that I'd been a bit ripped off by Noppi and the TAT place, and had spent so much more than I'd originally budgeted; I was just waiting for the good weather when I could spend most of the time laying on the beach, spending nothing. As the conversation developed, it seemed that they too had all booked through TAT and had blown their budgets. Being more of a long holiday for them than an extended trip, they weren't too concerned, going back to jobs in the New Year, but had all overspent. Our stories were the same: each of us had been told that the islands were fully booked and that if you didn't book via the TAT you would not find anywhere, and that you would pay much less anyway by booking with them. All of us had been sold tours which had brought us to Koh Pha Ngan for the Full Moon Party. Adam referred to us all as

'Thailand Rookies, TAT'd', as if it was a verb. Later they spent a day exploring the island, seeking out cheap accommodation; though it was too late for this trip, they found plenty of places, very cheap in comparison to our resort. They'd been sold air-con rooms too, which at least made me feel a little better, my fuss with Noppi having worked a little.

I went back to bed after failing to track down the mozzie that buzzed in my ear as soon as the light went out. I must have been asleep for the sudden pain woke me up, bewildered. My arm was in agony, though in the dim light that the hut bulb offered all I could see was a couple of small red marks. I searched the wall against which my arm had been laid, and noticed the hut was full of small holes and crevices which had been plugged with paper, small pieces of screwed up toilet roll. One such hole high above where I'd been laying had been unplugged. I guessed that it must have been a spider, perhaps just curiously investigating when my arm had moved and nearly squashed it; or perhaps it just fancied inflicting some pain on an unsuspecting farang. I blocked the hole, and looked for any other possible entrances, blocking those too. It was a painful and sleepless night thereafter, and my arm hurt spasmodically for days, occasionally twinging even some weeks later, but I did not die, and didn't feel ill from it. The girl in the reception laughed when I told her and assured me there were no poisonous spiders around, and that she hadn't heard of anyone being bitten before. I didn't exactly feel assured having now witnessed two spider incidents in such a short time.

On the subject of unusual crawling creatures, there

are several types of Thai ants. Some apparently bite, and some are extremely small. Here is an interesting fact that some might find disgusting, but it is true: these small ants will eat pretty much anything left out or spilt, from orange juice to snot. Yes, that's right, these small fellows seem to be natural clean-up agents who will even dine on unwanted bodily fluids. I know this for sure having woken up one morning with a bunch of snotty tissues pressed up against my nose, covered in these little ants. You can squish them away quite easily, but once the trail is known, there is an endless number of them, and they will return. I learned quickly not to leave any food or drink around unwrapped.

The snot bug had used up the one small toilet roll provided very quickly. I thought perhaps a maid would come round with more but this wasn't the case, so I was left sat there one morning unequipped. I hadn't liked to ask for more in case they'd thought I used a roll a day to wipe my arse, flushing it into their clean sea, so I had a go with the trigger hose; fortunately by then I had found out that it was for cleaning oneself, not the porcelain or an alternative method of flushing. Another small step away from western ways, I was amazed at just how much cleaner and easier this method is, removing both the need for chopping trees and the subsequent pollution during its disposal once soiled. As is too often the case, western standards seem to be set by big business, this time the paper industry, so that what is in fact the cleaner method is regarded as backward and indicative of shameful poverty, all for the benefit of the profiteering suppliers. It left the arse wet but I found the Chang beer bar towel from Chaweng most effective in dealing with this and just the right size.

It turned out that the Full Moon Party was cancelled, though the news only got to us after the sellers had come and sold travel tickets to those that wanted to make the fairly long trip to Hat Rin. I say long trip, it's not that far by western standards but too far to walk. You can hire a bike easily but the road is very winding, hilly, and not well signposted. Several people said it was easy to get lost, after all, the road infrastructure on the island was not only subject to the tropical weather, but had been developed in bits to try and keep up with the tourist traffic that had so rapidly increased over the last few years. Ironically it is the landscape and climate that draw us there which create such travel difficulties.

Since the weather had been so rough lately, the seas were unusually high and beaches had become dangerous. The night before the party some early revellers had taken to venturing in for a late-night drunken dip and had drowned. At first it was six, later it was confirmed as being four dead people. Subsequently the beaches on Hat Rin had been cordoned off, removing the area that housed so much of the atmosphere. The Aussie guys went anyway, taking the girls with them on the back of their bikes, and the taxis all turned up to collect people who had tickets. The weather was bad again, and the cost of getting to Hat Rin from here was more than from Koh Samui, so I stayed back. Though the big party was indeed cancelled, quite a few people had still turned up and many bars had opened all night; apparently there had been a heavy police presence keeping an eye on things.

HOW TO WIPE YOUR ARSE IN THAILAND

The Aussies had found a bar that sold buffalo shit mushroom shakes, where you could have a discreet smoke too. I'd heard of this place where the owners are said to have some deal going on that prevents their customers from being busted by the Thai police. That said, if you start acting like a goon then it could be game over for a while. I thought of hiring a bike for a day and heading off there for a treat but since I've hardly ever ridden, decided against it. Besides, I really didn't want to get arrested, especially before Amanda got there. I imagined her waiting at Bangkok Airport whilst I was trying to bribe my way out of jail, spending even more money I couldn't afford. Better to wait until another time, when the weather was better too, though I'd been smoking cigarettes just for the sake of it for some time when really all I wanted was a joint.

I tried practising my Thai but knew it was going to take some time. One morning, I passed someone who had given me a puzzled look after our very brief exchange of greetings in the native tongue: a few steps on and I realised I had said thank you instead of hello; about the only two words I hardly knew at all and I'd just got them the wrong way round. I walked on towards Thong Sala; every ten minutes or so a minibus went by laden with farang, tooting. I later found out that it wasn't because I was in the way, nor was I the missing passenger they were expecting, but that these are not designated tour minibuses but public buses. They will stop anywhere along the road, and their way of seeing if you need a lift is to toot their horn as they approach. When I found this out, all that tooting in Chaweng suddenly made more sense.

I passed by a roadside bar and diner called 'Rasta Bar' playing loud reggae music, and someone called out and waved. I waved back and walked over. A few people were sat around a small table, and the big guy that had called out, started chatting. He was Canadian and invited me to sit down with them. There was a young Thai barman and his girlfriend who was making decorations for a party. I watched her cut several shapes before she stood up and realised with surprise that she had been snipping through the tablecloth as well. This she found hilarious, and her boyfriend and the Canadian, called Ricky, evidently thought so too. Ricky roared with laughter and sunk the rest of his beer, slamming down the glass and ordering another. The barman looked at me and I asked for an orange juice, hoping that it wouldn't be long before something to smoke might appear.

What can I say, but you meet some strange people at times. Perhaps we are all strange, just waiting for the right environment for the strangeness to manifest itself. Ricky was in his late fifties and explained that he had first come to Southeast Asia during the 1970s for a holiday. He'd run a business in Canada with his wife until seven years previously, but with their children grown up and left home, the marriage had ended; Ricky had decided to forget western life, and had returned to Asia to live in Thailand. He'd lived in a hut in Koh Pha Ngan for seven years, knew this family who ran the bar, spoke at least some Thai fairly fluently, and dressed like a Thai too. The only thing was, I realised as our conversation went on, that until now Ricky had been living on his western savings, and that this was just about to run out. Further, Ricky had become accustomed to drinking vast amounts of cheap Thai beer. His plan, however, which would address several issues simultaneously, was to become a monk. Most Thais do this for some time during their lives, relying on charitable gifts and alms to get by. Ricky was off to Burma to begin his excursion into monasticism, where, I heard him explain several times to different people, the Burmese approach to monasticism was far more relaxed and laid back, and allowed one to consume alcohol, especially if, like Ricky, you happened to qualify automatically for a higher status upon entry due to age or, perhaps rather more cynically, if you can play the part well enough.

Along with Ricky was a Swedish guy with dreadlocks who'd been a monk in Nepal, and an Italian guy who spent most of the time practising his martial arts, which may have been something to do with the fact that he'd fallen in love with a Thai bar girl and was due to go back home in a few days' time.

Ricky showed me the family's pet monkey which they kept tied up around the back. They had a small puppy too and he took great delight in showing me how the monkey would hump the dog's face if the puppy came within range. He tried but failed to convince me that when the monkey, the puppy, and the children sat around playing with the monkey's dick it was all harmless fun, and that it was only a cultural thing to think otherwise. If I went to Rome I may not do what they do but I probably wouldn't be telling the people of Rome what to do either. I didn't say too much but walked back to my drink before taking one step further away from the west when using their toilet.

Back round passed the monkey, still safely tied up.

I steered well clear, not fancying a facial with a primate's penis (he was fast and agile, and this beast could have run right up me and clutched hold of both my ears prior to taking position before I had chance to move, given the opportunity). I found the shed-like construct which housed the dung hole, literally just a hole dug into the ground, part-filled with some kind of straw, next to which was a drum of water; floating on the surface of the drum was a small bowl. I must say that there is a technique to this that differs to a sit-down western version, and learning was made easier since I was only wearing shorts and sandals. I washed my hands in the same drum afterwards, seeing no separate tank: presumably any bits either sink or get eaten by the various insects that may breed in the vicinity. However, it has to be said, that overall the result is far cleaner and quicker than with a seat and toilet paper. For a start you don't want to be sitting there for a while, reading a book or newspaper, if you're crouched over a hole full of dung, so you're in and out quick. At home in the west, leisurely finishing the chapter or article whilst we have such comfort we have forgotten what it is we're doing, and can end up sitting in an atmosphere of bugs simply disguised by the smell of various chemical substances. When the hole is considered to be 'full' enough, they just fill it in and dig another, lifting and moving the shelter accordingly. Whatever it is that lives underground eats it away, naturally, and it turns back into the dust from whence it came.

I took the opportunity and asked Ricky directly what the score with the weed was. It seemed that everyone smoked but nobody had any, or most certainly weren't getting it out here. It is such an easy bust if you happen to be a Thai policeman that even after seven years living there, Ricky said he still didn't even keep his small stash in his own hut, but buried it outside somewhere. He said I could try one of the diners back up the street, and gave me a name; I'd passed the place earlier and walked back afterwards, but since my hut and all around it would reek if I smoked in there, and the beaches and bars were out of the question, I gave up on the idea.

That night Matt, Matt, Adam and I walked back to the Rasta Bar for the free barbecue. There were quite a few people around for a small bar, with mats all laid out and night lights burning. Ricky saw us arrive and the Aussies introduced themselves one by one. Ricky was pretty drunk by then and found it amusing when the second Matt said his name was also Matt, and that he was from Australia. So when it came to Adam, he said he was from Australia and his name was Matt too. Ricky roared, and roared again even louder when he realised it was just a joke. We had a free kebab stick each, which was difficult to identify but tasted good, and Ricky came over at various times and told us all about the monk plan. Reggae music played loud, flame twisters twirled fire sticks, a young Thai blew fire by holding petrol in his mouth and spitting it at the burning stick as it span, and people drank as much beer as they wanted, and still there was no marijuana.

There was to be a big party in Hat Rin on Christmas Eve, similar to a Full Moon Party (some people were even calling it this even though it was Christmas and not Full Moon). I went to the Pirate Bar party just five minutes' walk down the beach instead. It was a bar that had been built into naturally occurring caves right on the beach, an unusual shape, and the rocks formed a small natural amphitheatre. Since the weather was still very unpredictable, and heavy rain could move in at any time, it seemed the best option. Banging techno music blasted out as people danced on the sand drinking spirits from small buckets through straws: it could have been a small section of Hat Rin carved out and set down here, the scene being so similar though smaller.

I'd met a couple of young guys from Yorkshire who had arrived from Koh Tao, two Swedish girls and a German called Ben who'd moved into the hut next door when the strummer had left. The girl from the reception, Dare, had taken a fancy to the younger of the Yorkshire guys, Mark, so she was there too. It was amusing talking to Mark about it, as he feigned ignorance of the situation before admitting he was shit sacred for he'd heard that not only was her father one of the wealthiest men on the island, but that Thai fathers can be dangerously protective of their daughters, possibly expecting an official union should things get carried away in the heat of the moment. He was rather pale and puny, and would emit a low groan sometimes when she appeared, calling out, 'Mark, Mark, Mark,' to him in her slow elongated syllables.

When I spoke to her I found out that I was still ending my Thai words like a woman, still confusing the difference between the 'khap' and the 'ka', somewhat proving that learning sounds from a book doesn't really work, and that you learn the most from talking to people informally, even if it's something embarrassing to find out; maybe especially if it's something embarrassing.

I left the Pirate Bar just before the heavy rain began to fall, relieved that I wasn't stuck in Hat Rin for the night again. Those return taxi tickets worked fine for the people on the way out, but coming back is so often a different story. I heard people say how drivers refused to move until the vehicle was full, even if it meant sitting there waiting for hours. One guy said he'd had to pay another few hundred baht, chipping in to make up for the remaining empty seats because they were so fed up with waiting and just wanted to get back. Apparently many people had been put off by conditions and the party had only been small, pretty much ending when the rain came anyway.

I spent Christmas Day morning sunbathing, and the afternoon sheltering from a storm. The Aussies had all left, the girls to back home and the guys to the Chaweng Cabana on Koh Samui, where I'd stayed earlier on my TAT tour. This they found amusing, reminding us how we'd all been taken for rookies and sent round the same Cabana trail. A very large group of Scots had taken over their huts and several of the others nearby, and provided some entertainment, especially when I overheard the 'granddad' trying to book a boat to take everyone out on for the day. 'A boot, no a boot, a fishing boot,' he'd say, doing a little mime of casting a rod as he said fishing, as if the person on the other end could see. Comical to say the least, an old Scot booking and bartering with a Thai over the phone. They were properly on holiday, swamping the small pool as children bombed in, surrounding it completely. Even though the temperature was at least in the mid-twenties, I would have been disappointed if I'd booked my once a year two-week holiday with so much rain. Unfortunately, his trip didn't turn out to be a leisurely cruise over tranquil turquoise seas; after so much effort in booking the boat, the many phone calls and trips to Thong Sala, it rained and the sea was rough and grey, but I guess they made the most of it.

I left there Boxing Day morning, western bank holidays evidently having no impact on travel arrangements. I was feeling much better now the bug had finally cleared, and slightly more settled in this strange country, after all, not too much had gone disastrously wrong yet. Even the taxi to take me to the port per Noppi's tour plan arrived ok. Like many Thais I met, the driver was keen to practise his very limited English. Though conversations are tricky and take some effort, often with the need to repeat things, thinking of how to put things in comprehensible terms, it's better than sitting in silence. As we chatted he asked how much it had cost me to come to Thailand, translated into Thai baht, and how much it would cost him to get to England: like many Thais, he probably knew the answer to this already, and it merely acted as a healthy reminder that, regardless of effort or what we think we have earned therefore deserve, what is possible for us in the west is actually practically impossible for them to achieve.

CHAPTER 7

Off the Trail with Mr Lee

It was a warm, sunny morning and I was at the port long before the boat arrived. Though I was unsure of which port exactly I was at, or indeed heading to, the voucher and the ticket giving no indication whatsoever, with the change in weather and having now recovered from the fever, I felt so relaxed that it didn't seem to matter. It looked like Thong Sala except the driver had taken me on a fairly long journey through the island instead of following the coastal road. Maybe he had just felt like passing some time on a detour, for soon after we'd reached the port he'd received a phone call from his office wondering where he was. His job involved a multitude of activities, it so happened, and driving through the scenic island chatting was no doubt one of the preferable duties.

The boat came in and a call went out to waiting ferry passengers that we could walk the long walk down the pier and board. It had clouded over in a short space of time, sunshine turning to grey so quickly, and by the time we reached the end, far from the shelter of the waiting area, it began to drizzle. The ferry turned out to be heading to Koh Tao, not Koh Samui, so most of us didn't board anyway. The seas were very rough and the ferry schedules had been affected; this one was having real trouble even docking safely enough for passengers to get on and off. Several times the boat moved as a wave smashed up between it and the dock, making a thundering whoosh that sounded like if you fell in you might not get back out. Things became real interesting when a man in a wheelchair appeared; somehow, though, enough Thais managed to get hold of it and unload both man and chair with no harm done, even as the boat swayed and the gap changed size. A cheer erupted when the danger had passed, and it appeared from his expression that the man in the chair had kind of enjoyed the thrill.

Adjacent to the ferry, a smaller but more traditional-looking boat appeared, made of dark wood, natural browns weathered and in blend with the men who worked on board, bare feet, bare backed, tanned and tattooed rather than the shiny, coloured metal or plastic of the modern ferries, clinical and unfitting in a dirty world. Juxtaposed, it is the difference between a treasure chest full of old gold coins and a shiny plastic credit card with a bank statement full of printed numbers. The men offloaded old brown sacks full of rice as we farang headed off with our brightly coloured rucksacks, trainers, and travel gear. Under a small bamboo shelter propped up only by a few sticks sat a couple of men working out the due payments for the rice and other merchandise that had been offloaded. Quite informally these men sat around piles of money, not even thinking that someone might try and snatch it and run off. Not that there was anywhere for a thief to go, but it did look weird: in England, especially with its scope for anonymity which allows the spending of such proceeds, somebody would most likely have been happy to have a go anyway. The shelter though, came in very handy when the drizzle turned to torrential downpour, and a surprisingly large number of people managed to fit in quite a small area, bags too.

Fortunately the rain turned back to drizzle as the ferry came in so we didn't get too wet as we waited to play 'board the boat'. Someone nearly went in but was caught by a couple of Thais to the sound of much shrieking and talking. As always, the Thais turned it into a joke in what was a successful way of keeping people calm. I could imagine that in England people would have made such a fuss, refusing to board until proper safety equipment was in place: over here, people were glad that it had actually turned up, prepared just to get on somehow, even if it was a bit more exciting than planned.

The sun came out on the way back to Koh Samui, and lovely colours shone in the spray as we smashed through some heavy waves. I was heading to a place in Bophut, a quiet little fishing bay on the north coast. I'd looked it up in the book and on a detailed Koh Samui map I'd picked up in Chaweng but my place wasn't listed on any of them. There was no pretty flyer either, just a small business card in matt yellow and green: on it was written the name of the place and a mobile phone number, along with a very rough sketch of the coastline; a small arrow indicated the relevant point on the coast where Chalee Villa could be found.

It was sunny again when we landed on Koh Samui, another rickety pier that looked like it could collapse any moment but didn't, and it was yet another port different to either of the previous two from where I'd left the island to reach Koh Pha Ngan. Or maybe it just looked different in the sunshine. I had no voucher for this leg of the trip, and remembered that Noppi had mentioned the bus would only cost about 50 baht. I asked around a few vehicles but most were heading off in a different direction; one guy asked me how much I wanted to pay and I said 50 baht. He pointed over the street and said to wait there for a while. When he and everyone else had disappeared I realised that he had just pointed me to the right side of the road for the bus. I waited for a while, and noticing I was stood outside a travel agent, went in and showed them the card. They all looked at each other blankly, chatting in Thai until it became clear that one of them thought they knew where it was. They called a young guy who said he'd take me on the back of his motorbike for 50 baht, so I agreed.

This was quite an experience, for until then I'd not had to carry the bag very far even though it was designed for making the job easy. I'd opted for the every pocket is lockable canvas type bag that can be carried with a shoulder strap or converted into a rucksack. I'd not had cause for the big rucksack straps to come out yet so simply slung it on with the shoulder strap and got on the back of his small bike. I soon found that staying balanced was trickier than expected and we swayed our way along, me clearly more concerned about falling off than my driver who was keen to go as fast as possible. A couple of kilometres down the road and we reached another stretch of bars, resorts, and shops. I saw the Chalee sign as soon as he pulled up and was relieved that we'd found it so easily, so paid him and went in as the sunshine turned to drizzle again.

An Indian-looking older guy greeted me, seeming to be the proprietor of the place. It seemed ok, though not what I was expecting, more like a main building full of rooms rather than beach huts, but I guessed that perhaps there was much more behind some mystery back door. I pulled off the bag, tried to be cheerful and said confidently that I had a booking. He looked puzzled, saying he wasn't expecting anybody, and checked his book. He corrected his mistake to my relief, until he confirmed me as somebody else. We checked my paperwork and after a while the guy realised that I was looking for Chalee Villa, Bophut: this was Chalee Bungalows, in Bangrat. Outside the rain turned again to torrential, monsoon-like weather. I asked him if it was far, and he said I would need to get a bus, that it was too far to walk. He looked doubtful and concerned as he said he thought the track down to it might be flooded so a taxi probably wouldn't take me there either. I got the impression that he didn't think much of the place, and he said that if I didn't like it there then he had spare rooms here if I preferred. I explained that it had all been paid for already so I'd have to take a chance, but did manage to get a rough idea of where to get off the bus, avoiding the one major problem with taking public transport when you haven't a clue where you are. I bought a drink with a 500 baht note, having nothing smaller and needing some change for the bus, and he didn't seem to mind, allowing me to wait a while for the rain to ease. He pointed to a tree just over the road and said that the bus normally stops there, as if it was an official designated bus stop, perhaps to make me feel more at ease whilst standing at the side of the road where there was no sign, timetable, or shelter, like there would be back home.

The torrential rain continued to pour. I stood there under the tree making use of my poncho to protect both me and my bag. It is times such as these that one learns small details such as, though your bag may be sheltered from the falling rain, if it is on the ground in the wrong place then it will still get wet. Where the ground seems to dry so quickly in the sun, more rain brings unexpected and sudden small rivers as water volume far exceeds absorption rates: I moved to slightly higher ground quickly, hoping the bag really was as waterproof as the guy in the shop had said it was when I'd bought it.

When the songthaew came the rain was still pouring. I'd envisaged a detailed conversation with the driver where I explained exactly where I was going, and how I would very much appreciate it if the bus would just stop in the right place and tell me it was good to get off. Instead the driver simply wound down his window about half an inch and indicated that I should just get in the back. I tried showing him the Chalee Villa card through the small gap but some rain must have hit his face for he wound it right up and gestured through the rainy glass just to get in. I climbed on with the heavy bag, trying not to fall into any of the three Thai people in the back.

They stared at me and I tried to break the tension by smiling and giving my best 'sawat di khawp'; they nodded and smiled back politely, possibly wondering why I was getting on their bus on such a day, on my own. I tried to make conversation, hoping to find out where I needed to get off, but my English here was useless. The guy at Chalee Bungalow had said to tell the driver to stop near some place, but when I said it to them they hadn't heard of it. I showed them the small card with the map on it and they gathered around interested before looking at each other and shrugging. It was kind of pleasant on the bus out of the rain so I stayed on for a while, hoping that I might see a sign. After a while a girl, seeing me looking to see where we were, started pointing outside and said, 'Maenam.' I pressed the bus bell to get off, knowing I had gone too far; just how much too far I wasn't yet sure. I paid the driver 50 baht and guessed that I would have to head back again, feeling slightly lost.

Within seconds of standing there a motorbike driver wearing the vest of a taxi rider pulled up. I know that these people rely on their charm to make a living, but it always reminds me of something from a spaghetti western movie when someone I don't know addresses me as their friend, promising assistance even if un-requested. Perhaps the English way is simply suspicious by nature, which says much itself about both ourselves and our culture. Anyway, I was in truth quite vulnerable, Maenam being much less of a tourist place than say, Chaweng, and I felt a bit exposed as a farang amongst all the Thai people, especially not really knowing where I was or how to get to where I was heading. 'Hey, my friend, how are you today? Where you going, my friend?' I weighed things up in my mind quickly: had he noticed an easy target? He looked friendly and honest enough, if these things can be discerned at all by looking, and I knew I would have to ask somebody the way sometime soon, and that it might as well be him. I made out I was looking for a bank to change a cheque. He said he would take me, it wasn't far. I asked him if he'd heard of Chalee Villa and he gave me one of those 'that's miles away' kind of looks. Alright, how much was it going to cost me to get there? After a sharp intake of breath, a look at me and my bag, he agreed to take me there for 100 baht. Seeing perhaps the horror at such expense, he persuaded me that it was about four kilometres back towards Bophut, and then down a side road somewhere.

This guy was worth every single baht: not only did he take me to the bank and wait for me, but stuck my bag in front of him to make things better balanced. He drove all the way down an old dirt track flooded by the torrential downpours, weaving in between deep trenches and puddles that would have prevented many vehicles from passing, balancing the bag somehow with his knees as I clung on to the seat trying not to wobble us over, and dropped me off right at the door of Chalee Villa. He even waited until my booking was confirmed, to make sure I didn't need to go elsewhere.

Here it was much more rural, set amidst a plantation of palm trees several hundred yards from the main drag, sharing the dirt track road with just a few other dwellings. Like many resorts the reception and the restaurant were the same place, an area covered with a bamboo-type thatched roof with open sides and a view of the sea. Built on the beach itself, the sea was just a few yards away and you could have easily spun a beer mat into it, even at low tide. A young girl took my paperwork away, at first looking a bit concerned. After a while another lady appeared and assured me that everything was ok, sending the taxi rider away before instructing a young Thai to show me to my hut. He led the way across the restaurant towards what is best described as an avenue of huts running perpendicular to the beach, perhaps half a dozen raised wooden constructs in a row either side, all with balconies.

My hut was just across from the restaurant, right on the beach, though as with all of the huts the door and balcony faced the avenue rather than the beach. Up a few concrete steps, he opened the door and showed me in. I have to say that this was the cheapest of all the places I'd stayed in to date on Noppi's tour, and the one he'd been most reluctant to put me in, yet this was exactly the sort of place that I'd hoped for from the beginning. Just a small simple hut with a decent-sized bed, so big that it took up most of the space inside, leaving room only for a walkway to the small toilet and shower round the back. At the end of the bed were a few shelves to put things that might be needed; I slid everything else under the bed. Again it was a cold shower, and a semi-western toilet in that there was a seat and it looked very similar except there was no cistern nor flusher. Later I found out why there was a very large bucket next to the toilet, under a tap. The ubiquitous trigger and hose hung on a small clip on the wall behind, though there was a brand new toilet roll on a rack. It was still wrapped up and I couldn't help but wonder whether they give you a new one so that they can count how many sheets you use per day. A small window looked out onto the beach, and a larger one out onto the balcony. Outside there were a couple of chairs either side of a table; as in the restaurant, everything was made of bamboo. A blue and white rope hammock was slung from the heavy wooden beams, resting at about the same height as the balcony's small wooden safety fence.

The rain seemed to stop as soon as I reached this place, and the sun came out. In the heat everything dries out very quickly and I spent the afternoon sat on the beach, getting used to the new surroundings. The small bay was quite beautiful, stretching round almost in a semicircle so that you could look across the water and see the other end curling round, a narrow band of golden sand that the sun lit as it arced its way around. As the tide came in, the narrow strip disappeared in places, and I soon found myself moving to the higher sand.

We were at the western end, just before the point where a headland juts out, sort of tucked away in the corner. To the north, out through the channel across the open sea, the big, dark rock of Koh Pha Ngan can be seen, if the view is clear. Small fishing boats were tied to long ropes attached to anchors hammered into the sand, some tied around palm trees in the few places that they grew. These boats were like wooden canoes, often with exaggerated ends, and were most often paddled out by hand using a single oar. Thai fishermen wade out to their boats fully clothed, and since virtually everyone – even the builders – wore flip-flops everywhere, there was no worries about getting wet feet. Sometimes a small motor chugged them along, presumably depending on how far out they were going. I sat on the beach gazing out to sea, listening to the waves still agitated from the bad weather earlier that morning. It was a much calmer beach though than Chaweng had been after the rain, this beach being far more sheltered physically, and because of its position on the island. The sand was quite coarse, like brown sugar, quite harsh on the feet, and there was much evidence of the storm still washed up, but it had a real tranquil feeling. As I sat gazing out to sea I heard a low voice nearby slowly say: 'Hello, how are you? Do you smoke marijuana?'

I looked around to see a Thai wearing bright Bermuda shorts and flip-flops; he was probably about the same age as me, a few years younger perhaps, with short dark hair, and was surprisingly big for a Thai person. Wearing no shirt, he showed a large tattoo that spread across his chest, shoulder, and back. It was some greeting, and I had to laugh. 'Are you a policeman?' I smiled, hoping to make light any suspicion. He laughed, denying such a possibility and explained that he worked there, at the resort, and had been out when I'd checked in; many people who were there smoked, it was ok. Normally he would have been there to show me to my hut and would have asked then but he'd been having his hair cut. I was unsure, being fairly close now to the Bangkok rendezvous date, but time was wearing me down. He said just to let him know, I would see him in the restaurant later that evening.

The huts were all built on top of raised block foundations so that there was a gap of perhaps three feet between the floor and the ground. No doubt the layout designer had been aware of likely water levels, for the sea had evidently reached right up the avenue, sweeping the sand away and exposing areas that were usually covered. I watched the beach guy and the Thai who had showed me to my room fill buckets with sand from the beach and carry them back up to cover the exposed tree roots, hut borders, and any other holes that needed filling. 'Good exercise,' he called out to me, tapping his stomach and laughing. It reminded me of when I worked on a building site, and I noticed that he soon got bored of the whole thing, eventually discarding the shovel and just scuffing the bucket along the ground to fill it, holding it close to his stomach instead of chucking it up onto his shoulder.

After much thought, and a cold shower that was surprisingly good, I went over to the restaurant for tea. Sure enough, the beach guy was the waiter too, and when he asked if I wanted anything I gave him the nod. The food was good, there was no hassle about paying for it, the guy waving it away almost as if it didn't matter, insisting, 'You can pay later.'

I went back to the hut to meet him as arranged. Waiting, slightly apprehensively, I got some money out and put it away a few times, wondering what was the best approach, to have it out ready or rummage around and get it out after the deal was agreed, when there was a knock at the door. It was dark outside now and I opened it to see the waiter stood there with a large knife in his hand, the sort that a pirate might use to slit a throat quickly. He muttered hello softly and walked in. For sure, I was wondering what was going to happen next, particularly what was going to happen with the knife, when he pulled out a block of compressed weed and asked if I had a book or something to cut it on. I was just relieved that it wasn't going to be my throat so fumbled around quickly to find something. I pulled out an old plastic sandwich box that I was using for medical stuff. He looked in through the semi-transparent side curiously but I assured him there was nothing worth anything in there. Even the St John's Wort/ Diclofenic/ Solpadeine combination with a slimming pill and alcohol that I'd tried on the Half Moon Party night hadn't really done anything but make me feel slightly sick.

We haggled and bartered a bit on the size and cost, and I explained that I was heading back to Bangkok by plane in a week so didn't really need much, and we agreed on a deal. He didn't even want paying for it then, assuring me that any time over the next few days was ok. I pushed him for reassurance that I wasn't about to get arrested, knowing I was somewhat committed to any consequences now anyway, and he explained that in the hut, out of the way was ok; sometimes on the balcony, if nobody was around; but not on the beach. 'Up here is ok, but on the beach,' he explained with caution, almost in a drawl, 'you don't know who's who.' We shook hands, he said his name was Lee, went back to work, and I shut the door to sample the goods.

There were a few sticks and seeds but the weed was sticky and did the business. It was the first smoke for several weeks so the effect was quite something. Inside the hut I realised I was quite a sitting duck, not being able to see what was going on outside, or underneath for that matter. I was playing around with the fan settings (something I'd only had the need to use in Koh Pha Ngan, and that had just been to annoy the mozzie, not to cool things down) so that the smoke blew away, when I heard a loud shriek of what sounded like a large monkey-bird right outside, and nearly jumped out of my skin. I took a quick look out there but could see nothing: truthfully, though, I didn't look too hard and was never sure if it was a strange creature or someone playing a trick on me, messing about beneath the hut. I felt strangely isolated, somewhat at the mercy of unknown people in a foreign land; thankfully human nature tends towards respect for life, and it is hopefully not just the fear of the consequences of getting caught that prevents barbaric shredding akin to a pride of lions welcoming a lost and wandering goat.

I smoked another, knowing I only had six days in which to get through it, before having a go at laying in the hammock. On the balcony I was in full view of the restaurant, though without the balcony light on I was amongst the shadows. By now most people had eaten and had wandered off somewhere, except a small group of men who seemed to be getting plastered. Lee was with them, chain-smoking cigarettes. Whether they were watching me or whether it was purely coincidence, who knows, but they roared with laughter the several times that I nearly fell out of the hammock. I couldn't see too well – the combination of the darkness, the smoke, and being short-sighted – and felt happy enough that it didn't matter if I happened to be brief episodes of entertainment for them. I got the hang of just lying there without moving quite quickly, and was ok as long as I didn't try getting in and out; one wrong move and I was out of the hammock and over the balcony, though the small fence was just about high enough to hold me the right side, so long as there wasn't excessive momentum from a side swing or misjudged wriggle.

The skies were clear and I could see a small section of stars from my position. Warm, relaxed, and laid out, I felt a long way from anywhere, very far away. As I drifted off and perhaps the effects of the smoke intensified, in the dimness on the beach I could make out the silhouette of a large cockerel, similar in shape to what might have been found carved into a 1970s suburban bush. Nearby, in the shadows, a monkey joined it, and though I knew it was just a trick of the mind, the longer I looked the more vivid they became.

After an excellent night's sleep I awoke to the sound of waves lapping on the beach, calm yet audible, and once heard, their continuous presence is noticed. I looked out of the window onto the beach. A beautiful sunrise over the bay was made perhaps even better by the girl right outside sunbathing topless. It was a view that I found difficult to turn away from, but not wanting to be a secret starer I did my best to refrain. Later that day I went for a swim and watched her pick up a couple of floating coconuts and hold them to her now covered chest as she asked her friend what she thought of her coconuts. I'd seen the real thing but resisted comment.

I spent most of that week smoking, swimming,

sunbathing, and eating. Breakfast had already been paid for, and catering for the farang, like most places, you could get eggs, bacon, and toast for breakfast. In Thailand they call this an American breakfast, presumably much to do with the historical US military presence not too far away, and not a 'Full English'. The food there was good: the eggs, small piece of bacon, and toast were well cooked to the point of being crispy, unlike on Koh Pha Ngan where they seemed to have difficulty in leaving the eggs in the pan long enough to cook, so that they were barely solidified. At times back there I'd quickly stuck them between two pieces of toast just to give them a bit more heat, not that the toast was all that hot either; the Koh Pha Ngan toasters took forever just to warm the bread, often queues formed and waiters enquired politely but knowingly to see what was holding things up. Koh Samui, with its more developed infrastructure catering for tourists' needs, maybe had better electricity supplies. Mr Lee had served, recommending the American breakfast with mango juice and coffee; he explained that here there were no time limits for breakfast, I could come over at any time, it was never too late. An older-looking Thai wearing only shorts and flip-flops strutted around as if he owned the place. He was shaven-headed, covered in tattoos, and had a few teeth missing, such that he had a somewhat fierce appearance and would have looked quite at home on a pirate's ship. I found out later that this was Mr Tong, and he did in fact own the place, proving that one should always be careful how one approaches even the unlikeliest looking people around.

The morning before New Year's Eve I was sat

around after breakfast drinking coffee and smoking menthol Thai cigarettes (cheap and not as rough as normal ones) when the family, waiters, and the waitress all sat down around a table and started feasting on a mass of freshly caught seafood. After a while Mr Tong got up and insisted that I joined them, along with an old guy from Switzerland, also called Pete. He had long white hair, a long white beard and moustache, and being fairly small in stature would have looked at home fixing clocks somewhere in the countryside, perhaps with some elves to help. He was staying here for a month or so before heading to Bangkok for a few weeks. I couldn't help but wonder why an old Swiss would want to spend a few weeks in Bangkok, knowing some of the depravities so easily obtainable, so found it best not to think about it. We tucked into various types of shelled creatures that had been cooked in lots of Thai herbs and chillies, Mr Lee providing an invaluable service of doing the shelling for us. When I thought they were nearly all gone, and the family began to wander off, the cook (who I think may have been Mr Tong's wife) brought out another panful and poured them out. Mr Lee, Swiss Pete, myself, and another guy who looked a bit like Mr Tong but spoke pretty much no English, finished them off. It was a most unusual meal but quite delicious, and an honour to have been invited.

There was another big party due in Hat Rin the following night, and the place began to get filled up with people using Bophut as a place to stay; here was within easy reach yet away from the madness of Koh Pha Ngan on party night. The people at Chalee Villa were happy to arrange travel to and from the party on one of the many speedboats that departed from

Bophut beach. On the day itself the bay was filled with motor-cruisers lined up ready to fill up with as many people as could fit on board. I decided to stay back at Bophut, having a bag of weed and the safety of the hut. Swinging in the hammock, looking at the stars and listening to the waves lapping at the shore was good enough for me; besides, all along the beach there were small gatherings going on. I noticed too that none of the Thais were heading for Hat Rin, including Mr Lee who made up the excuse that he was working the following day. Since he'd already told me that he spent most nights smoking until three or four in the morning I figured that Hat Rin parties don't particularly interest most Thais. Having already witnessed farang drinking excessive amounts of cheap Thai alcohol, dancing to banging techno music and flashing lights on a beach as Thai bar girls provide services for the right price, I decided that I would stay here where I had pretty much all I needed.

A Norwegian guy, Frederick, turned up to warm greetings from the family who clearly recognised him. I found out that he'd stayed here a few times before, and that he'd been here a few weeks earlier during the big storm. There'd been so much flooding that he'd stayed in the main house with the family for a few days, such was the atmosphere of the place, and hence the familiarity. It was talking to him that I found out the Thai guy who said very little and looked like Mr Tong was actually Mr Tong's brother. He lived in a hut at the very top of the avenue, and was apparently in Mr Tong's bad books today already for drinking a bottle of Sang Thip with his breakfast, and was well part through his second bottle before midday. Although strange, Frederick assured me that he was harmless enough: I hadn't really noticed too much other than that he stumbled from the restaurant to his hut and back every so often, virtually ignoring everyone as he went.

That evening the family and the few people who worked there set out a huge table for their own celebrations. I wasn't there for Christmas so couldn't compare, but masses of food came out. I'd already eaten but after a while Mr Tong invited the few of us left in the restaurant to join them. There were spring rolls, soups, curries, rice dishes, and all kinds of seafood, including a large whole fish. I sat in between Mr Lee and Mr Tong's brother, not that hungry but sampled some of the food anyway; Mr Lee ate both the fish eyes, its fins, tail, and head, inviting me to share in it. I passed on the eye though ate some brain or whatever it is inside a fish's head. Mr Tong's brother had made it through the day after having had his second bottle confiscated for several hours by Mr Tong, but was making good headway into yet another now. He appeared somewhat agitated and Mr Lee explained that he wanted one of my cigarettes: I offered him the packet in which there were only two left, and he took one with a very pleased look. I would have a friend for life now, Mr Lee assured me.

Mr Tong was in a good mood now too, and took great delight in showing me the fireworks on the beach right outside the restaurant, due to go off at midnight. It looked just like a large pallet of upright tubes sealed in with a wrapping. Apparently, Mr Tong explained, the large hotel further down the beach had bought them, but because of the bad weather and high tides they had been unable to set them up outside their own place; instead they'd had to use the beach outside Chalee Villa. Mr Tong laughed and said that though he hadn't paid a single baht, everyone around would see when they went off and think they were Chalee Villa fireworks.

I went back to the hut and got very stoned, and watched the myriad of small red lights make the trip over to Hat Rin, their engines humming in the distance. My big spliff to see in the New Year had sent me off to sleep and I woke suddenly to the sound of loud exploding fireworks right outside. I was so stoned I had to make an effort to drag myself off the bed, convincing myself that it would be worth a look at least. When I stepped outside the entire sky was lit up, banging continually. Mr Tong, his brother, and several others stood nearby the fireworks, though the people who had paid for them had lit the fuse and were stood just that little bit closer, all watching Chalee Villa light up with the explosions right above us. There must have been a firework pallet on every bay around the island: to my left, in Maenam; to our right, in Bangrat; several from behind us in what may have been Chaweng, Lamai; and a clear view of Hat Rin. There must have been six or seven firework shows high in the sky clearly visible. After ten minutes or so the banging gradually calmed down, as if everyone had had the same type of firework pallet. After a couple of hours the small red lights began the make their repeated return journeys bringing people back from Koh Pha Ngan, and it was all over.

Even at the start of December when I had booked the tour with Noppi, the night train back to Bangkok had been fully booked, so I was due to fly back instead. The night before I left, the resort lady called the taxi that Noppi had booked; in the morning, sure enough, it turned up, no problem. Mr Tong asked where I was going, and when I explained I was meeting a friend in Bangkok before probably coming back to Koh Samui, he assured me that if I wanted to come back to Chalee Villa then to book direct with him as it would be cheaper; I thanked him and said maybe I'd call him from Bangkok.

Time had slowed right down, the weather had stayed good for the week, and it was sad in a way to leave such lovely people, such a lovely place.

CHAPTER 8

Samran I

It was a pleasant drive to the airport in the sunshine and we passed the Big Buddha. I call it an airport, it was really just a large thatched bamboo hut with a runway. Security was simply pushing the bags through an x-ray machine situated near the 'official' entrance before slapping some security tape on it. It was a Thai Airways flight, and they brought around a delicious breakfast meal even though we were only up in the air for about forty-five minutes.

Landing at Bangkok Domestic Airport was a total contrast and instantly I felt the change in atmosphere, pace, and attitude. Everyone was more hurried and busier as I made my way over to the connected (as it was then) International Arrivals area, trying to retain the relaxed mood of Chalee Villa. This time I'd had good opportunity to make sense of the guide book and didn't want to be paying 700 baht for a taxi, so headed for the airport bus stop.

I don't want to say that Amanda was disorganised but when I'd left England she still didn't have an email address up and running. Time had run out the day I'd met up with her in town, and the plan of setting up an internet account using the library computer had been replaced with Vic agreeing to email me confirmation of Amanda's flight changes; Vic had emailed as agreed, including details of the hotel that she had booked for three nights. In Chaweng I'd set up an email account for her and put the details in a letter. To make things more complicated, my email account had expired when I'd been in Koh Pha Ngan: I'm no computer expert but I think this was because the email address had been connected to a land telephone line; though I could access it over the internet, not having used it from the designated landline address for some time had led to the account being closed. So I'd had to set myself a new account up as well, and email the new address to everyone I needed to, including Amanda's newly set-up address. Though I'd not checked my emails since a few days before New Year, I'd not heard from her at all at this time.

The Number 2 airport bus stopped right outside the Samran Hotel and cost 100 baht to get there. I spent the journey trying to note landmarks to make it easy for the following day; Amanda had booked the Asia Hotel which was just around the corner from the Samran, deliberately chosen by Noppi as a nearby but cheaper alternative. The plan was to check out of the Samran in the morning, take my bag round to the Asia for storage, and get the coach back to the airport in time to meet Amanda who was due in sometime late afternoon. There was absolutely no time pressure at all, though I'm fully aware that sometimes this can make things as likely to go wrong, being too relaxed.

The Samran was situated on a busy street, and the front entrance meant walking through the elegantly laid tables of the empty restaurant to reach the reception. It was smaller than the Siam Beverley where I'd first stayed but was quite classy-looking with its shiny laid-out glassware and large Buddhist statues in the front window. A water feature bubbled peacefully away just round beside the reception, and Thai music played lightly in the background.

The room was as clean and tidy as the ambience of the downstairs reception suggested it would be, though it was only for one night anyway. I went for a walk around Siam Square, a place jammed with shops, stalls, and eateries, located the Asia Hotel, and bought some food from a street-side diner, feeling more at ease with the crazy Bangkok pace after a month on the islands than that day I'd spent at the train station. Yes, of course I'd have chillies with the barbecue kebabs. I nodded to the chef when he offered them, after all, I was practically Thai by now. It served me right when I took a bite of meat with half of one of these small green things that were meant to be chillies; I braved it out, refusing to spit but needing half a bottle of water to cool it. I ate both the kebabs kind of wishing that perhaps I should have tried one before committing to two, and didn't feel like eating much else that night.

The next day all went as planned. Leaving the bag at the Asia was no problem and I even managed to find one of the cheap Siam Square diners in the guide book for lunch. I found an internet place and checked my email. Quite a few had built up over the days; I could see by the titles that the tone of the most recent was becoming a little concerned. Evidently my silence had not been interpreted as me being too relaxed to bother walking into Bophut town and checking emails. Amanda, it seemed, had sent about ten in the few days prior to her departure; my letter which had also included details of where to meet at the airport had finally reached her just after Christmas. Apparently she'd been wondering whether to change her dates again but not knowing where I was, hadn't been sure of what to do. I guessed that she must have left anyway for the messages had stopped and she hadn't said otherwise. I wondered momentarily if the Asia would still let me stay, even if she didn't turn up, but quickly put the thought out of my mind.

After a couple of hours wandering around the airport, watching planes come in and take off, the flight arrival was confirmed. I'd tried to explain in the letter that there were two queues, a quick one for visa holders and the slower one for visitor applicants, and waited near the exit, as described in the letter I'd sent. Time passed and so did large numbers of people. I tried looking at the tags to see if any were from London, but couldn't really make out the detail as the suitcases hurried through. Lots of people, all looking very different, heading to Thailand for whatever reason. Occasionally I'd see old overweight western looking men travelling alone, maybe just a small suitcase, and couldn't help but wonder what they were here for. But then we were all here for something, and if not here, then somewhere.

Time went on, it was just beginning to get dark and as I was wondering if Amanda had gone out of the other exit by mistake, amazingly she came round the corner. Not only did I see her long before she saw me, but she hardly recognised me until I stepped out in front of her. It's strange because sometimes we see things in our minds how we expect them to happen, and I'd often wondered whether she would appear wearing her bag as a rucksack or whether she'd wear it like I had, as a shoulder bag (for she'd bought hers the same day as I'd bought mine, it was the same type). As it turned out, it was neither: instead she'd slung it on a trolley along with the armfuls of carrier bags filled with stuff that she hadn't been able to cram into the bag. A slight sinking feeling overcame me as any plans of light-footed island hopping were made quite sticky when she admitted that actually the big bag alone was too heavy for her to carry. In her hand she clutched an English newspaper which, to make things a little tense from the start, had a front page story of a British girl raped and murdered on Koh Samui on New Year's Eve. Apparently it was all over the news at home, yet I'd not heard a word about it on the island.

Still, it was good to see her, and we took the airport bus back to the Samran. I carried her bag (thankfully having stored mine I didn't have to try and carry both of them) and Amanda just about managed the remainder, and we walked the five-minute walk around the corner to the Asia. I reckon she probably would have preferred to have turned up in one of the plush-looking taxis right outside the door instead of the two of us stumbling across to the busy entrance trying to avoid being run over, but never mind.

CHAPTER 9
Bags, Big Gun, Boats, and Buses

The Asia Hotel was huge, and the large reception area was filled with guests, bags, and porters. Chandeliers hung sparkling from the high ceiling, and after checking in we sat in one of the plush bar areas for a complimentary cocktail, delicious but small.

Our room was in the centre of the building so that the large window of one side looked out onto the quadrangle far below which housed one of the two swimming pools. It was clean with a beautiful bathroom and soft white sheets that look even whiter somehow when smeared with the red of a squashed mosquito. Amanda unpacked her things as we chatted and caught up. The girl who had been murdered had come from Wales and was only eighteen; it had apparently been all over the news in the UK, the first information saying that it had happened in a quiet fishing village on Koh Samui. I found out much later that my family's concern had been because they knew I was staying on Koh Samui, in a small fishing village, and they hadn't heard from me for over a week: fearing the worst, they hoped I hadn't been caught up in any of it. Later, the details had confirmed that it had happened in Lamai whereas I'd been staying in Bophut, putting their minds at rest. Unfortunately, however, the spa place where Amanda intended to go for her health course was also in Lamai. I tried to convince her that Lamai was probably quite a large place, and that the spa was most likely some distance away from the scene. The murder, I assumed, most likely happened in the night-life area, and the spa was unlikely to be in such a place. But, Amanda insisted, there was the mention of the quiet fishing village, and that was exactly how the spa described their location: her concerns remained.

We ate in one of the hotel restaurants after being hassled by several tuk-tuk and taxi drivers all wanting to take us to Patpong for the night: for food, a show, entertainment, and the fare included, all for next to nothing. Nothing is for nothing, and I'd heard a few tales already about some of these scams, where many 'extras' are added to the bill and must be paid for before you are brought back from some unknown back street. It seemed there was a zone just outside the hotel that was fairly hassle-free (though not completely); a few yards the other side of the imaginary line and it was a free for all, and everyone who stepped into it from the hotel was assumed to be going somewhere, needing something that they could offer at a bargain price. We found the swimming pool up on the roof instead, and looked out across the lights of the city.

I'd given Amanda my copy of the *Rough Guide First Time Around the World* which I'd read, and hoped she would have read it too. Even though there's nothing quite like doing it to learn, it was a useful book and makes you feel like you're away travelling for the few days it takes to read. I'd bookmarked the pages that emphasised the need to travel light: unfortunately, Amanda hadn't actually read it, including the marked page which said that one small camera is quite sufficient. She brought the large and heavy Nikon with detachable lens, as well as a small digital camera. The first problem was that Big Gun, as I named it thereafter, needed some batteries: and no sight-seeing was worth undertaking without it.

After an enormous breakfast that was possibly even better than at the Siam Beverly we headed out to the shops around Siam Square. I'd learned how to say 'no thanks' or at least the equivalent in Thai after watching a girl on the beach in Chaweng: said with a smile, most Thais give up trying to sell you something, figuring that you've probably been here long enough to know of the scams if you pronounce it right, so we easily passed through the tuk-tuks and taxis that lay in wait outside the hotel. Somehow I knew it was never going to be easy but eventually we found a place that sold the right batteries, deep inside a huge building that was about four floors of brightly lit shops and restaurants that sell just about everything, cheap but not necessarily authentic, hardly any two items made quite the same, even copies of replicas. After a while in Thailand the ubiquitous T-shirt phrase 'same-same but different' not only makes increasing sense, but becomes gradually more and more meaningful.

We took a tuk-tuk to the Grand Palace after a lengthy discussion with one of the drivers. I made it clear we wanted to go directly to the Grand Palace, that I'd been in Thailand for five weeks, knew of the silk and diamond shop scams, and didn't expect a crazy detour. Turning down his ludicrous offer of a complete tour of the city for 20 baht, we agreed on a price and he delegated the job to one of the others stood watching, dark eyes low, deliberately moving slowly, smoking, much like a bad character in a western movie. After a while of driving through streets completely unfamiliar, he pulled over and showed us his brochure of shops he would like us to visit, that we need not even buy anything. In Chaweng the couple I'd met who'd spent too much and were going back to change flight dates had told me they'd gone on the tour anyway, just to keep the driver happy (who gets a petrol voucher just for bringing farang to any one of the shops); the guy had ended up buying a handmade silk suit that he hadn't really wanted. Even back in England some time later I worked with someone who'd done the same, and hadn't worn the thing once since getting back. Both gave almost lame justifications that the material was really top quality, and the workmanship professional, but in a cold moment of honesty both admitted that it was the sales pressure that had persuaded them in the end, and that alone. I told our driver we weren't interested, and that we had a deal to go direct. Moodily he continued, several times stopping on the way and tapping his petrol tank. In the end he dropped us just around the corner from the palace entrance and I gave him what we'd agreed.

As soon as we got out we were approached by one of a group of drivers nearby. In disbelief I pointed to the tuk-tuk we'd just got out of, indicating that we were hardly likely to need a lift somewhere. It is times such as these that it is wise to remember that people tell lies, and if the benefit is sufficient for them, do so with considerable ease, quite convincingly. This guy assured me that today the Grand Palace was closed to western visitors, explaining in great detail how there was a special ceremony involving monks going on. I pointed at the many people heading towards the entrance around the corner. They would soon find out it was closed, he assured me, pulling out a map of various Buddhas and monuments that were open, and where he would happily take us to, for a very reasonable price. I let him say his pitch and told him we would go and see for ourselves. This scam is even in the guide book: if I'd had it on me I would have shown him. Even between him and the entrance we were approached by another guy saying the same story, even more well-dressed than the previous guy. These people do not look poor or underfed, so you can be sure that at least sometimes one of their repertoire of scams must pay off.

Amanda took many pictures as we walked around the palace: it is an area of outstanding architecture filled with statues and carvings, if you like that sort of thing, and we saw the Emerald Buddha wrapped up in his gold winter tunic. Is it truly Thai culture or is it simply for the tourist industry, similar to Buckingham Palace in London? I guess it's a matter of opinion, and consider me uncultured if you like, but I still prefer laying in a sunny hammock on the beach listening to the waves, perhaps the sound of fishing boats.

On the way out we were approached by yet another Thai who told us that the palace was shut for the day. When I told him I knew it was open because we'd just been in there he just smiled: what can you do but smile back? I remembered Daryl's words of advice that day at the train station, that the Thais are lovely people and will be really nice when ripping you off; as he said, just be nice back and walk away, they will not hassle too much. It had worked well for me so far; once you begin to engage or argue with them they have an answer to soothe each and every concern that you may have, and before you know it you'll have been ushered into a taxi or tuk-tuk heading for who knows what it will cost.

Surrounding the area around the palace, far beyond the royal walls, the buildings continued to have that typically oriental design, with pointed roofs, fire-breathing beasts, and the appearance of a temple about them. We wandered around for a while, without hassle, through back streets where farang were neither catered for nor expected, seemingly lost until we found a canal and took a boat trip back to Siam Square. We were the only farang on board, most seats being taken by either school children or people on their way home from work. The boat had wooden boards that spanned the width for seats, perhaps eight benches in total fitting four of five persons on each, depending on the size of passenger. It was ridiculously cheap, something like ten baht each for the journey, and the ticket sellers walked up and down the outside edges, leaning in, taking money and handing back tickets and change whilst balancing on the swaying boat as it chugged along the canal. If there was more than one boat on the same stretch of water – as there was now, it seeming to be rush hour – then the boat rocked even more as it hit the wash of the boat in front. And these Thais love water so much that this fact seems to encourage the driver to go even faster. To the sound of a few small screams, the ticket collectors changed activities and rolled down the rain shields to stop too much splash from soaking the passengers next to the open sides, and we passed through parts of the city where the not-so-rich Thais lived, where laundry swung freely in the wind and barely dressed children dived into the urban water.

That night we had a swim in the pool on the roof of the hotel. Bangkok is so smoggy you can hardly see the stars, and as warm as it was, the smell of chlorine combined with traffic fumes and air-con unit outputs acted as a reminder that we were not in paradise. That said, swimming outside in January on the roof of a luxury hotel beats sitting in some office somewhere doing a pointless job that is simply a means to an end.

We had to start thinking about where to go next. Like me, Amanda hadn't slept on the flight at all but she had seemed to sleep well for her first two nights. One problem we had was that her plan of staying back to get more money together hadn't really worked; it had cost another £400 just to change the date to early January, having to upgrade the first leg of the multi-stop ticket. The fact was that we both had less than a grand each which had to last two and a half months; I then had about fifteen hundred which I'd converted to Aussie dollar traveller's cheques which would have to last both of us a month in Australia; as for Bali and Singapore on the way back, well that was just too far away to think of even.

After the peaceful week in Bophut I couldn't stand Bangkok and really just wanted to leave and head back to the islands; or any island. The next problem was Amanda's health: details aside, trekking through the mountains was out of the question. Since she intended doing the course fairly soon, she didn't want to start taking antimalarials so big Koh Chang, where the weather was good but the mosquitoes a potential sickness-inducing nuisance, was ruled out. Eventually we agreed that perhaps it would be good to go back to Koh Samui and at least check out the spa place; Amanda was ploughing through 400 duty-free B&H and was adamant that she didn't want to start the course until she had given up, and she didn't want to do that right now. Then there was the fact that the spa place was pretty much fully booked for block bookings long enough in which to complete the course and recuperate; because it was January, it was real busy with people from the west on a new year health drive whilst getting away from the cold. Come March, however, it became quieter, and a bit cheaper. Finally, since the health problem was a hindrance to pretty much all other plans (other than staying on in the Asia and taking lots of photos of Bangkok, money being the real issue there) we went off to try and book a night train ticket to take us down to Koh Samui.

We took a tuk-tuk to a TAT office near Central Station; since all of Noppi's transport links had worked out so well, it seemed a safe way to book the tickets. The lady was delighted to help us until she realised that we weren't looking to book accommodation as well, but she did try to get us train tickets. All sleeper tickets had been sold, she told us after a phone call; we could go the night after instead or go by coach. We were put on the spot for a decision, no doubt the tiny commission she'd receive made the amount of thinking time allowed very minimal. The place was very busy and to be fair there were plenty of people waiting, most likely happy to be spending much more money. It would have been good to have got the train, but in the end, after convincing us with a picture of a large luxury cruising coach and assuring us that it wasn't one of those hot, crammed, and uncomfortable buses you hear of, we booked. She asked if we had somewhere to stay, suggesting that without her assistance we would find nowhere, adding that being January the whole of Koh Samui was fully booked; except that she happened to know of somewhere that would be able to fit us in, as a favour for a family friend.

I told her that I'd just come from Koh Samui and there were plenty of places to stay. She gave a small grunt as if she had been caught bluffing but didn't really mind, and phoned the spa for us to see if there were any vacancies; she confirmed there was a room for two nights but that it couldn't be booked by phone. She assured us it would be far safer to let her book somewhere, but knowing she'd been partially rumbled, didn't push the point. She passed us the tickets, pointed to an area just outside in the street and told us that the coach would be leaving there about ten o'clock the following night. She gave me her business card and I noticed it was the same tour company as Noppi's, only with a '2' after it. I laughed and asked her if she knew Noppi but she was already greeting her next keen customers. Outside the tuk-tuk driver looked disappointed when I said that all we'd booked were two coach tickets.

After yet another superb breakfast Amanda took a final luxurious bath before it was time to pack up and check out. For her this was no easy task, partly because there was so much stuff but partly, I'm sure, because she didn't really want to leave there. Added to this was the fact that she'd had second thoughts about the coach as soon as we'd booked it. I was just glad that we were going somewhere, and that at least we had somewhere to stay that night, even if it was just on a coach. Eventually all the bags had been repacked, the big rucksack and the many plastic bags for the overflow: I wondered how on earth we would manage to get on and off the buses and boats involved in any island excursion. Amanda assured me that much of it was just creams and lotions with only very little in them, and like the cigarettes, they would soon be used up and there would be much less to carry. Minutes before being late for checkout we found a trolley and wheeled it all to a storage place for the day whilst we roamed around Siam Square for the last time, drinking coffee, eating Pad Thai and watching some of crazy Bangkok life carry on as it does, no doubt, every day.

CHAPTER 10

The Man in the Pink Shirt

The tension began even before the coach left Bangkok. We were all crammed on board, bags stuffed all around us in the humid heat, waiting to leave when an argument began downstairs. It did not look good when the driver and one of the passengers began to scuffle. It soon calmed down but there was a slight air of unease, and people began to get off, some to smoke, some just to walk about. We got going only to stop an hour down the road; apparently this would be the only stop between Bangkok and Surat Thani, being the only place open at night on the way. It meant a long time without a leg stretch, something that the sleeper trains offered, and with the humidity increased by so many people in such a small space, it was far from the comfort that been suggested by the happy faces in the TAT photograph. I guess we always knew it was going to be like that, but that didn't make the journey any less tense.

We reached Surat Thani just as it was getting light to much relief from everyone on board. As always in Thailand, everyone needed to pee as soon as they got off but had to pass the person demanding ten baht for entrance into the facilities. This is ok if you have change though slightly annoying when you find out it's just a tent around a hole dug in the ground; really irritating though, if you have no change and they won't let you pee without paying. I guess they know that if you have to go you'll find ten baht somehow for nobody visiting there really has no money. Sometimes people try to sneak by and I guess it depends if you feel like fronting it out with a loud Thai happy to cause a scene in front of everyone. Mostly I noticed people just grumble and pay up.

Neither of us had slept on the coach and we both felt a bit groggy. There were touts selling accommodation on Koh Samui, all saying the same story as the TAT lady, that everywhere was fully booked except a few places that they knew about. When the crowds had dissipated we asked one of them if he knew of the spa: in the guide book he drew an arrow on the map, saying that he knew of a couple of places nearby that were much cheaper. We explained about the course and he said it would be no problem, many people did the course whilst staying at these other places, saving money. Though these touts, situated at nearly every farang stopping point, make their money by selling accommodation for commission (I heard somewhere that they get 20% of the first two nights) this guy called the spa for us to confirm that there was still a room available for us. He took no payment but knowing we were on our way, and so close, they agreed to hold the room until lunchtime for us. He reluctantly took our tip for making the call, and wrote down the names of the places he'd recommended in case we ever needed them, marking them too on the map. It was a relief to know we had somewhere to stay, and his help was a welcome lift to the mood after the night on the coach.

Another coachload of farang arrived and unloaded. Then both coaches went off and two other empty ones appeared, one heading to the port for the islands on the east coast, one heading west. We all loaded back on and headed for the port, us with our very many bags, before loading them off the coach and onto the boat.

It was a different port to when I had come down on the night train, I think something to do with the fact that this one had been flooded out back then, and it seemed quite a bit busier too. The boat was jammed with people and piles of bags in the typical Thai style of cramming in as many farang as possible. A couple of farang clambered over a pile of bags and sat down heavily on the luggage pile, indicating why it is a bad idea to put anything at all breakable anywhere but close to yourself.

The sea was still quite rough, and it looked as if the weather had taken another turn for the worse since I'd left less than a week before. A Thai in a bright pink shirt was walking around the boat selling taxi rides direct to resorts. With our number of bags, and not knowing exactly what the spa looked like or where to get off of any public bus, we booked a couple of seats for 150 baht each. It is a problem, even if you have a map, for marrying up marks on a piece of paper with the outside world is not always that easy at home, let alone in Thailand. After my motorbike taxi, then bus, then motorbike taxi experience to Bophut, with our luggage it seemed like the best option. He gave us a ticket and made a joke about running off with the money; I said I'd know where to find him because of his pink shirt to which he laughed and said he had a different one to change into in his bag. In moments like these you can never be sure but simply have to hope that it really is a joke; sure enough, when we arrived at Nathon, after a walk down the pier, the man in the pink shirt appeared and directed us to a minibus, and a group of us all squeezed in with our bags, somehow.

As we headed towards Lamai we chatted with an English couple who had moved to Cyprus and were here on holiday. There was some concern on the bus about the weather for it had started to drizzle, but most had heard that the forecast was ok. I confirmed that the weather had been good for the week I'd spent here before the few days in Bangkok, somewhat hoping it would return, as much as anything to convince Amanda that coming down here really was the best plan.

On we went, feeling very tired from no sleep, and weird from the boat trip which always seems to leave me feeling like I'm still swaying about on the water for weeks afterwards, and just as we appeared to be leaving Lamai the minibus pulled over and indicated that we had reached the spa. Finally, after all the discussions, the views back in England of the website, and the failed attempts to book by email from back home, of course made pretty much impossible by not knowing when we were likely to be there, we had physically arrived.

The Cyprus couple were staying in Chaweng, not far from where I'd stayed before, so remained on the bus, and when we said goodbye they kindly replied that if we were passing by at all then to look them up. Of course, people say this sort of thing not really expecting to meet again, but it is a pleasant way to part anyway.

CHAPTER 11

Lucky Lime Green

When the spa had first opened some years earlier, when the whole of Koh Samui had been less built-up and had fewer visitors, it had been like everywhere else on the island: cheap, simple, and laid back. After an increase in tourism, along with an extremely affluent western culture keen to purchase some good health to offset an otherwise unhealthy lifestyle, the spa was now very much a successful commercial enterprise; not so laid back or simple, and certainly not cheap. Amidst the many busy staff around the place in their uniforms, the computers behind the reception, and the various areas selling food, freshly squeezed juices, herbal nutrients, saunas, massages, and all kinds of homoeopathic remedies for all manner of western problems and ailments, you could almost hear the sound of money chinking in by the second. There were even tip boxes in the rooms to encourage daily generosity towards the maids. That said, it was situated within a very pleasant setting and after Amanda had asked just slightly more questions than the receptionist had felt needed answering straightaway, we went up to our room.

Inside the room everything was just seeming ok when Amanda noticed one of her bags was missing. As well as the big stuffed rucksack with its detachable day bag (and the many plastic carrier bags) she also had a small rucksack, an old faded nylon thing which was tatty-looking but still lockable. After searching the area around reception several times, including the pile of bags that had been left for temporary storage, and more questions for the receptionist, she realised that it was most likely left on the bus. The fact was she couldn't remember seeing it when we got off, though she could remember me putting it in the back of the minibus in Nathon. It had been one of the first things on, and had been buried once the minibus had filled up. As people got off at various stops (not necessarily in the same order as packing their bags) things inevitably got moved around a bit. Of course, not being totally familiar with the entire bag count at that point I hadn't noticed it not coming off either, and to be honest, I reckon both of us being tired and a bit stressed after the bus trip, heads swimming from the boat journey, just glad to have got there, had not been paying enough attention.

After some complicated but futile endeavours with the Thai receptionists whose earlier relief when we had left them soon dissipated when they saw us return, Amanda found the manager of the place, an older-looking Thai guy called Ty, and tried to explain what she thought had happened, hoping that it hadn't really been left in reception and picked up by a stranger. She showed him the small piece of paper that we had been given by the man in the pink shirt. It was nothing more than a blank ticket with a few fields to complete and he'd handwritten it himself, but there was a small piece of Thai print that we hoped might mean something significant. It didn't, it just meant 'ticket' or something similar, and after reporting it missing, as helpful as he wanted to be, there was really not much he could do other than suggest we somehow try and find out the name of the bus company.

Of course, the bag turned out to be the one with both cameras, Amanda's mobile phone and charger, and several other valuable items. In a moment of panic it seemed that suddenly the bag was vital, and that she would be unable to continue the trip without it. Maybe it was because I was more settled in, perhaps had a different perspective, and for sure it wasn't my bag but I thought being unable to continue was being a bit dramatic, after all, I hadn't needed any of the things that had been lost in the six weeks I'd been in Thailand to date. However, as much as I tried to assure her that we would manage somehow anyway, finding the bag was the only thing that would lift the dark atmosphere that had seemed to engulf us; even the sky was grey and looked somehow foreboding.

We headed back to Nathon, taking the public bus back on the same journey that now seemed much longer and slower than on the minibus just a few hours earlier. There was a chance that the man in the pink shirt was around, or that the minibus driver might come back to meet another boatload of farang to deliver around the island, but we saw neither. There wasn't even much activity going on there so we gave up and got another bus back.

The beach looked quite pretty with the small area of fishing boats, and the flat soft sand was good to lay on; it was much finer than on Bophut, and lighter in colour. However, the sea was also much murkier; when swimming it was practically impossible to see through it, and on the sea bed was a layer of fine silt that felt a little slimy and unpleasant. After a while we got out and lay on the beach, and I could see that this was not the paradise that Amanda had hoped for.

The spa had its own restaurant but since it catered specially for the vegetarian or raw food vegan, and both of us felt like having a decent meal after the events of the journey, we headed out along the main road towards the busier area of Lamai. Just a few hundred yards up the road was a large well-lit place set back slightly from the road, and we went to have a closer look. It appeared quite empty other than a guy who walked out towards us, warning us not to eat in there, doing the slit of the throat miming action. He appeared to be drunk and we were curious to know why he would say such a thing, so pursued him for more information. A large group of Thai police had gathered outside of the place, perhaps twenty in total, all armed, and we all hurried on by, him refusing to speak, waving us away as if he'd said too much already. Out of range of the policemen's hearing he started muttering about a girl who had gone there and been murdered, but all he could say was for us not to go in there. He went on his way so we continued on ours until Amanda did that freeze and gasp thing where someone suddenly stops and grabs you, making you feel alarmed instantly before you even know why, and pointed to the lit-up New Hut Beach Resort sign. For a second I hoped it was just a streetside advertisement, or a slightly different name, but Amanda had it etched in: it was beyond sight down a small pathway just off the main drag, but this was the place the Welsh girl who'd been murdered had been staying at. She turned straight around and marched back to the spa, past the group of policemen as inconspicuously as possible for someone who is really panicking inside. As if the spa was some kind of sanctuary, when we were back there she whispered, slightly out of breath: 'That was the place.'

We ate in the spa after all, later than they really liked serving, and the waiter brought out the ice cream and bill whilst we were still eating the fake chicken. That night we made a plan, after all, if the bag was to be found then it would need to be quickly if at all: if tomorrow proved fruitless then we'd have to give up, but for now there was still hope. Though the room was very clean and comfortable, we both slept quite badly.

Next morning we went out and hired a bike from a place just down and over the road, since the bus was actually becoming quite expensive, two of us going backwards and forwards to Nathon. It was a small bike and the lady gave us a slightly strange look when she knew we were both getting on it, but after a very quick lesson in how it worked, she took my passport and 150 baht and gave us the key and a couple of crash helmets. She asked if we wanted petrol, confirming that the tank was virtually empty. If she would sell us some, I replied, and she poured a small bottleful carefully measured out into the tank: the needle on the gauge didn't move and she said that there was also a petrol station just down the road, leading me to wonder why I had bothered.

We headed towards Chaweng on our new vehicle, the small lime green moped with its little shopping basket on the front, hoping to track down the Cyprus couple who we'd met on the bus: the bikes for hire on the island generally had a number, and ours had the number 7; we hoped it would be lucky. Just a couple of miles down the road we reached a particularly hilly section and the bike started misfiring, popping small explosions before cutting out. I'm not sure what sort of fuel she'd sold me but we managed to coast down the hill to another street-side vendor and bought another litre which seemed to solve the problem, even though the petrol gauge still read empty. These places can sell virtually anything, and sometimes the most unlikely looking small roadside hut will have a couple of drums of fuel set up in the sunshine with heavy dispensing pumps that look like they may have looked in England over thirty years ago, with numbers on cards that seem to flap round instead of the orange-lit digital lights or LEDs of today's western world.

The day before, Ty had managed to track down the name of the resort where the Cyprus couple had been staying. To be fair to him, he had gone out of his way to make several phone calls to possible places before a receptionist at a resort on Chaweng beach confirmed that yes, yesterday around lunch-time an older couple from Cyprus had indeed checked in, but that is all she would say, refusing to give out any other details. The plan today was to find them, or at least leave a message at reception for them, to see if they'd seen the bag or if they knew anything about the minibus, anything that could help. We'd written a letter with details of where we were staying, just in case. As it was, the resort was within a complex of several large luxury hotels, and finding the right reception was not easy. However, by chance, just as we came out of one of the buildings we happened to see them walking down the road towards the beach. Like a scene made-up in a comedy sketch we got back on the bike to speed down the road before we lost them again. You have to bear in mind that I've hardly ridden a motorbike in my life, and that the last time had been many years before and I'd nearly crashed then, and that was without anyone on the back. So when we wobbled to a halt beside them with our crash helmets on they wondered at first what was up. Anyway, they knew nothing that could help but were very sympathetic, and we headed off on to the next phase of the mission with the consolation that the weather was good today, providing a feeling of positive enthusiasm to the point of perhaps unfounded expectation.

There was a chance that the man in the pink shirt did the same run every day, selling tickets to farang on the boat from Nathon to Koh Samui. Amanda was probably more hopeful than I was, for I couldn't help but think if he did the same run then it might be every other day, using the day in between to get back to the mainland. Back on the bike we returned once again to the port of Nathon, well before the boat from Surat Thani was due to dock, hoping that when it did we would find the man in the pink shirt.

Nathon was busy this morning and we ate a decent breakfast in a place on a corner that overlooked the pier, just to have a good view of things in case a boat suddenly appeared. We asked around a few drivers, showing them the small ticket in case there was anything they recognised, but to no avail; we asked the official boat ticket sellers on the pier but they couldn't help either. After a while, the traffic in the waiting area began to increase, and a boat arrived. Our fear at missing it if it came in quick was amusing, considering just how long it takes a large boat to pull up and offload, and we waited, eyes peeled for our man. Thankfully the mozzie deet had cleaned the sunglasses enough for me to be able to see during the day, even if my spectacles were useless.

It was a long shot, and he was hardly likely to be wearing the same pink shirt again anyway, but amidst a small crowd heading for the car-park, was the man. Amanda had seen him, pointing him out with an urgent, 'That's him.' A Thai in a blue shirt; sure enough, it was him, though he looked quick to deny being anyone when we suddenly pounced on him. We showed him the precious little ticket, I mentioned his pink shirt and his joke, and he remembered who we were. Amazingly, after a series of phone calls whilst we waited nearby, wondering what was being said as we heard one side of a Thai conversation, he came back and confirmed that the bag had been found: all we had to do was to get to an arranged meeting point not far from Chaweng and a driver would meet us there. He indicated on a map exactly where the petrol station rendezvous point was located, taking quite a liking to my Parker pen. I kind of liked the pen too so gave him a tip instead. When he'd gone, our relief at our fortune was such, however, that I hurried back before his bus pulled away, waving him down with his second alarming intrusion that day, and gave him the pen as well: he eyed it carefully and took it as if he'd expected that to happen all along.

I'd tried to explain that it might take me a bit longer than anyone else but we'd arranged to meet up in forty minutes, plenty of time for an average bike rider to make the trip, so we got straight back on, wobbling and weaving our way out through the busy but small streets of Nathon towards Chaweng. It's pretty much one road, even if very bendy and narrow in parts, and eventually we found the petrol station, hoping that we weren't too late. After about ten minutes of scrutinising every possible-looking vehicle, in pulled a minibus similar in colour to ours from the day before: as it veered its skewed course over towards us, weaving through the gaps between the pumps, we could see the driver holding the bag up in the windscreen. His smile showed he was as happy as we were, possibly just happy because we were happy. Amanda tipped him and checked the bag: it hadn't even been opened, and to our amazement as much as delight, everything was in there that should have been.

We headed back to the spa where once safely stored, the bag could be truly classified as retrieved, as if until then it was still at risk. I was kind of getting the hang of the bike, and starting to enjoy it a bit; the semi-automatic gears needed no clutch so were quite forgiving of my many errors. There was a small panel of lights on the dashboard indicating which gear the bike was in but I couldn't always see it in the bright sunshine; several times I held up a bit of traffic as the bike struggled to pull away with the two of us in third gear, sometimes stalling. I know for a fact that Amanda has been on the back of bikes much faster than this, though with far more competent riders, so each time something happened she would cling on tighter half in a panic, half embarrassed.

When we showed the receptionists the bag and told them the story they seemed to force a smile before talking to each other in Thai, as if they thought that we were really quite strange people. One of them looked like they could have been a boy turning into a girl, but we could never be sure: even he/she spoke to us with a slight tone of condescension after that, in a way that one would laugh politely at the jokes of a psychopath just to keep him happy.

Since we had the bike for the rest of the day we decided to go for a ride around the island. On the map it's virtually one road, and the only road that follows the coast, and even if you take a wrong turning and head inland you will soon reach the coast on the other side.

Into the sunshine in the fresh air, so much cooler when riding along but easily warm enough with just a pair of shorts on, we headed around through the scenic views of the coast to the left and the mountains and forests to the right, tooting our way through like all the other bikes, though we were about the only ones to be wearing crash helmets. On Koh Samui apparently the law is that you should wear one but it is only enforced very occasionally when a policeman might decide to stop everyone riding without one. I never saw this happen but was aware that I was still fairly new to all this so kept it on, just in case. We ended up in Bophut village and I pointed across the bay towards Chalee Villa, hoping Amanda would feel the lure of the tranquillity before heading round to the Big Buddha just round the bay. The bike made exploring so much easier and was great fun until, as so often happens so quickly in such situations, before becoming too relaxed, my complacency was checked with a patch of rough road. It was actually more like a stretch, the surface of the road having been worn away by flooding, so that instead of just bumping over and through it, hoping for the best, this time the bike nearly swerved out of control. The front wheel, at one point, was bumping along sideways so that the contents of the small shopping basket bounced out; somehow the bike stayed upright and when we skidded to a stop Amanda got off, declaring that she wasn't getting back on again. It must have all made good viewing for the people watching from the shops and diners at the side of the road. I got off too, feeling a bit shaken up, and stood a little bit away from the bike, distancing myself from the offending embarrassment: where before some of the near-misses had been in a way exhilarating, realising just how close we had come to crashing then was more shocking.

I promised to be more careful and we got back on and had a quick look at the Big Buddha which appeared to have some scaffolding around it. Time was getting on and Amanda wanted to get back before it got dark, so we went on. I suggested a route around the coast, through Chaweng, which I thought would be well lit-up anyway, and then on to Lamai; unfortunately however, I had forgotten just how quickly it gets dark in Thailand. Within about ten minutes it was dark and, without glasses and unable to wear my sunglasses any longer, I could no longer see where we were going. Still, the route had looked so simple on the map, and I kept assuring Amanda that I thought we were heading the right way. The road became very narrow and very dark and when we reached a crossroads in the middle of the forest, I didn't have a clue which way to go. I pulled over, much to Amanda's horror who thought that either someone would see that we looked lost and take us as hostage, or that someone was just about to jump out from the forest and grab her, like some scene from a Hammer House of Horror story.

I took a chance and headed onwards, eventually hoping to reach a junction back onto the main drag. Unfortunately, in this corner of the island the road structure is such that you have to turn off the main drag to stay on the coastal road and avoid going back round in a small loop; at some point I took a right instead of a left, or missed a left turning and continued when I shouldn't have, and before long we were heading back past Bophut village in the wrong direction. I had a hunch as we passed it but had lost all sense of direction, all the time trying to make out to Amanda that there was no problem, that just around the corner it would all become clear and we would know exactly where we were, probably only yards away from the spa.

It was as we passed through a street of shops that

all had Maenam in their name that I knew we were in Maenam. At night many of the stretches of the island looked similar to me, and I could hardly read the road signs before it was too late to change direction. But this was Maenam for sure, I'd even been there before, though I didn't say anything. Not long after that Amanda noticed the signs indicating we were heading towards Nathon, which meant she knew too that we had gone the wrong way back; but it also meant that it would be quicker to continue. By the time we got back it felt like we had been on the bike for days; indeed, there were times during that last hour when it felt like we would never get off, like ghosts destined to rev along forever on the whining machine through the darkness, lost.

I took the bike back that night to the place we hired it from before any real damage could be done. The lady gave it a real good look over, much more thorough than the brief scan before she'd loaned it, but was just about content. It almost seemed as if she would have preferred some damage, perhaps knowing the bike engine had seen better days. For sure, our demands that day hadn't helped prolong its life.

In what was most certainly a combination of many events and circumstances, we ended up arguing that night. The tension was not helped by the fact that no matter how often Amanda asked the reception people, they did not have a room available for the time needed to complete the course before March; added to this was the fact that our two nights were nearly up and we had to check out and find somewhere else. It felt like we hadn't really relaxed in the whole time there, and though the setting is very pleasant with its piped flute music and yoga tents, it seemed there was an unexplainable air of oppression about the place which I was glad to leave.

CHAPTER 12
Mr Tong's Brother

Packing up and checking out was never that easy with all the bags, though fortunately Amanda hadn't unpacked everything this time. We left them in the reception area for safe storage and headed down the road to one of the places the guy in Surat Thani had suggested. It was fully booked, as were a couple of other places we passed that looked ok. Not wanting to go too far from the spa, we turned back and headed in the other direction. Conscious that this was in the same direction as the New Hut Resort we opted for an alternative plan of heading back to Bophut for a week just to chill out and relax. I remembered that the sea had at least been cleaner than at Lamai, the food was good and the people were lovely and friendly, and hoped that after a week there Amanda might feel as settled in as I had done.

As we walked down the road in the now oppressive heat of the day, the thought of lugging the bags around without knowing where we were heading seemed almost impossible, and it was the best place that I knew of, so Amanda agreed.

Right nearby was a travel agent so we went in and the lady phoned Chalee Villa for us, to make sure that they had a hut available. She confirmed a week there was ok, and though she would take no money, not even for the phone call, she was curious to know what we were doing. Explaining that the spa was full but that Amanda wanted to do a course, the lady said that she had huts available; many people had stayed there and simply walked up to the spa each day. She showed us the huts which actually looked better than those at the spa, and booked us in after our week in Chalee Villa. If we'd known this first we may not have booked Chalee at all, who knows, but then since Amanda was also happy to smoke and drink coffee for a week it seemed that things had worked out ok after all.

I guess it was perhaps an indication of how things would continue when the taxi had slid as far down the slippery track as possible, the same track that the motorbike taxi had swerved down before, and we had to carry the bags for the last few hundred yards. Laden like a camel with the two big bags strapped across me, Amanda carried the remainder. It wasn't until I emerged from under the hat and luggage right in the reception of Chalee Villa that they recognised me. Pleased at my return, they welcomed us with coffee at one of the tables by the seafront.

Mr Tong apologised that I couldn't have my hut

for a few days because some people were staying in it; however, he assured me that as soon as they left he would move us into it. I had no claims to it as my hut, but had happened to mention before I left that I'd liked it right on the seafront: until it became ready we stayed in one halfway up the avenue. It was larger than the hut on the beach, with two single beds. As before though, there was no hot water and no flusher for the toilet except the large bucket and small water bowl facilities for manual assistance. I suppose the cold water shower would have been more acceptable if the flow had been more than the tiny trickle not quite strong enough to implement the effect of the shower rose, so that it was more of a randomly directed dribble than a nicely spread array of tiny jets. To be honest, it just about did the job and wouldn't have bothered me too much, I mean I wasn't there for the washing facilities: however, when it stopped working altogether with Amanda still covered in soap, for her it was more of an issue. My joke at finishing off using the trigger hose did not go down well.

Mr Lee was still around and assured me that now he had some weed that was much better than before. I suppose in hindsight it must have been weird for Amanda because she hadn't seen the weeks of turning down opportunities, nor the week where all had been safe and well. To her, I think she thought it was taking an excessive risk, and though she was ok about it, I knew she felt a bit uneasy at first.

Frederick the Norwegian soldier was still there too, and always happy to converse. He was hoping to head off to China but needed to sort out some visas somehow so was staying around for a few days. His

English, as most Scandinavians that I've met, was excellent, and since he also enjoyed talking he was a good person to speak with if you wanted to know what had been going on. He knew, he told us, the people in 'my' hut actually hated it and wanted to leave: they were on a honeymoon and apparently the newly married wife had been expecting something a little more luxurious. I said I wondered what people expected when they came to a tropical island, and Frederick agreed that as long as all the physical needs are met with a reasonable standard of cleanliness then surely that is all that matters. Later Amanda let me know in no uncertain terms that she could see exactly why she would have hated it.

The weather had turned sunny again and we spent much of the week laying on the beach reading the book designed to be read just before embarking on the cleansing course. There had been a time back in England when I'd suggested that maybe it would be beneficial for me too: however, a bit like the giving up smoking plan which had lasted about three hours one night in Chaweng (finally giving in to the craving after all the shops had shut so I'd had to use part of an old bank receipt for rolling paper), I wasn't quite so keen now. This was partly due to feeling so much better anyway, perhaps from the diet, the climate, or just the slower pace, and partly because I felt too thin not to eat for a week. Amanda was ok with this since she thought that it would be best for one of us to be mentally alert after the previous events. So we read the book that explained how all the toxins were killing us and needed flushing out. After smoking in the hut it all seemed interesting enough as we laid there in the sun, and Amanda was happy since I think she felt that in reading the book she was doing something positive towards the course, all the time still being able to enjoy the wonderful breakfasts, coffee, and banana pancakes with honey served up in the restaurant, and the cheap cigarettes.

When the honeymoon couple had left, placed somewhere else by the tour company that had put them in Chalee Villa, we moved into the hut on the beach. It was much smaller but at least the shower worked and there were no gaps in the floorboards. I omitted to mention the four cockroaches I'd found crawling over my toothbrush the first time I'd stayed; I had after all thrown them outside and thereafter kept everything wrapped away when it wasn't needed, and didn't see that it would be a helpful story. This hut had a hammock too, though of course we had to take it in turns.

I felt very relaxed again, partly knowing that we had somewhere to stay for now and the next few weeks, and partly because Amanda was very close to being able to complete the course, after which I hoped all would be well and we could continue on the trip in good health. Having somewhere to stay was one less very important concern to worry about, and finding somewhere when it is hot, when all is unfamiliar, and when laden down with baggage, is not that easy. You end up taking a chance anyway, no matter what it looks like, even if you have the opportunity to see it before you check in, for who knows who else may be staying there, out of sight when you check it out; often people make all the difference, and so often people look at many places only to return to the one they first thought was right anyway. You may as well take pot luck, or at least go with your instinctual feeling.

In a moment of candid honesty back on Koh Pha Ngan, Ben the German had admitted that the whole travelling around thing had not been the adventure that he'd hoped it would be, that there were no groups of hippies sat around campfires smoking pot on the beaches, singing to gentle guitar music, and it was not the spiritually enlightening experience of finding oneself he'd expected, but quite hard work. If we are honest then we will admit to ourselves, we are simply tourists spending money in a country of people we cannot truly understand; and what we find is that we have been born, by chance, into a different world to them, made so by the vastly different possibilities that circumstances allow.

It was during this week that I became aware why Frederick had made his comment about Mr Tong's brother. Where the hut on the beach was further down, he had no need to pass directly by: our hut further up the avenue, however, that we'd been in before the honeymooners had left, was on the much-walked path from his hut to the restaurant. In the mornings, before people began to eat, Mr Lee and the waiter guy would tidy up the avenue, picking up leaves, and would always say good morning if we were out on the balcony: Mr Tong's brother, however, would never reply, and the only people I ever really saw him speak with were Mr Lee and the fisherman who hung around. However, though he'd never reply, he often made a strange sound as he passed. When he began to raise his arm simultaneously with the 'pa-choo' sound, it could have been construed as being a shooting action. After possibly too much speculation, Amanda and I guessed that perhaps he had been involved in a Southeast Asian war of some kind, like Apocalypse Now, and with the tense, harrowing memories in a setting blurred by strong Thai alcohol and marijuana, was somehow lost in a different world, in a different time. Amanda said she felt uneasy around him, and if I'm honest then I have to admit I was glad when we were back in the hut on the beach, off the path, out of range.

Chalee Villa got busier as the week went on and the Full Moon party over in Hat Rin approached. This time it was a proper full moon, not a Christmas or New Year version, and the weather had improved. Chatting to several people made it clear to Amanda that nearly everyone here had been visited by Mr Lee, which put her mind at rest. One girl even spoke as if it was practically legal, and planned to take a pocketful of pre-rolled over to the party; we told her about the undercover police likely to be there, showing her what the book said, just so she didn't get tricked, and she was much relieved to have been forewarned. In the end we didn't go, for many reasons, one of which was that we were due to check out the next day.

The morning after the party the restaurant was busy with stories from the night before, which had seemed to go well for most. We checked out and Mr Lee assured me that he was due to be getting something even better; I said I hoped to get back and see him soon, and we headed off to Lamai. The fisherman who hung around the place and was friends with the family became a taxi driver and took us; after a three-way discussion in Thai with Mr Tong and Mr Lee, he explained on the way that they had been arguing about which was the quickest way, since there were three possible routes from here, and not much difference in terms of travel time. He opted for the route that cut across the island, giving us a new and pleasant view of the forest scenery in the morning sunshine on the way.

CHAPTER 13
Colonic Irrigations

The fisherman dropped us off, and after a thorough count of the bags to make sure we had everything, we checked into the Surat Palm Beach Resort back at Lamai. The nice lady who'd made the phone call greeted us with a kind smile, as if she recognised us, but then throughout my time I could never tell if Thai people just smiled like that at people anyway. A huge German Shepherd dog lay on the reception room floor, happy to do nothing in the heat; alongside him was a much smaller dog with long, white fur. When Amanda happened to mention a slight concern at being so near the New Hut Resort the lady simply pointed at the dog and said if we had any trouble then he would hear it; better than any policeman, she assured us, pulling back his jowl and giving us a quick look at his teeth. When I asked what his name was she said something I couldn't understand; seeing my puzzlement, she kind of flexed her muscles in a weight-lifting pose and repeated, 'Rambo.' He was a well-built dog in every area imaginable, and the name seemed fitting. Just as it had done at Chalee Villa, the fact that these people openly cared for and looked after their animals well did much to put Amanda's mind at ease.

The hut was a cold water shower but the western-style toilet had a flusher this time. The lady had fully empathised with Amanda at her relief at this fact, and I felt a slight indication of the, *Yes, see, how could you have made me suffer such deprivation?* With the benefit of experience and investigation, it seems that this sort of thing is more of a big deal to ladies than to men. Or maybe that just happens to be because of who I've spoken with; I'm not a girl, I don't know.

It was a beautiful setting amidst the palm trees, set back from the beach but only yards away from it. The huts all faced towards the sea and had been somewhat randomly placed so that there were many different pathways leading through. We'd bought a couple of hammocks from a beach seller on Bophut so we'd have one each, even in places where they didn't have their own: unfortunately there was nowhere on the structure to tie it safely, but never mind, it seemed a lovely place.

We went for a walk down the road and found an excellent roadside diner called the Ninja. The restaurant at our place did breakfasts and snacks but closed in the afternoon. It meant walking past New Hut Resort to get to it but the road was busy and well-lit at night even. The Ninja food was good and very cheap, they stuck a fried egg on top of pretty much everything, and there was an internet area round the back where we could check for emails. It all seemed like it had worked out, maybe not as planned but certainly as required, though who can tell what will happen before it does?

The first morning was beautiful and sunny, and sat on the beach in the early, peaceful tranquillity before people began to do whatever it was they did, everything felt at ease. Looking at the beach at a time like this, it was hard to imagine it could have been the scene of such a hideous crime. The huts at New Beach were right on the beach itself, small, thatched, wigwam-shaped and raised above the sand on stilts to minimise chances of flooding. At night the place was lit up with small lights like a Christmas tree. Between us and it was a gully that led into a swampy area: this was passable by following a pathway through the sea when the water was low enough, when the tide was out; if it had rained or if the tide was high then it became quite impassable. Some said a huge lizard lived in the swamp but no-one ever saw it. To our left, in the other direction, the short walk along the beach through the palm trees led to the spa; when the tide was high it meant getting wet feet in a few places where the waves swallowed up the beach but was still traversable. A strange old totem pole stood amongst the trees, weathered and battered but still standing.

We ate breakfast at our resort, another excellent American breakfast of eggs, bacon, toast, coffee, and juice, and headed to the Ninja to check the emails. Amanda had some matters to sort out which she hadn't been able to do before she left, to let her family and friends know the latest plan, which gave me a chance to catch up too. Though I'd sent a few emails by then, I didn't really like sitting indoors on a whirring computer in a tropical country; somehow it didn't seem right to be clinging onto the world back home when the idea was to be getting away from it, into a different world and culture. But then it is a useful way of keeping in touch with people, and easy and cheap all over Thailand.

Normally you might find several terminals all lined up along a wall inside a shop, each with its own seat but not too much elbow room; and almost certainly there is an unspoken etiquette that although one could easily read what the person next door is writing, most people tend to keep their eyes focussed on their own business only. It's weird that you can detect when someone else is looking over, even though all they have moved is their eyes. Anyway, in the Ninja they had an entire closed off internet area round the back of the restaurant; and each computer not only had its own private booth – a personal cubicle – but had a big comfortable armchair in it as well. I must say, that particular morning I was glad of the privacy.

Back in England, before I had left, my gran had been very ill with the second bout of double pneumonia in three years. I knew I was going away, and so did she, and knew that it was most likely that if she was still alive when I left then she probably wouldn't be when I got back. The illness had left her frail body as not much more than a loose bundle of bones, denying her even the strength to turn over by herself. You cannot wish somebody would die just to fit in with your plans though if she had passed on when the illness was at its peak then it would have been over and done with long before I left, and in truth would have made things, in a way, easier. However, for a small lady she was very tough and did not want to die, so she had fought through it and hung on. I had said goodbye, making her promise to help the nurses so that she would be there, back in her armchair in the living room back home where she had lived ever since I had known her, when I returned.

My dad had sent an email telling me the bad news. No doubt this must have been a difficult email to write, and never a preferred delivery option, but then there was no other way of contacting me. So I felt very sad, and when I went outside for a cigarette it felt very strange to be upset in the heat, surrounded by Thai voices carrying on their daily business. I read the email on the morning of the 17th: she had died early in the evening of the 15th, waiting for the full moon to rise before giving up her spirit. My dad had sent it in the early hours of the 16th but with the time difference there had inevitably been a slight delay. There was talk that the date of the funeral may be the 20th but it hadn't been decided fully yet. He suggested that it would be proper to remember her at the time of the funeral but that he did not expect me to come back for it. If it was going to be on the 20th then it was unlikely that I would be able to get back anyway.

Amanda was very sympathetic and perhaps it was better that it had happened after she had come out rather than when I was there on my own. However, she was also very much concerned at what I would do next since this very much had an impact on what she would do. The newspapers that had plastered the story of the murdered student had also ran the story that the men responsible had been caught: two Vietnamese fishermen were being held and were due to be executed, just to put everybody's mind at rest; they had even confessed to it. This didn't really do much for Amanda's peace of mind, and staying where she was alone for a week or so whilst I returned was not an option. Yet having left her own flat and put everything she had into getting out here, it seemed that to forego the opportunity of completing the course that might put an end to the years of ill health when it was so close would be such a waste. Being January, flights were not only hard to get but were very expensive: I could barely afford to go back alone, and this would have meant maxing out a credit card and juggling money for the next few months, so paying for the two of us was out of the question.

It turned out that the funeral was delayed until the 27th, but having realised that it would mean the end of the trip for both of us I decided to stay in Thailand. It had been a difficult decision to make, and the few days whilst it was hanging in the air had been very tense for both of us; after all, this was not like some distant relative who I had hardly ever seen but rather someone who had practically been like a mother to me when I was young, and over the years since. However, she was gone, she would not be there, and there are times when I believe the needs of the living come first. My family all said that I would be missed but were supportive and fully understood, and I think Amanda's family were relieved to know she wouldn't be left out there on her own.

For the last week we had been getting up early to

check emails for news and had been eating breakfast as well as dinner at the Ninja. Now things were more sorted we realised that we should go back to eating breakfast at our own resort. It must have looked weird walking past the restaurant each morning and then coming back after breakfast. Admittedly the first occasion we ate at the Ninja was because we were up before our restaurant lady had opened up. But the book says it, and I reckon it's true, that you should eat at least one meal a day at the place where you are staying: if you don't, they will wonder why. At least you get to know the people you are staying with, staff and guests, and it's undoubtedly the best way of finding out what's going on immediately nearby.

Both the reception lady and the restaurant lady were lovely, friendly people. Sometimes you had to go and find them if you wanted something; out of sight and out of the heat, the sound of laughter gave away their whereabouts as they chattered and cackled away at something. As well as the two dogs, who seemed to bark at everyone who was not staying there quite viciously, like they knew who were guests and who weren't, there was a small black and white cat that roamed about the place. It looked like a kitten but being Thai was just a small cat. We like cats too, so she soon realised she was welcome and even began to sleep in our hut. Her greatest pleasure was to chase the small lizards that she was quick enough to catch with ease, letting them go only to catch them again straightaway. The lady in the restaurant fed her dry food, and when I asked what her name was she said in her Thai voice: 'Meow Meow.' Often Rambo would chase her for his own amusement and she'd end up in a palm tree somewhere, hissing at him from a safe distance until he got hot and bored and wandered off, with little Scamp following close behind. One day in the restaurant I could see Meow Meow had had enough of running and fronted him out. Rambo was so taken aback that when she hissed and swiped at him he backed off, totally perplexed. For a while she strutted through like she was Queen Cat but in truth I think all involved knew it was only for as long as Rambo felt like playing along. When a stray beach dog turned up and broke the rules, Rambo had him pinned to the ground with his teeth, whining in seconds.

A German guy called Colin moved into the hut next door. He had a guitar and was happy to smoke weed sat outside his hut, so I joined him a few times. I hadn't gone back to see Mr Lee mostly because of the bad news from home and needing to sort out what to do, so it was a welcome smoke. He'd been over to Koh Lanta where he said it was much hotter, and the sea much clearer and bluer, and had found a place where you could sleep in a treehouse overlooking the jungle. I know Germans have a reputation for being organised, but this guy was on a quick four-week tour of Thailand to find the best places to stay for when he returned with his girlfriend the following year. He'd been to Krabi, Koh Lanta and Koh Pi Pi on the west coast, and was visiting Koh Samui, Koh Pha Ngan, and Koh Tao before heading up north.

When I'd been staying in Chaweng first time round on the King's birthday back in December, from the beach I'd seen a stream of floating lights from over the bay somewhere in the distance rise up into the sky and drift away. They seemed to stay in the sky for ages, lanterns that somehow stay burning but are lighter than the air. I thought that it would be a good idea for Gran's funeral ceremony that we were going to have on Lamai beach. We asked everyone we could think of where we might find some of them. It took some describing as well, for whenever I spoke of floating lanterns most people thought I meant the type that floated on water. As so often is the case, it took a series of mimes to find out that they are actually called 'chom loy'.

We spent one rainy day wandering around the whole of Lamai town in our ponchos looking for the 'chom loy' to no avail. It had ended up being a much longer walk than we'd thought; to make matters worse Amanda's poncho had begun to leak. She had planned to get one the same as I had, a basic model, not too expensive but that seemed robust enough: instead, in my absence she'd bought an alternative in a sale from a camping shop, a much more expensive piece of kit that had been reduced so that the price was the same as mine had been. When she'd shown me she was very pleased with herself, for it was indeed a plush-looking poncho and the material felt pleasant to the touch, kind of silky. Tired from trudging around, wet from the leaking material and disappointed with her purchase, she was now not nearly so pleased.

That's how the weather was at the time, maybe a day of rain and then a day or two of sun. When the roads had dried out we hired a bike again for the day to undertake a proper search of the island for the now almost essential 'chom loy'. It seemed like a wild goose chase around the island, starting in Nathon. When we managed to explain what we were looking for, and then when we managed to find the specific shops to which we had been directed, still there were no chom loy for us. I couldn't help but wonder whether this sort of thing just isn't sold to farang, and that perhaps the Thais see it as somehow disrespectful to be allowing such things normally reserved for special occasions to be let off any old time. In a way it surprised me that Thais, being as fun loving as they are, didn't let these things off more often. We ended up in a small store in Maenam; as with most places they were happy to sell us firecrackers, just like were in a mysterious box we'd bought in Lamai that we'd hoped might have been the right things; not being able to see inside or read the description, it had been difficult to tell. The shop person had smiled and nodded reassuringly when I'd described what we were after; however, where there is a possible sale there is an element of Thai optimism ever present and we'd taken a chance. Firecrackers are not expensive but these seemed hardly appropriate for Gran's funeral ceremony. In Maenam instead we bought a bunch of windproof candles and some incense.

On the way Amanda had seen a stray dog and wanted to stop and get some food for it. I must admit I thought attempting to feed every stray animal on the island was an impossible mission, but I guess she thought that feeding just one was something, and hadn't really come to terms with the general Thai attitude towards stray animals. Getting back to the bike I could see it had been moved so had a quick check to see there was no damage, and that it had been moved by hand rather than nudged by the heavy-looking truck collecting glass now parked there:

it all seemed ok but I was puzzled how he'd moved it with the steering lock on; a further check showed that the lock was no longer on, and didn't seem to be working. For a while I thought that it had been broken just to move it, and could hardly believe that a Thai person would have done that. Typically when we had parked up, there had been a line of bikes along the road; when we'd returned it was just ours left. I puzzled in my mind why he hadn't just dragged the bike out of the way, and wondered if he'd either seen us or guessed by the hire bike number that we were farang, so that he'd simply broken the lock instead using some special know-how; I felt somewhat affected by it all evening.

The following day was funeral day. Calculating the time difference it meant that we'd have our ceremony at nine o'clock in the evening so it would be synchronised. The weather that day was a clear blue sky, and in the morning I took the bike up the garage to replace the petrol we'd used before returning it. We'd hired it from the nice phone call lady at our resort and I knew I would have to explain about the broken steering lock. Away from their view, I took the chance of having a good look at it whilst at the garage, not that I had any tools to fix it anyway, but at least I could guess how much damage had been done and how much it might cost. It had been a failed mission anyway, and we'd not found the chom loy, so I took a look just to see. There was no visible evidence of any breakage, and we hadn't seen any pieces of metal on the ground at the scene of the supposed crime. I'd even taken it to a roadside workshop in Maenam for them to check the day before; they'd looked at it for a few minutes, having a conversation in Thai before saying that they might be able to fix it but would need to keep it for a while. They were very puzzled as well but then I found out why: messing around with the key, I realised that in order to put the steering lock on you had to turn the key even further round than the off position: unlike, say, a car in the UK, where the lock just comes on anyway when the key is removed. It appeared that I hadn't even had the lock on, and the glass truck driver had only had to wheel it away. There had been no damage done, no broken metal, no animosity towards farang who park anywhere, and there would be no expensive repair bill. In the bright sunshine I felt like a whole load of imagined worry had simply disappeared.

That evening we went down to the beach just in front of our hut. It was dark by then and in each direction small areas of lights lit the beach. Having been sunny all day and for a few days, the sand was warm and dry, and with the low tide the waves hardly made a sound as they lapped gently at the shore. We built a small floating boat out of things that had drifted onto the beach; onto this we placed a small candle, some incense, and tied on a plant with a piece of red ribbon made into a bow. Amanda threw on some tobacco which she said was apparently the custom in ancient days. My gran had hardly smoked at all, if ever, but in her life had been surrounded by tobacco smoke and open fireplaces so I'm sure she would have felt at ease with it. Around the boat we put more incense sticks in the sand, and made a circle from the big candles we'd bought in Maenam. These were like sticks of wood with red candle wax wrapped around most of it, leaving part of the wood exposed much like a lollipop, to stick into the ground. There was hardly a breeze anyway but these candles were designed to burn even in the wind.

When the time came we lit all the candles and the incense and just sat there for a while thinking, while the funeral went ahead back home. She spent most of her life being late and I couldn't help but wonder if she'd got there on time. I'm sure most people would say good things about their grandparents, especially on an occasion like this, so this is nothing unusual; however, my gran was a person with a loving heart, generous with kindness, and a pleasure to have known, and would be always be remembered with great fondness. Amanda had known her for a short while too, and thought the same of her.

It is odd how such things are timed, for I don't recall the date being a special occasion otherwise, but as our candles burned on the beach in the centre of the bay, at both ends, simultaneously, fireworks began to go off. It was as if they had been timed especially, with her small flames burning in the centre of the show. When it was all over, and our candles had burned out, we put the small boat out to sea with its small candle just about still alight. The little waves slowly took the boat out, the flame died, and we went and sat back on the beach, placing a small rock where the boat had been.

For a while we just sat there looking out to sea, all quiet. I heard a small splashing sound and in the distance it appeared that somebody was walking through the water. Through the dimness I could just about make out a figure in the bay, maybe forty yards out. It was odd because I'd swam out there and thought it was deeper than that; this mysterious-looking figure, wearing a white dress, appeared to be walking across it, barely ankle deep. She looked like she was wearing small white Wellington boots, the ladies' type that finish well below the knees, just like my gran used to wear when she took us for a walk across the forest when I was very young. Odd to say the least, and Amanda saw it too so I know I wasn't imagining it; we watched the figure walk the entire length of the bay, always staying the same distance from the shore, until she went past the spa, beyond the far headland and out of sight.

The next morning I went down to the beach. It was early and there were only a few people around. The stone was where we had left it even though the incoming tide had just about reached it at some time during the night, dislodging the sticks that had remained after the candles had burned out. I walked down to the water to see if the boat had been washed back up: I found the ribbon, still tied in a bow, but no sign of the boat, and comforted myself by considering it an indication, like a message or receipt confirming she had reached her destination safely. The stone stayed where it was, long after the sticks had all washed away, until one particularly stormy night some time afterwards.

What with the events, we extended our stay at Surat Palm; the nice phone call lady gave us an even cheaper rate since we would be there for so long. It was a lovely place, felt quite safe, and we got to know a few people around. Down at the spa, however, things were not quite so simple.

The restaurant, like in most places, is open to anybody, and you don't have to be a guest to eat there.

Amanda needed to prepare for the course first by eating special foods for a few days, so we went there quite often. In a way it was a fairly clever marketing technique, recommending a diet before, during, and after the course, a special diet that only they served locally. The bag incident had been somewhat unfortunate, and so had not been the best of starts; it had, however, caused us to be remembered.

One evening we ate a meal, and there was some confusion over the bill. It wasn't unusual, for as much as the place was clearly a commercial enterprise, there seemed a distinct lack of organisation or enthusiasm from the staff. Sometimes we had to wait for ages to be served and then ages to pay, almost as if it seemed they didn't want us to eat there. So on this night when we came to pay we asked the first waiter who happened to come by for the bill, glad we wouldn't have to wait too long. When he eventually came back the amount was wrong, but it was only fifty baht or so, so we simply paid up instead of arguing about it.

The next day, as we arrived there, I saw the waiter who had served us point us out to another lady who worked there. At first I just thought that they had recognised Amanda, and knowing she was on the course would serve us quickly, like some unspoken preferential treatment for regulars. The lady came across and explained that, though she was sure it was just a mistake, we had left there the night before without paying. After much discussion she accepted that we had paid, though it always felt that she didn't believe us. We thought about paying again but the place was so commercial anyway that I couldn't have done so without resentment, especially knowing how much money we'd both spent there (for both the course and the food were expensive); besides, I knew that sooner or later the waiter that we had paid would appear and the matter could be resolved. As it turned out he never did reappear; either that had been his last night or he had not actually worked there at all, but just appeared to be dressed as a waiter. It seems that he may have picked up a ticket that had already been paid and pocketed our money, which would explain why we had paid the wrong amount and why our ticket had remained unpaid at the end of the night, pinned to the 'outstanding' board in the kitchen. Oddly enough, he looked very much like the waiter on the night train who'd played the change game. It made things awkward thereafter, unfortunately, although the lady was nice about it and to us became known as 'Nice Spa Lady'. Someone told me later that the owner of the place deducts unpaid bills from the staff's already small amount of wages: by the time we stopped going there though we more than made up for things with the tips we left, and hoped the owner didn't take a cut of those too.

Amanda went to see a hypnotist to stop smoking. He was associated with the spa but only as much as he had a card pinned on their wall advertising his services, although he often treated guests who stayed there. Amanda hired a room at the spa for an hour, as he'd suggested, and she had her first session. Should the extremely unlikely event happen that the treatment failed, he stated beforehand that he would return for free. I must admit I was intrigued to see if his results matched his confident assertions and promises, and wondered how many sessions he would give for free before he broke; I felt sure Amanda might be a challenge for him. It was an expensive treatment, and I knew she had smoked for years, and had never been able to give it up before, even after hypnosis. She was, however, convinced that Dr Neil was worth a try.

To be fair it had seemed to work for a while, though not without its pains. One day we were in a restaurant in Chaweng for lunch; she was insisting that she needed to be especially careful what she ate, but didn't like to see me eat what she couldn't. Normally I ate at the resort or at the Ninja on my own, whilst she did things at the spa, so didn't really feel like eating anyway. I ordered some chicken satay with peanut sauce, just for a snack; Amanda ordered some kind of salad. When the food arrived she took one small taste of the dressing, got up, and said with plain disgust there was sugar in it as she walked out. The waiter saw it happen and when I'd finished the chicken he came over and asked if everything was ok. I drank both drinks, apologised about the virtually untouched salad, paid up and found Amanda drinking the contents of a coconut through a straw in another Ninja restaurant, this one owned and run by the sister of the one in Lamai.

By chance a room became available at the spa for Amanda to stay in whilst she did the course. It meant paying for two places for a while but at least it gave her the privacy she wanted, and the close proximity to the facilities, herbs, yoga, broth drinks, special foods, and anything else they were selling as healthy. It also meant being with people on the same course, and the spa set things up so that people began the course at the same time, so they could help each other through it as they faced the same difficulties of not eating for seven days together. The spa seemed a safe place at least, and there was a security person watching all night, which lessened the effect of the close proximity to New Hut. So while Amanda was with her new set of spa friends I thought I could hire a bike and go off exploring the island further, visit Mr Lee, and relax for a while.

It didn't go well from the start: the first night Amanda was due to stay on her own she had a bit of a panic attack. It was quite late and I was in the hut when I heard a knock at the door. I nearly had a panic attack myself until I heard Amanda saying, 'It's me, can I come in?' She'd got the security person to give her a lift down here on the back of a bike, being too scared to stay on her own but too scared to walk the short length of road in the dark. That was when I made a careless assumption of thinking that if Amanda wanted to stay in the hut instead, knowing that I still smoked, that she would be alright with it. Partly though, I guess I thought I'd put myself out enough already, and didn't feel like getting up and going outside for the last smoke of the day knowing it would wake me up. But there is a proverb about going the extra mile, and there is good reason for remembering this, for it is at a time when one feels least like making an effort that extra care is so often needed. Though Amanda stayed in the hut, we had a bad argument and it seemed that it would be pointless continuing the trip like this.

In the morning she went off down the beach towards the spa, not wanting me to go with her; she reminded me of a character in a children's tale and looked as if she should have a small bamboo stick on her shoulder with her belongings wrapped up in a handkerchief. Even though we argued too much, I was fond of her and felt a bit sad as she disappeared into the spa grounds, especially knowing that none of it had gone according to her hopes and plans. I spent the day on the beach thinking it best if I was at least around. It was about four o'clock when Amanda came to the hut, hoping we were still friends, which of course we were. Unfortunately she'd hurt her toe at the spa when her flip-flop had got caught in a loose paving brick, scuffing the toenail into the flesh. I suggested she should perhaps wash it but she explained she didn't have much time because she had to get back to the spa where there was a free yoga class on the beach, which was specifically to help with breathing: it was essential for her to get back. In hindsight, maybe I should have insisted but I prefer to be easy-going and let people do what they want to do. So instead, we walked back along the beach to the spa, to the class that had already started. When Amanda went to join in the instructor told her she wasn't allowed to, for she had missed the beginning.

Things kind of settled down and I spent most of the time on the beach. I didn't bother with a bike or with going to see Mr Lee, mostly because I thought it best to be around in case something else happened. One afternoon Amanda came back in a state. Not only had she started smoking but there had been a major confusion over the change when she had bought the cigarettes. It was odd because the next time I went into the same shop the lady counted out my change in a very strange manner, as if she had known that something had been up. Amanda called

Dr Neil who came back and gave a second session, 'deeper' than the first.

I'm no expert on hypnosis and I wouldn't want to have it personally, so I can't imagine what it was like, but Amanda returned to the hut again that night in even more of a panic, thinking she was either going to die or go mad at the very least. What can you do in a situation like this? You can say don't worry as much as you like but what does that do? You keep calm and hope the feeling is transferred the right way before you catch the fear yourself, but this can seem as if you don't care or aren't taking it seriously. The night passed, no-one died and I didn't make the same mistake as before by smoking in the hut (though Amanda did follow me outside when I went out there).

After a few days of walking up and down Lamai beach Amanda's toe began to look as if it had a slight infection. I'd given her some cream which she said had probably made it worse, and wanted to go to get it checked. We walked in towards Lamai town and found a chemist who gave it a clean and dressed it. The next day, convinced it could develop blood poisoning any minute, Amanda insisted on going to see a proper doctor. There was a surgery in Lamai town where farang could be seen as well as Thais. Of course, the spa course made taking antibiotics a complicated matter, and took some explaining to the doctor, after all, the spa ethos was very much against this sort of medicine and blamed it for a lot of the problems for which they were in the business of offering a cure.

These surgeries are very clean and hygienic, better than perhaps one would imagine in Thailand, and as a farang you simply pay for the treatment as if in a shop. After a long wait we saw a doctor, a Chinese man with excellent English, who agreed that an injection would probably be best, and to return for another if required. He shook his head when he heard that she had been walking through the Lamai sea with an open wound, as if he knew just how polluted the water really was. On the other hand, he was a very pale white colour, appeared never to go in the sun, and may have had the whitening treatment that seems to be so popular over there yet is so weird to me, who spends as much time as possible soaking up the rays.

Before the toe had had its final treatment I developed a painful ear infection, so when we saw the doctor again I got him to take a look. I've had trouble with the ear for years, possibly since a bit of muck flew out of a mixer and landed in it when I worked on a building site a long time before. Ear drops never seemed to work, even the Hopi ear candle had had little effect: I imagined this guy was just going to give me some drops, knowing how much doctors seem to dislike syringing out ears. Not him, he was straight in there and had it all washed out within minutes. He showed me what came out, and even he as a doctor looked quite disgusted at it, and gave me some antibiotic drops to clear away any remaining infection; within days it had all cleared up. After such acute pain it was great relief, and I've not had a problem with it since. Amanda's toe healed up as well but for her it meant buying even more herbal medication from the spa to replace any good bacteria that the antibiotic jabs had killed off.

Amanda finished the course and finally checked

out of the spa, though not without the hassle that was inevitable after our brief history with the place. They had sold her the use of a 'zapper' for a week, designed somehow so that you hold a couple of electrodes and some kind of current 'zaps' bad things in the blood. I saw it as ridiculous and a complete rip-off, and we had tried to take it back after her first session using it. It so happened that the owner of the place was around and I guess he didn't want a scene for so little money, so in the end they didn't push for it, after all, as I had pointed out to them, we had spent quite a lot of money there as it was.

There was still the special dietary requirements for the course aftermath, so we stayed on at the Surat Palm. By now we had got to know a few people around. There was another guy staying long-term who'd been a milkman, sold his business, and come to live out here for at least six months. I'd seen him jogging on the beach when I'd stayed in Chaweng at first, for he was quite recognisable since we looked very much alike; I had thought it odd when I'd seen him again and had mentioned it to Amanda. I called him Mike, imagining that was his name, and even when I found out much later that his name was Andrew, I still referred to him as Mike. He had a Thai girlfriend, a bike on constant hire, and a cheap rate for his hut so was pretty much set up for a while, spending his days sleeping or sunbathing and his nights in bars.

Since our stay in Koh Samui had been longer than expected, I needed to renew my visa. The conversation I'd heard on the bus that first day I'd come to the island came back to me, when I'd thought how we would be long gone by the time the sixty days were up. We found the immigration office where you could apply for an extension. It is a strange process which I found slightly unsettling, for you have to apply and pay for the visa extension before they will let you know whether it will be granted. I wanted to check somehow whether there would be any problem without jeopardising the application by appearing to be suspicious; a security lady must have read my thoughts and indicated it would be ok, and it all turned out to be straightforward, no problems. Though it is slightly stricter than the initial visa application in that you have to provide a reason for being there for longer than planned, they will extend it once in Koh Samui; after that, you have to do a run to the border which consists of sitting on a minibus for about a day, just to get your passport stamped. Some suggest that there is no need for this at all because as long as you are spending money they are happy for you to be in Thailand, suggesting further that the whole visa business is just another means of getting money out of the farang; on the other hand, western countries seem to revel in administration of their own these days that is at least as onerous as a visit to a border once a month.

The beach sellers came by each day with their various wares. Like taxi drivers, they have to apply for a licence and if successful are supplied with a numbered vest. Most days there were a couple of Thai ladies that came by, always together: one sold spring rolls and donuts, carrying a large covered plateful as a waiter might carry a tray; the other carried a stick on her shoulder which balanced on one end a basketful of fruit and sweetcorn, and on the other a portable barbecue to cook the corn. It weighed some, for I had a check of it myself, and the stick bent slightly under the strain with each step taken. The lady who sold the spring rolls (with a small dish of chilli sauce) was young and very beautiful, though somewhat hidden beneath the large hat and white cloth to fend off the scorching sunlight; the sweetcorn lady was older, and was, I'm sure, as glad of the rest as much as the sale when she stopped to serve someone. She would cut up a pineapple or a mango there on the beach using a large knife with considerable skill, perhaps shaping the pineapple as she cut. It was all delicious, but these ladies walked a tough path along the beach all day, in bare feet, carrying their loads for beach sunbathers to sample, just to try and make a living from farang who invariably wave them away like an irritating fly before they even know what they are selling, as if they are just a nuisance, preferring instead to pay vast amounts of money to tour operators back home for the half board or the all-inclusive.

Sometimes there was an ice cream seller with the ladies, though mostly he only appeared at the end of the day when they were on their way home. The ladies had vests but he didn't, so for him it meant taking a chance. He explained that he couldn't get a licence because there were limits to numbers issued: if he was to get caught he would be fined 2,000 baht. Considering how little he earned, this would take some time to repay, especially if they confiscated his stock as well. These are lives so far removed from anything imaginable in our country, yet knowing we were customers of the ladies (one of whom may have been his sister, we were never sure since their English was only slightly less limited than our Thai), he one day insisted that we had a free ice cream. I don't eat ice cream unless it's made from coconut milk, and had to explain that the reason I didn't buy any was because of that; Amanda tried to explain about the spa course and the special diet. The next day he brought a coconut ice cream around especially, and Amanda and I shared it. He got me some Thai tobacco too, at a Thai price, which was virtually nothing; I made him accept payment, though he wanted to give it to me for free. In shops it seems that there are two prices: one is in Thai, that Thais pay, so without knowing the language farang do not know what it is, and one is in English, the price that farang pay. Is it fair, you may ask? Some think not, expecting the price to be fixed regardless: it is odd though, that the world has many people all happy to earn different amounts for their time and effort, yet still expect to pay the same for the same thing.

Since tourism is the main source of income, at least down on the islands, there are many beach sellers trying to earn a living. I bought a necklace in Koh Pha Ngan made of a leather tie with a shell as a pendant, and a tie for my wrist in Bophut. We bought two hammocks in Bophut as well as a few other items, so by the time we met Dan on Lamai we were already sufficiently stocked up. The easiest way to turn away a beach seller is to show them that you've already bought something from someone else; they will try and sell you something to take home of course, but they seemed happier at that rather than an outright refusal at first sight. And if you can say something in Thai then they know you've been here for a while, so don't persist too much. Dan the man, as he even called himself, was worth seeing just for the entertainment he gave. Though small in build, he had a large presence, mostly due to his loud, happy greetings and the ability to talk very quickly for quite some time; so much so we thought he must be on ya baa. He carried a big bag over one shoulder, a large cotton sack stuffed with wares, and several items wrapped over his other arm, and would go through the same motion of revealing each item over his arm, one by one, holding it up at various angles in the sun, catching the light and the best view; then he'd do the same for each item in the bag. To each shake of the head his eyes would look sad before he pulled out something else, showing it off with fresh admiration in his own eyes, as if it was perhaps better than he'd even thought. When he'd gone through his entire stock listing, with great elaborate movements he'd put it all away, taking his time, flapping out the sand and folding things carefully in an exaggerated display for all to see. To his delight we bought a couple of tie-dyed sheets and some silk cloth with an elephant pattern on it, and after that he would stop by and speak every day. His English was fairly good, and he tried teaching us some Thai, as well as explaining further what life was like for a Thai person. He would show us his new wares, just in case, but didn't push for it, happy just to chat as he looked for new customers.

I guess one of the reasons why westerners feel aggrieved towards the sellers may be because really we know that it is unfair, and we don't want to be reminded of our fortunate situation. Maybe we think that really they are fortunate to live in a tropical paradise, how we'd love to walk up and down the beach all day if we could for a job: well, perhaps try carrying a bag across the sand all day long in the heat, along with enough water to see you through, and see how tired you are after just one day under the scorching sun; and if it's not hot, there's no-one there to sell to so you'll have no money. If it is hot, most people are going to turn you away, some annoyed, most wishing you weren't there. Yet when we spoke to people such as the beach sellers, or the waiters or porters, they did not seem resentful in any way, accepting that it is how it is.

It was good for a while just to watch the ordinary world go by without going out looking for entertainment, especially since the ordinary was really something new. The life back home was being left further away as time passed and the everyday items I'd brought with me ran out. Small differences such as buying Thai toothpaste and a toothbrush act as constant reminders of being in a foreign land, though in tourist areas much from the west can be bought, at least the Thai replica equivalent, more or less the same, perhaps slightly different. If you want to find and look there are stores such as Boots and even McDonald's catering for the needs of farang, feeding the need for the familiar. On the other hand, maybe you can see a family of four on one moped, the father holding a child with one arm whilst steering the bike with the other; or young ladies on mopeds in the rain holding an umbrella as they ride; or twenty men stretched out in the back of a pickup truck, piled on top of each other on their way home from work. Such sights make the picture so mixed up that even what is familiar to westerners can seem so out of place to be curiously alien.

One evening we went to a place just up the road with a sign saying 'Thai barbecue'; most of the writing was in Thai except for this one phrase, and the price, which was very cheap. It seemed a busy place, full of Thais eating, so it looked good. A waiter showed us to a table and said we should help ourselves to the large array of food spread out buffet-style on two large tables in the centre. The salad and vegetables included some unusual items, but was mostly vaguely recognisable; the meat, however, was not. Though there was much of it, and I only realised that it was still raw when Amanda pointed it out, it was difficult to know exactly what it was. I took a selection anyway, and back at the table the metal dish sat on fiery coals that the waiter had brought over earlier made more sense. A quick look around showed how to cook it all, so we got stuck in. Actually, I should say I got stuck in for Amanda was a little reluctant, especially with the meat. It all tasted fine, and neither of us were ill afterwards, but even when cooked none of the meat tasted like chicken, pork, lamb, or beef. I would guess, from knowing the types of animal found on the island, that likely possibilities include goat, monkey, and lizard, perhaps various parts of each. I probably wouldn't rush back for another, and we were two of the very few farang amongst the crowds of Thais, but it was worth it for the experience. The waiters seemed glad we'd come too, were very hospitable, and gave us some coconut ice cream with Thai sweets for pudding.

Now that the spa course had been completed, there was no longer any need to stay around Lamai. In truth it had not been the instant miracle cure that perhaps we'd hoped for, and Amanda worried herself into thinking that the antibiotics had messed it all up. But then, who can say what would have happened anyway, for we noted that many of the spa's customers were people who had been here before and had felt the need to return to do it all over again. One day in the restaurant there were a group of men on their fifth or sixth visit, practically competitive about who could fast for the longest; one or two were on their twenty-first day, or so they said. It led me to wonder just how often or for how long one needs to fast in order to cleanse 'thoroughly' and detoxify 'effectively'.

We continued to visit the Ninja, checking emails and keeping up with people back home. It seemed that Amanda's finances hadn't worked out, some cheques hadn't turned up, and she was having to sort that out; I had problems back home too, for it seemed that my gran's death, or more accurately the events preceding and directly after it, had caused much family trouble. Divisions had emerged, people took sides, and things had been said that could never be unsaid. It was a final ironic cruel twist that such a small family should end up fighting over something that my gran had never had in her life, and sad to hear about. It was a worry not being able to do anything from so far away, for some things take more than just a few emails. As well as this, my dad had been having heart problems and needed to go into hospital for surgery. So when he sent an email saying that he wanted to scatter Gran's ashes before his operation in order to help his health, I immediately agreed. A couple of uncles had suggested waiting until I got back, having missed the funeral, but I figured that the least I could do to make things easier would be whatever made him feel better.

It's odd that when I sent my reply, typing out quite a long email, carefully phrased to avoid sounding uncaring, when I tried sending it, it failed and I lost the entire letter. I nearly walked away in annoyance, thinking that I should consider what had been said overnight; and maybe I should have seen the failure message to be an indication to pause, and think. Instead I'd rattled out the reply again as best as I could remember it, only to spend the whole night wondering if I'd done the right thing.

The following day I sent another email, this time saying perhaps it would be good if we came back for the scattering after all, having missed the funeral largely because of circumstances that were now different. Given enough notice the flights would be cheaper, and if the scattering could be delayed until just before his hospital date then we would still have time to see a bit more of Thailand before cutting the trip short. If the date was to be sooner, however, then I would need to know quickly in order to act in time.

By now the weather had turned unsettled again and a big storm flooded the beach, leaving a mass of washed-up wooden debris, trees or pieces of wood that had been floating around somewhere out to sea since the damage from the previous storm. Gran's stone was finally washed away, and we decided to head over to the west coast where we'd heard it was hotter and more settled. So we said our goodbyes to the lovely people of Lamai and headed off to Krabi.

CHAPTER 14
The Pink Suitcase

It was still dark when we got up, and only just light when the minibus picked us up to take us to the port. Amanda had spent hours packing the night before: the potions, lotions, and stuff still overflowed into plastic bags. The bus filled up around Lamai and then headed to Nathon where we got off and onto a different coach. Waiting amidst the confusion, it seemed there had been a last-minute change in departure points, and we headed out of Nathon and boarded the ferry further up the coast.

After all the unsettled weather it was a hot and sunny morning when the boat left Koh Samui for the mainland. It looked like an old rusty tin can and stunk of diesel fumes, a large vessel that rocked its way through the choppy waves with a hypnotic sway. The journey just added to the swaying in my head that was still there from earlier boat trips, and after this one never really went away. Amanda had it too, a feeling that words cannot quite capture, as if there is no such thing as a fixed foundation. I imagine that people who witness and survive earthquakes never truly have the same sense of security again, for once the stability of the ground comes into question there is very little left that can be relied upon as firm.

It seemed to take hours to reach the mainland, and we docked in yet another unfamiliar part of the coast, as if perhaps the Thais don't want farang to know exactly where they are, preferring us to feel lost. There had hardly been a cloud for the whole journey, and it was very hot now. The sunlight was so bright that it was almost blinding. A small wooden walkway perched upon stilts that looked far from stable, though proved itself to be safe, formed a bridge from the boat to the dock for passengers, and I was glad that our bags were on the coach. Nobody knew quite where to wait, and when our coach came off the boat there was a scene as if from a comedy where it pulled up for a few seconds only to move on further around the corner, inciting the queue to chase it as it went, each trying to keep their place in the queue. As usual, and I noticed this most of the time that I was there, I could join a queue and be near the front yet still manage to be one of the last to get on somehow. I guess I don't push forward enough but what does it matter? If there's not enough seats, someone's got to be the one to stand up, which is what happened here. I didn't mind too much, in fact it was more comfortable leaning against the bags than being jammed into a seat, though I couldn't help but wonder how long the journey would take.

I needn't have worried, for barely an hour down the road our coach stopped and we all got off for breakfast at a roadside diner. I guess both the heat and the number of farang that had passed through had increased now we were further into the season, and we paid the 10 baht fee to use one of the curtained-off holes dug into the ground that a haze of flies hovered above; in Thailand it seems everything is either much bigger (like the spiders in Koh Pha Ngan), or like these flies, much smaller and very fast, similar but nearly always different.

The coach that dropped us off reloaded with passengers heading south, down towards Trang and Malaysia. A lone pink suitcase sat in the middle of the pavement, and we watched as the driver had a quick check around to see who owned it. Nobody did so he assumed the owner was on board; he loaded it back up, assuming it had been offloaded in error, closed the doors and drove away. As we sat on the pavement I watched my faded hat go off down the road on the coach where I'd left it, jammed against the window in my attempt to try and dry the sweat that had soaked into it so many times that a white salt mark had appeared. It didn't really matter, there were hats everywhere for sale. We waited for the next pick-up, surrounded by our many bags that continually reminded me that we wouldn't be island hopping so much as staggering. It had been a bit of a feat just getting them this far, and in the heat, wandering around laden looking for accommodation would continue to be difficult. But then you have to put these things out of your mind and accept that somehow it will all work out. Whether or not it is as you planned, that's another matter, but something will work out. A few minutes later a girl appeared looking for her suitcase. When she found out it had been reloaded by mistake she was furious and created quite a fuss. The Thais all tried to calm her down and reassure her that they would get it back but I guess she thought it was just talk and it did little to ease her mood. We watched on, intrigued, wondering if it would actually be found and brought back as they claimed it would be, no problem.

After a phone call to somebody ahead on the route of the coach, who presumably intercepted the coach and found the right case, less than twenty minutes after it had vanished the suitcase reappeared. It was an excellent moment which gave us a lovely lift, and we gave a small cheer; unbelievably the girl hardly looked pleased at all, sulkily leaving it on the pavement where the driver dropped it off as if to say it shouldn't have been moved anyway.

There were touts selling accommodation for all of the west coast islands but having spoken to Colin and a few others who'd been to Koh Lanta, we had intended waiting until we got there, especially since they had all said that there was plenty of places available. At the port there would be many drivers waiting to take farang to their resorts, and we could just have a look at their flyers. Obviously we knew that the picture would exaggerate everything good about the place, and typically Colin had been unable to remember the name of the best place he'd found, only giving us a description of how to get there by motorbike, but he had given us the name of the best stretch of beach. Unlike Koh Samui with its sandy bays, Koh Lanta was surrounded by coral reefs which were sharp on the feet and made swimming impossible if the tide was low.

When the crowds had dissipated we decided to have a look at some of the Koh Lanta flyers out of interest. We were convinced that one of the touts was the same guy that we had seen in Surat Thani who'd called the spa for us on our way down, but couldn't be certain. We spoke to him about the beaches and he admitted that you had to be careful to pick the right place for swimming. In the end we booked a couple of nights in a place on Ao Phra-Ae called New Beach Resort (eerily similar in name to New Hut) and a couple of nights further down the coast in the jungle.

The coach came and we all just about managed to fit on board, and headed for Krabi. It was similar to one of our National Express coaches in that it stopped at several places on the way, mostly picking people up from the side of the main road. However, unlike our coaches, it seems that so long as you're willing to get on, it doesn't matter if there are no seats. For the Thais who boarded it seemed an everyday occurrence for two to share one seat, especially since they tend to be fairly small in size, and the aisle was full of people sitting on the floor. Almost as many were without seats as with, suggesting that the driver may have been benefiting from this somehow.

The weather turned monsoon-like again whilst we drove west and we wondered if it had been a mistake in direction. Since the Gulf Coast was also unsettled, we decided to see what would happen, possibly heading south where it might be hotter, if necessary. With the rain, the humidity, and the number of people in the crammed coach, it got uncomfortable after a while, and one is reminded that a journey that seems so easy when read in a guide book, and so cheap in a country such as this, has its drawbacks as well as its benefits. The scenery, however, was quite spectacular, and the change in vegetation matched the change in atmosphere. All the plants looked much bigger, more tropical, green and lush so soon after the monsoon season that hadn't actually properly finished yet. We were glad to get off when we finally reached Krabi bus station, where it was still wet and grey from the rain that had just about stopped.

We had a couple of nights booked in Krabi in a place called KM Mansion. The lady at the Surat Palm had called them for us after we had read about the amazing sunset views from the friendly ambience of the rooftop bar in the guide book; our tout en route had called them for us to see if they would pick us up from Krabi bus station which is actually a short distance outside of Krabi town. He told us they would send a driver there to meet us, and to look out for a sign with my name on it. It seemed far-fetched, like something that might happen in a film or in a book, but not in real life, though you do see those sorts of signs at airports. Of course, there was no-one there, no-one with a sign, and we waited a while before a tout at the bus station offered to call them for us. Apparently they were on their way. Eventually we gave up waiting and got on a songthaew, loading our bags with us into the back. A couple from London got on too: the guy had been to Koh Samui ten years previously and was amazed at just how much it had changed in that time; they were heading off to Koh Pi Pi where no doubt they would see even more change.

Once in Krabi town centre we found out how to get to the KM Mansion and opted to walk it, after all, it was how we had planned it to be when we'd bought the rucksacks. Though not quite as planned, since Amanda carried the once lost camera rucksack and the bundle of bags, and I carried the two main rucksacks. They were both set up with the shoulder strap, so I slung one on each shoulder, the two straps crossing over my chest. It was further than we thought, and walking laden in flip-flops that slipped as my feet began to sweat, we stopped every few hundred yards for a brief rest. It is at times like this, just when you think that things can't get more difficult, that something happens to prove otherwise. Now I'm not saying here that Amanda had put all of her heavy stuff into the rucksack by design, but it clearly must have weighed quite a bit for as I picked it up off the floor the strap broke. Fortunately I used to be a hod carrier, so know a bit about carrying things, and managed to hoist it across my shoulders balanced by my own bag which was slung round on my back. It wasn't easy but after a long hill that forced me to wonder if we should have just bitten the bullet and paid for a taxi out of our rapidly diminishing funds, we reached our place.

KM Mansion was a very oddly structured building, quite high but each floor had only a few rooms. We were up on the fifth floor and for me it was the final jump and uphill finish after a long steeple chase, up round the twisting narrow staircase, knees nearly buckling every now and then. It was laid out in a way so that you could only reach your room by using the appropriate staircase; otherwise, you could see it across the landing but couldn't get to it. Once while we were there we got lost, and in the confusion tried going into another room. Fortunately our key didn't fit and the room appeared to have nobody in it to freak out. It was all clean and comfortable enough, as nearly everywhere in Thailand had been, and we checked out the rooftop for the promised views and atmosphere. It was still afternoon so we figured that the lack of anybody else was due to the bar being closed, and that things would no doubt liven up towards the evening when it opened.

Outside, across the street, was a Thai court house, formal in appearance such that its neat organisation, fences, and architecture, so deliberately ordered amongst buildings and life otherwise generally haphazard, had a foreboding look. It was made worse when I witnessed a truckload of prisoners being brought in for trial. The term 'monkey-house' could be no more apt, as shaven-headed young men, bare feet and bare-backed, clung to the bars of the cage in which they were crammed, cuffed, and chained. It was a chilling sight to see in the heat of the day and I shivered at the thought of being so constrained, claustrophobic and trapped.

We had a meal in Krabi town at a place recommended by a Canadian guy we called Jake, who pulled up alongside us on a motorbike as we walked down the street, and tried selling us some CDs. He was friendly enough, especially when he thought he had a bite, but lost interest almost rudely when he found out we had no intention of buying anything. I'm fine with Thai people in Thailand approaching me to sell things, after all, they are at home and I am visiting their country. However, when it's farang who are just trying to extend their holiday lifestyle by selling to fellow farang then I suppose I'm less understanding and tolerant. I was happy to waste his time looking through his collections of cheap replica copies that he'd made on a PC, even to the point of engaging in discussion as to why I wasn't going to buy anything (something I would not have done if he'd been Thai) just because he'd insisted on joining us for food in a place he'd recommended, inviting himself to sit down, a place which turned out to be ok but nothing special.

Back at the Mansion sunset was not quite as we'd hoped. The sky was fairly hazy, the bar was shut, and the only other people up there to share the bites from all the mozzies were a couple who were clearly sharing a private time. The book, it seemed, was as reliable as the resort flyers, though to be fair perhaps it was like that on the night that the person who wrote it stayed. Anyway, it was pleasant enough and the food there was excellent. We booked transport over to Koh Lanta which would pick us up from just outside the hotel to save a walk back into town, leaving us with just the simple task of carrying the bags back down the twisting staircase when we checked out.

CHAPTER 15

Washed Away Dry Remains

The port of Krabi, with its clean and modern-looking building and neat and orderly road infrastructure, looked different to anything on the Gulf side of the country. The boat was newer but much smaller than the big ferry from Koh Samui, and we were much closer to the water which appeared significantly clearer than the Gulf, more of a turquoise so often associated with tropical countries. We passed small uninhabited islands, sometimes just spikes of rock jutting upwards, strange shapes formed by unknown forces. A while into the journey we approached a larger island that looked like a dense jungle with a single strip of beach along which we could just about make out a row of huts.

A long-tail boat headed out and intercepted our route. These are basically small wooden boats with an old car engine strapped onto the back: the prop shaft has a small propeller welded onto it, and a lever lifts this shaft up and down, in and out of the water; the entire unit turns on a pivot which determines the direction of travel, and the exhaust pipe system has been removed so that the noise made is very loud, and stinks of burnt petrol fumes. We watched on in amazement as bags and people swapped vessels, carefully stepping across the gap in between, some heading to this remote island, some coming from it. In another time or age it could have been a pirate boat trading lives, robbing us. I imagined us trying to undertake the same manoeuvre, passing all the plastic bags over one at a time, hoping they didn't split and spill the contents into the sea, hoping that the small smiling Thai didn't get dragged in by the sudden unexpected weight of Amanda's bag as he caught it.

When we reached Koh Lanta there were so many boats in the port that we couldn't actually dock but just pulled up alongside another, so that in order to reach the dockside we had to walk from our boat, across a plank to another boat, and then over it and another plank to dry land; I wobbled once or twice, interesting for the crowd who were watching on, but we managed.

The port was full of resort buses which had come to deliver and collect guests, very hot and real busy. Though we had accommodation, we had a look at a few of the flyers to see if we could find the treehouse place Colin had mentioned. The fact was reinforced, that it doesn't matter if you see it back in England on a computer, or on a glossy flyer in a Thai port just down the road from the place, everywhere looks good in pictures and you only really know by seeing it for yourself. To be fair these drivers will take you to their resort just for you to see with no commitment, but to see somewhere and decide to walk away might mean a lot of hard work walking about in the heat with a heavy bag searching for a better alternative, one that you may not even find. This wasn't an option for us, so we found our resort's truck which took us to the Lanta New Beach Resort.

I think every place I had stayed at until now had been a Buddhist place, discernible by the miniature piece of architecture, often brightly coloured and at times quite intricate, built somewhere in the vicinity of the main building, to house the spirit of the place said to have been displaced by the human intrusion. On this side of the country I'd read that there were fewer Buddhists, and our place here in Koh Lanta had no such tiny house. After checking in at the reception with the bar and restaurant on the beach, we walked the several hundred yards back towards the main drag, passing the small bamboo huts to an area built of concrete rooms in single-storey blocks. We'd opted to pay less and just have the fan, and when we checked in they told us if we wanted air-con then we could pay and they would switch on the machine that remained fixed to the wall but powerless. The room was very clean, though without a doubt I would have preferred a hut, and wouldn't have booked the place had I seen it first, but never mind. Our small area – like a cul-de-sac off of the main avenue of huts – looked as if there had been much construction work going on. A swimming pool that had been shown on the flyer back when we'd booked looked like it hadn't been used for some time; instead, they'd built another out the front near the beach. There was an odd, lonely, and forgotten atmosphere that the pool of uninviting stagnant water helped to preserve; there were no people sat around it, none even outside any of the rooms that were set back on three of the sides that formed the small cul-de-sac. A white plastic chair was still submerged in the middle, and it may not have been fish but some small creatures were visible, swimming around, breeding well in the wet heat.

Koh Lanta had been hit by the tsunami and we wondered just how much this place had been affected. Certainly the people who worked there didn't seem too happy but then I'd read that these west coast islands had been so popular and busy that resorts didn't need to be polite, a feeling worsened by having such a different culture to the many farang who came and did little but damage by bringing western rubbish with them. Maybe it had had an oppressive feel even before the wave.

It was a bit of a walk to the beach and we passed the diving school tucked round the back near our room. A couple of Thais were stretched out in the shade of a palm tree and gave us a friendly, lazy greeting. It was a clear blue sky, a deeper blue than on Koh Samui, and much hotter. One of them, seeing our towels, asked us where we were going; when I said to the beach he smiled and said, 'Aah, barbecue,' stretching out even further. Was there a barbecue down at the beach? I hadn't seen any sign of it earlier and it seemed an odd time of day to have one. After some confusion Amanda explained that he meant us, we were the barbecue, not so much for eating but just burning. Sure enough, when we got to the beach the midday sun was far too hot for sunbathing. Besides, the beach wasn't exactly as described, and whilst the coral reef looked beautiful it was no good for swimming in, being either too shallow or too sharp on the feet to get out to deep water. Further investigations proved that we weren't actually on Ao Phra Rae at all (as the flyer and the tout who sold us the accommodation had said), but Had Khlong Khong: even the guide book said that this beach was no good for swimming. We saw a few jellyfish washed up on the beach and I recalled Colin's story of seeing someone get stung as they walked out into the water, hopping around in agony wondering what to do. I thought it best not to mention it in case it made the mood worse.

One of the attractions of the west coast was that the sun would set into the sea; it was indeed a spectacular sight, with the low tide exposing the coral reef which formed pools that reflected the many colours in the sky, the shades of pink, orange, and fiery red. Amanda had both big gun and the small digital pistol out and indulged herself while I sat around smoking slyly, just out of the way, watching the sunlight gradually fade as the sky became starry with its clear constellations, views never seen back at home.

We ate some fresh barbecued snapper in the restaurant on the beach, excellent food in an idyllic setting. To our amazement, as we finished eating, a few people gathered on the beach and lit a couple of chom loys, the lanterns we'd searched for in vain for Gran's funeral. They were much bigger than I'd imagined, like a paper cylinder the size of a diesel drum with wire inside that supported a kind of wick which burnt. The top was sealed so presumably the heat acted like a hot air balloon; it was a tricky manoeuvre lighting it and needed someone to hold it whilst someone else lit the fuse. When the flame began to burn properly, the bag filled with hot air and the whole thing floated off into the sky over the sea. I thought of finding out where we might be able to get some to bring back but they were far too big to carry around; still, it was good that we saw them. It would have been good fun too, to let a few go over the New Forest, though I'm unsure what the people back home would think, or the fire brigade.

Next day we hired a bike from the resort to explore the island. We wore the safety helmets since my riding was still far from proficient, a fact Amanda remembered as soon as she got on the back and we wobbled off down the road. It didn't take long though and I felt I was getting the hang of it again. A brief look at the map and it seemed it was one road that would take us down the coast to the southern end of the island, where the beaches were said to be beautiful, quiet, sandy bays. I have to admit that in the heat of the day it felt good to be riding along, keeping cool from the rushing air in just a pair of shorts, and I loosened off the strap of the helmet for a bit of comfort. Not far down the road my head felt a little strange, lighter somehow, but I could still feel the helmet on. Amanda tapped me on the shoulder and I pulled over to discover that I was actually only wearing a small moulded piece of white polystyrene: in the air flow the red plastic outer casing had separated and blown off. We went back to get it but the truth was out now: these helmets would do very little to save your head in a crash so I took it off and let it bounce around in the small shopping basket. This felt even better, to be riding along with the breeze flowing over the bare head.

We saw a sign for a treehouse bar and stopped to have a look. It was up a steep and winding track into the trees, and after nearly falling off the back Amanda decided to walk up there instead. I rode some of the way but lost it on a sharp bend near the top; for a moment I had visions of the bike sliding all the way back down, bouncing through the trees and ending up a smashed wreck down below, but fortunately both it and I just ended up laid out on the forest floor. A Thai who worked there saw what happened and kindly gave me a hand to get the bike back upright again so we stopped for some coffee.

The treehouse was like a platform about twelve feet high around a large tree near the edge of the hill top, with a rail around it, like a wooden scaffolding. It was quite a precarious walk up a steep wooden ladder to reach it. On the planks there were small cushions around small wooden tables so that people could sit and drink coffee whilst viewing the scenery below. Set high up in the rainforest and overlooking the sea, in the bright, hot sun it was truly beautiful. There were a few others up there including a guy who had a similar but better camera to Big Gun; he and Amanda talked technicalities for a while, and no doubt she was pleased to find someone who saw cameras as more than just a weight to carry: it is strange how we seem to meet such appropriate people by chance, people more apt than random chance would seem to allow.

After a few coffees we went down to pay and Amanda went off to use the hut round the back. As I chatted with the guy who helped me with the bike, the inevitable question arose: did I smoke marijuana? I explained that I did in England but in Thailand I knew it was dangerous. 'No, no,' he assured me, 'you can come smoke now,' at which he led me round the back to their private hut. After a few bongs from a coconut shell we went back round the front where I remembered Amanda would be waiting. It was a welcome gesture and we went off feeling somewhat lifted after the strange subdued atmosphere that seemed to hover over the New Beach Resort.

A bit down the road, just as I was enjoying the free feeling of riding in the breeze, through the trees, I noticed the coast again, except that it seemed to be on the wrong side, to our left instead of our right. Could we have gone back on ourselves without me realising? I was puzzled since I'd made an effort to stay on the one main road, sure that it would simply take us straight down the coast. It reminded me of the night ride back on Koh Samui, and it wasn't long before Amanda was tapping me on the shoulder asking me if I thought we were going the right way. We continued on anyway, partly because I remembered Colin saying something about the treehouse hut resort being down here somewhere and partly because it always seems to be preferable to continue onward rather than turning around and going back over old ground. The road got narrower and more pitted so that it was tricky riding along and eventually we decided to turn round, spooked at being funnelled into a dead end after having ridden past the police station. However, we did see a couple of elephants under the trees at the side of the road and we stopped for a closer look. They weren't wild elephants and were used to humans, unperturbed by our presence, for they just looked back at us through grey wrinkled eyes that were sad, as they nearly always appear to be, as if perhaps elephants see something in us that we do not.

On the way back we passed an old Thai pushing along a small cart full of brushes made from sticks and cane. Obviously there are no carpets and lots of sand on the islands so brushes are without doubt the best tool for sweeping floors. They are made from local materials by local people, and when they wear out they are not only simple to replace but easy to dispose of since the environment is naturally designed to absorb such materials. He appeared to be either delivering a load he'd made or was peddling his wares along the road, or maybe both; it reminded me of when I was very young, for in the England of those days the rag and bone man went by regularly on his horse and cart, and occasionally men knocked the door offering to sharpen knives, tools, and lawnmower blades. Nowadays I suppose we might get an Amways seller trying to force us to buy enough chemicals to clean the Med, products that epitomise the world of centralisation and pyramid selling, far, far from the world of the man making home-made brushes. At times it is incredible to think that two such different worlds exist on the same planet at the same time.

Back at the resort we checked a map to find that the main road actually cuts across the island about halfway down, and if you want to stay heading down the coast then you have make a right turn, down what looks like a side street. So we headed back out, found the turning and followed the coast down through the forest to Ao Kantiang to have a look at Lanta Marine Park View, our next resort. This was partly to arrange a lift to get there, and partly to see if it looked ok, for if it didn't then we could make good use of the bike and find somewhere else.

The place was beautiful, set amongst the rainforest right above the small white-sanded bay of clear turquoise sea. We ate some food in the restaurant built into the top of the cliff side overlooking the water, relieved that we only had one more night in New Beach. The people were lovely and agreed to collect us from our resort the following morning, slightly puzzled that we had ridden all the way down and spent the afternoon there when we could have easily phoned. However, it seems you never know who knows who so we didn't say it was because it felt so weird and uncomfortable back at the New Beach.

Compared to Koh Samui, Koh Lanta was much quieter, and on the way back we stopped off at a few places to walk along the coral reefs. There was hardly anyone else around, and the whole world felt very distant.

That night we went out on the bike to find somewhere to eat and ended up in what seemed one of the few places left open that late; it always surprised me how early Thais ate, and many times it caught me out. It was part of a luxury complex that had only just been completed, but for such a posh-looking place the menu was still very cheap compared to somewhere similar back home. I tasted delicious freshly cooked blue crab for the first time, along with a superb Masaman curry. We were the only people eating and after the meal the manager gave us a tour of the resort, showing us inside one of the many luxurious rooms that remained vacant. It was all very marble-looking, very posh and no doubt very expensive, designed for honeymoon couples flying to Thailand for a couple of weeks in the tropics who not only want to retain similar standards to those back home but wish to exceed them for their special holiday. We looked, knowing that we wouldn't be booking up even a few nights, though no doubt the manager hoped we might have been persuaded just by seeing.

CHAPTER 16

Pink Shorts and the Girl Who Got Stung

We checked out of the New Beach and waited in the restaurant by the reception for our lift to come and pick us up, as arranged. We'd have rather walked up to the main road but the bags would have been an ordeal in the heat, besides which it would have looked strange. The breakfast the day before had not been good so we planned on waiting to eat until we got to our next place. Time passed and the people in reception didn't seem too impressed that we didn't want to eat there. It was very hot and a few kittens roamed around, mewing. Amanda thought one looked undernourished so bought a small bottle of milk; when the reception ladies saw her open it and give it to the cat they roared with laughter, scornfully hysterical. It was an awkward wait and when the lift finally arrived it was much to our relief.

Arriving at the Marine Park View was like stepping into a different world after the glaring exposed concrete of the previous place. Sounds of the forest birds filled the trees above us as we were led through a stone path up the mountain, some of the steps having been placed there intentionally, some carved into shape out of the mountainside so that the path weaved and twisted according to the terrain. Our hut was set back too far into the trees so we didn't have a view of the sea, however the scenery was still stunning. Inside the wooden hut we had a bed each, both with a large mozzie net hanging from the ceiling. So long as you don't close it up with a mozzie inside these things are excellent, and after using one for a few nights, eliminating the buzzing in the ear as well as any potential bites, I couldn't help but wonder if it would have been better to buy one of these instead of using deet at night (which cannot possibly be good for the body). Not that I suffered too much from mozzie bites, especially now I was tanned, though in Koh Pha Ngan I'd seen a guy who appeared to have fallen asleep with his shoulder exposed, which was covered, I mean hundreds of bites; he'd been a slightly plump chap, pale pink and full of western ingredients, a formula that seems to be the mozzies' elixir.

We ate in the restaurant overlooking the bay, the sea just as blue and beautiful as the day before, and were served by the same waiter, an Indian-looking guy who wore his black hair tied back into a very long ponytail. His English was very good, as if he was not born in Thailand, but always carried an air of mystery about him, as if being aware of an entire world that we could not see. At first he seemed a bit standoffish even though faultless in his serving, almost aloof, but after chatting a few times it became easier to get him to talk. We asked about the tsunami, for the shape of the bay suggested that an incoming surge would be funnelled in so that much damage would have arisen, depending on the direction of the wave when it had hit the island. He confirmed the worst, explaining that he'd had to climb up the rocky path from the beach up to the restaurant to escape from the water that came crashing in. All the bamboo huts that had been down at beach level in the centre of the bay were still listed in the guide book but had been washed away, leaving only a gap as a trace that anything had ever been there, a gap slowly being filled by a replacement concrete resort, the foundations of which had already been laid. He'd seen the fate of many people and when he spoke of it there was still a feeling of puzzled shock, a vague disbelief in the reliability of the world to be the same in the next moment as it is now.

The scene itself seemed almost perfect, a small sweeping bay of soft white sand lapped by small turquoise waves. There were coral reefs either side but most of the bay was sand and the gradual slope led into water plenty deep enough for swimming. It appeared idyllic, if a little breezy, and the water was so warm that getting cold would never be a reason for getting out. However, it seems that even in a place that appears to be paradise there is something, even if it is very small, which will put enough of an edge on things to undermine total comfort. After a few minutes in the water I began to feel a few tiny nips, like flea bites. I said nothing until I saw Amanda flinch a couple of times. Some kind of sea lice or other biting creatures, it seemed, were there to annoy us. We got out in time to catch our towels which had nearly blown away in the wind and moved up to the sun loungers outside of a posh-looking complex built into the mountain behind the bay.

The beach was pretty much deserted which in a way made us even more exposed to any passing onlookers. After a short while of sunbathing, a Thai dressed in an official-looking uniform approached us. He was from the hotel and wanted to know our room number: we told him the number of our hut and he said the hotel had no such room number; we told him we were staying at the Marine Park View, pointing to the huts in the trees, and he said that we were not allowed to use the sun loungers since they were reserved for the hotel guests. We gestured around us, laughing, for there were no other guests, but he was adamant that we had to move. It was then that we noticed some kind of waste pipe that led from the hotel down into the bay and figured that perhaps the small creatures fed on whatever flowed through the pipe: we moved to the far side, partly amongst the coral but with enough sand to access the water easily; away from the pipe, the biting creatures vanished.

Our hut was built so that we could tie both hammocks onto the frame of the balcony. The whole structure gave a bit of a creak when we both got in, and I'm sure I heard something move somewhere but it all stayed upright so we were able to relax amongst the trees in the evening. It would have been perfect for a bit of a smoke but I didn't feel I knew the waiter well enough yet. There was an English couple staying in a hut near ours that we'd seen in the restaurant. The girl was quite loud and reminded me of an ex-public schoolgirl who had perhaps more confidence than experience, but she was funny to listen to and pleasant enough. The guy was a chef, quite large in build but always wore the same pair of pink shorts. In the evening Amanda and I were on our way to the shop when she suddenly turned back. I carried on and whilst I waited for her the English couple came past with the waiter. 'You wanna smoke some marijuana?' he asked quietly as he walked by. Amanda had gone back to the hut so when he said it was just down the track I followed on. It was actually a bit of a longer weave through the trees than I thought it was going to be but felt somewhat committed now. Another waiter joined us and we had a couple of bongs each, chatting for a bit before I thought I'd better get back.

I wouldn't say the waiter was especially friendly after that, for he still retained his air of mystery, but he seemed much more relaxed. He asked us what we planned on doing the next day and suggested a four-island boat tour. We asked him if he knew the people who ran the boat, and he said that he had a brother, it was his brother's boat. It was a good chance to see a few islands and do some snorkelling, so we agreed. Back at the hut Amanda mentioned that snorkelling might be tricky for her since it was that time of the month. I light-heartedly commented about having to look out for sharks which she didn't see as a joke so much as a real possibility.

In the morning we made our way down to the bay to meet the boat. The guy in pink shorts and the girl were booked on too, and there were about a dozen of us in total. The boat was a long-tail, a bit like a large wooden canoe with a canopy supported by a few poles creating a shelter for passengers. To the delight of the boat-man, who looked on with admiration, Amanda took a photograph of the engine in its naked glory, pulleys and cam belt all exposed.

It was a calm, hot, and sunny day, blue skies and blue seas, but even still the long-tail boat trip to the first island was fresh to say the least, especially when the boat hit a wave head first and a wash of spray smashed over us all. After a while one had to wonder if they were deliberately steering into some of these waves for the two Thais took great delight when the crowd who were huddled inside got wet and let out a scream.

The first stop was more of a rock sticking out of the water rather than an island, for the sides were pretty much vertical limestone preventing anyone from landing: a pretty rock nonetheless, formed from coloured stones of pale pinks, sandy yellows, and creams that change with the reflection of the sunlight during the day. We arrived as another boat was leaving, and it seemed that we were on a well-trodden tourist circuit, although perhaps there is much sense in keeping visiting farang all within an enclosed area; much like one might restrict dangerous animals, or perhaps contain a virus. Just as we all got kitted up with our snorkels and flippers I happened to see one of the Thais get a coconut bong out. I laughed as I saw it and he asked, 'You smoke marijuana?'

'Back in England,' I replied, and he smiled and nodded. I'd just got into the water when Amanda called out from the boat, and when I got back on board, the Thai guy passed me the bong to smoke. It was a strange feeling on the water, even stranger when I got back in it amongst the blue and yellow tropical fish and the weird corals all around. Amanda got in as well, equipped with spare necessaries to change into as required. I suppose the truth is that if the spa course had worked effectively straightaway then the problem would not have been anywhere near as bad, but things were ok so far.

The next stop was another beautiful rock though this time more featured in its shape instead of a vertical jutting. Shoals of fish gathered around the shady edges, and again we all got out for a snorkel around. Pink Shorts was not only first in but the first to notice some of the fish bit, nipping like a small pinch. The Thais assured us that they were harmless and definitely not piranhas, which kind of put our minds at rest. That was when I saw the Thais throwing bread in the water right next to where someone was swimming; all the fish would swim straight over, the person would start by looking uncomfortable before thrashing about and trying to stop the nipping, and all the time the Thais were on the boat laughing away. I had to laugh too when I saw what was going on, when I caught one throwing bread next to me, which made them laugh even more. Then one of them happened to see Amanda changing and made a joke, which she heard, about sharks to his friend. And that was that for Amanda's snorkelling, which may not have been such a bad idea considering what happened at the next island on the four-stop.

Emerald Island, as it is called for farang, looks like any other rock jutting out of the Andaman Sea except this island has a hidden centre. We pulled up alongside an opening in the rocks, a mysterious-looking cave in which the sea became darker until it blended with the blackness of the shadows. Our boat people provided each of us with a floating jacket to aid the swim through the cave into the island. There were a couple of other parties here too, one lot also going in and another lot on their way back out. Amanda was unsure, especially after the shark jokes, but I tried to persuade her that it would be ok. Comments from the swimmers coming out made it clear that whatever was inside was worth seeing, backing up the encouragement from the Thais on the boat. Everything was ok until we reached the darkness of the cave: the water became much colder and the ceiling of the cave much lower; as we swam further in, the light not only disappeared behind us but, since the route in was curved like a banana, the light at the other end could not be seen. Before I knew it Amanda had turned back, spooked by the darkness and the thought of strange underwater creatures that preyed on unsuspecting farang as they swam through, who knows, perhaps taking the odd one in a deal set up with the Thais who deliver a meal in exchange for their own safety.

I swam on alone, Amanda now out of sight behind, and the rest of the group out of sight in front of me. There is a small stretch that is in complete darkness: no visible light in front or behind, which was a little disconcerting but over very quickly; noises helped to direct the way. Turning the bend into the light, the water leads up into a lagoon of turquoise green set in an almost perfect circle within the rock, open so that the limestone rock walls form a cylinder shape; above, the sun high in the deep blue sky shone down inside. The lagoon shallowed off into a small sandy beach edged by tropical shrubs and bushes. It was like a small hidden paradise, and unsurprisingly, it had a history of being used by pirates to hide themselves and their plunder.

Once most people had turned back, and the mass of bright orange floating jackets had dissipated, the place had a peaceful ambience so that it seemed separated from the outside world, a lost solitude strangely relieving. When there were only four of us left, including Miranda the posh girl and her friend in pink shorts, we thought we ought to head back, reversing the journey through the darkness of the passage through the cave. I followed on last, and in the darkness, not wanting to get left behind, got slightly tangled up in Miranda's legs as she swam. I heard her say something like, 'What was that? I just felt something,' and I thought, *It's ok, just clumsy me who can't see*, and stayed back a bit before getting accused of a sly fumbled groping.

Back on the boat it seemed that Miranda had a mark on her leg. At first I thought, *Surely not, surely I didn't scratch her with a toenail.* I checked to see how long they were. A small group gathered around her as she showed a mark off on her inner thigh which can only be described as a mouth mark, oval in shape, purple-red in colour, with a raised outline. I imagine a jellyfish sting would look similar, except for the mouth shape. I must say that this was a time when Miranda's personality did her a major favour: instead of making a fuss she took great delight in the injury, telling a story of a time when she had been stung for real by a jellyfish; this, she noted almost with the pride of an earned trophy, was far better looking. The Thais took a look but admitted they hadn't seen anything like it before, at least that was what they said. At lunch time she placed a piece of cucumber over it, partly to cool it down, and partly to compare size and shape. She noted, for the purpose of future reference, that it was pretty much exactly the same shape: so if you ever see a slice of Thai cucumber, which is larger and more oval than ours at home, then you will know the size of the bite, for by now the general consensus, driven mostly by the shape, was that the mark/sting was actually some kind of bite, possibly a poisonous one. She stayed remarkably calm about it for the whole trip but we found out later that she got it checked out by a doctor back on the island, and everything was ok.

After the excitement of Emerald Island we headed for the final stop on an island called Koh Ngai, larger in size so that there were several resorts along a stretch of sandy bays, but small enough so that the only access to the island was by long-tail boat. As we approached the beautiful white sand, the water turned completely clear revealing amazing shells, corals, and coloured tropical fish. On the beach the thatched bamboo huts amongst the palm trees gave the place a typical holiday brochure appearance, so picturesque that even with the clever trickery used in photography and advertising it would have been difficult to have improved that which we saw with our own eyes. For a while we sat and drank coffee, gazing at the beauty of it all, feeling momentarily immersed.

Returning on the boat, it was flat out all the way

now the four islands had been toured, although we passed by more that were just as spectacular in appearance, including one shaped exactly like an octopus, aptly named (presumably for the benefit of us farang) Octopus Island. When we landed on the beach near our resort the ground continued to sway and it was good to get back up to the hut and the hammocks. Amanda took a shower and the water stopped halfway through; after several visits down to reception it came back on, as if for no apparent reason, and we couldn't help but wonder if this was just someone having a bit of fun: the Thai humour seemed to enjoy little tricks like this, especially where water was involved, and their delight in seeing us each time we went down to reception indicated that it was possible they were turning the water off just to get us to go down there, like it was a fun way of getting to know us better; for there is little more revealing about a person's personality as when they are deprived of something expected, unexpectedly.

We stayed on there for a couple of extra days since it felt so relaxed and peaceful amongst the trees, even with the continuous buzz which we could never decide if it was birds singing or the electric cables; and they were all such lovely people, who of course assured us it was small birds. We saw plenty of cables but the birds were too well hidden so we were never convinced until one day later when we heard the sound in a place where there were no electric cables. We saw a wild monkey run across the track and quickly vanish into the trees, only small and grey in colour, but wild all the same.

Miranda clearly made a full recovery for we heard

her laughing at Pink Shorts the morning after the sting/bite incident. It appeared that she had been taking the piss out of his pink shorts and he'd decided to put on a pair of grey ones instead. Seeing this, she had shouted out through the trees, 'Oi, where's your fucking pink shorts today?' followed by peals of laughter echoing through the trees.

It was a comical scene to watch as he tried to shrug off the insult, but it clearly got to him for he actually turned round and went and changed, reappearing ten minutes later in his beloved pink shorts, as if he'd thought, *No, I don't care what she says or thinks, I like them so I'm wearing them*, and with that, strutted off down the track to wherever he was going. His name was fixed, and thereafter I only ever heard her call him Pink Shorts, even when she was being nice.

After much deliberation of where to go next, especially since the plan needed to incorporate a border run to renew the visa within a week or so, we decided to head back to the seemingly near-paradise island of Koh Ngai. It seemed whilst we were so close we could stay there for a few days, even though it was expensive; at least it was beautiful water to swim in, and there was a chance we might regret it if we missed the opportunity. It was as if the snorkelling trip had been partly to show us the island as the next stop, so we booked up with a resort just down the beach from where we had landed a few days earlier; another brother of somebody had a long-tail boat which would take us so we booked that too and said our farewells.

The Indian waiter, mysterious to the end, gave me a tin of Thai tobacco, insisting he intended giving it up; a most beautiful vanilla-smelling tobacco, coarse but smooth to the taste, and Amanda took regular deep breaths from the tin as small compensation for not being able to partake in it herself, which I know she would have loved to have done.

CHAPTER 17

Red Bandana Man and the Fat, Naked Intruder

It was a beautiful morning as we boarded the long-tail for Koh Ngai. Getting the bags on was a bit of a mission since it involved walking through the water and holding them high enough to stay dry. On today's boat a guy took care of the engine and a girl took care of the passengers: as I passed up Amanda's bag I tried to explain that it might be a bit heavy but she just smiled, inviting me to offer it up; to be fair, when she hauled it up she was a little surprised at the weight, giving out a little grunt, but hardly flinched under the strain considering her small size. We headed down the island coast, stopping off at a couple of secluded bays to collect more people so there was a full load by the time we left Koh Lanta. We'd picked up an English family on the final day of a two-week holiday, a couple with their three young children, all very excited, and everything went well until we hit the open seas.

There always seems to be a strong sea breeze on the open water even on the calmest of days, but today it had picked up so that the sea was quite choppy. We hit one or two big waves face on and a spray of water swept over the boat to the sound of shrieks and screams. Getting wet was ok because you knew it was hot enough to dry almost straightaway back on the beach, but the booming crash as the boat's nose lifted and then smacked back down was too scary for the children, and suddenly it was not so much fun for them anymore. The small boy had had enough and wanted to get off, which may have spoilt the Thais' game of splash the screaming farang a little bit. The girl was good about it all and quickly climbed up onto the side of the boat, unleashing the tarpaulins and tying them into place as a shield from the spray. She was most agile, moving along fearlessly as the boat was tossed about in the rough water, made more difficult by the guy steering who seemed to look for waves to steer into, and would not slow down until the girl perhaps told him enough was enough and he had to. She covered all the bags too, and when she noticed that one of ours was exposed and getting wet she clambered all the way back to cover it properly.

The approach to the beach was not nearly as tranquil as it had been a few days earlier; the crystal-clear water was more opaque so that the fish and corals were blurred and barely visible until we reached very shallow water. We clambered off, wading through to the beach several times to retrieve all the bags; each time we went back for more, the girl on the boat looked surprised at the amount we had. On the beach a very dark Thai wearing just a pair of black shorts and a red bandanna watched the guests arriving before disappearing through the trees and around the back somewhere.

It was further along the beach from where we had docked for coffee, and much less holiday brochure looking. There were a few bamboo huts around, and several large single-storey terraced blocks set back a small distance from the beach. Instead of thatched roofs, everything here was corrugated iron, and as we walked through the grounds to our room, even with the small flowers growing on the bushes there was an air of dried deserted death about the whole place. Apart from a few people in the restaurant there was hardly anyone around, barely a sign of anyone even, although it appeared from a couple of towels that there was at least someone staying in the room next door. Inside our room, which was on the end of the block, the two metal-framed single beds on the white-tiled floor reminded me of a hospital, like a psychiatric ward, too clean and too bare. Amanda knew I wouldn't like it even before I'd looked in, but the beautiful beach was much consolation.

We checked in provisionally for four nights, and the people seemed friendly enough, if a little detached. Maybe they were just intrigued at the visiting farang who came to a place looking for peaceful simplicity, that which is really free, yet spend so much money getting there. In a mercenary way I suppose to them each boatload is simply another arrival of baht, and you might wonder why they would want to swap their remote paradise for cash which jeopardises its very nature and attractiveness. A little research indicates that, just as there is very little, if any, free land left in our country, and probably no such thing as a free person, the Thai authorities have likewise imposed themselves upon the free people of the islands via citizenship and taxation.

We read in the guide book about the chao ley, the people who'd once lived on the sea like gypsies, and how they'd been forced to comply with the regulated system imposed from the capital. Of course, there is also a history of piracy associated with these areas, so true chao ley no doubt found themselves caught up in the mess as the authorities attempted to make passages safe for global trade. Typical of human behaviour though, as the military might of the authorities increases, the pirates simply take advantage of the same by stealing it; only very recently a ship was taken by pirates and its weapons turned and pointed towards those who had made them. The sad impact is, however, that families who may have lived the free sea life for generations have been somewhat grounded, and no doubt end up like the girl on the long-tail boat, ferrying farang around from one island to another, spending their baht on fuel and engines, and paying their taxes.

Our position on the island was such that there was a flat strip of land between the beach and the mountains, dense tropical jungle rising up a steep incline, without evidence of any path, track, or road. With the sea in front, and this mountainous barrier behind, this small area of dry, arid, inhabited land felt strangely enclosed. It is difficult to explain but our resort had an empty, desolate feeling around it, and sitting on the plastic chairs on the seating area outside of our room, it felt exposed in the same way a stranger in a western movie would feel upon entering a town via a soulless road.

Since the sea was choppy and uninviting we went for a walk along the beach to the resort we'd visited before. There was evidence of storm damage, some debris washed up that had now dried from the hot sun and lower tides, and the beach was very narrow in places. It seemed that there were no other resorts in between ours and the coconut paradise, although there was a long stretch of space, perhaps half a mile. The area was overgrown with trees, although there were many masonry sections left standing, the only remaining part of a bamboo hut that invariably houses the shower and toilet area, the rest being made entirely of wood; a style of hut that seemed typical on beach resorts everywhere. These looked long empty though; at first we wondered if the tsunami had washed the wooden structures away and just left the empty brickwork sections. It seemed too overgrown, however, to have been washed away so recently, since the trees were some ten or twelve feet tall; if not the tsunami though, we wondered why such resorts would have ever closed.

Further along the beach we came across a large stone monument, broken in half and lying face down in the sand. Only a colossal force could have broken such a large stone. Since it had clearly once been facing the sea it seemed the only possible cause for its demise was from the sea itself: the slam of water required for such breakage was plain, and we knew then that the tsunami had hit here too. In hindsight, knowing just how fast vegetation grows in tropical climates, the trees must have grown that tall in a short space of time, showing just how quickly nature can remove all trace of human life.

We walked the length of the beach, beyond the next resort, as far as we could, and sat down for a while. The sky looked grey, reflected in the choppy water, and even though it was still a beautiful tropical island, we couldn't help but feel in a way subdued, which at the same time felt wrong since we'd spent much time, money, and effort getting here. Perhaps we expected too much, or perhaps it was just realising that life isn't always sunny when you want it to be; bad moods, however, rarely, if ever, make things any better.

On the way back we found some rope and a tarpaulin sack washed up amongst some debris which proved to be ideal for keeping all the overload plastic bags together, even though Amanda wasn't over-impressed at first sight. Hardly designer label admittedly, not even pretend fake, but it's funny how small things can give you a lift, for I thought instantly how much easier it would be getting on and off boats with this new piece of free tackle: lifted like Robinson Crusoe might have felt upon finding something left by providence.

The following morning was bright and sunny, the water was calm and clear, and after a decent breakfast with plenty of coffee, everything felt ok again. We sunbathed on the beach for a while, dipping in and out of the warm water whenever we felt like cooling down. The water was quite shallow and meant a bit of a wade out to be able to swim; pleasant though with the soft sand underfoot, the clearly visible small fish that darted around, and the nearby small islands and rocks jutting out of the sea that caught the dazzling sunlight, the same features that the day before had looked so foreboding and sinister. The clear blue water gradually got deeper until it reached a shelf, evidently dropping off suddenly to whatever mysterious depths as indicated by the change in colour to dark blue, a shelf that stretched along the coast of the island so that a line ran through the sea where the two colours met.

We borrowed masks and flippers from the resort and spent the afternoon snorkelling, marvelling at the amazing corals and multi-coloured fish. The flippers not only enabled a lot of distance to be covered quickly but offered protection from some of the sharp and poisonous-looking things on the sea bed. There were some strange spiky creatures that had a tiny blue dot in the centre from which sharp, jet black needles jutted out at all angles; whatever it was, it looked like if you stood on it then it would hurt real bad, and they were everywhere once the water reached about eight feet deep. We swam around, amazed at all the different fish for several hours, and met a Chinese man out there who had a floating jacket and remained semi-submerged for most of the time. He was a friendly guy when he spoke, delighted that he'd seen Nemo, though not being much of a film watcher I didn't know at the time what he meant, or what I should be looking for to see it too.

After a while out there I began to feel brave and went for a snorkel over the ledge, across the coloured line into deep water. Straight away the water felt colder, less inviting for sure, and I could see it was very deep, dark before I could see the bottom. A large fish that looked like a small shark with a squashed blunted head swam nearby and spooked me enough to send me back to shallower water where things that swam around were much smaller and more friendly-looking.

It was weird how the sea then changed so quickly; I suppose being out there in the water looking down we hadn't noticed the change in weather going on up in the sky. The wind had picked up, the clouds had moved in and the water quickly became choppy and much less visible, so we got out and got changed. A long-tail boat pulled up and some new arrivals got off; back at our room, having got changed, I saw them again heading to a room in a block to the right of ours behind some trees. There were four large men who looked Eastern European, possibly German, being led by one of the Thais from reception, slender and small-looking alongside four big middle-aged guys with fat stomachs.

We went and sat back on the beach to watch the sun set before eating. The four big guys, unperturbed by the weather and the waves, splashed about in the water, and it struck me as strange why four grown men should want to come to a deserted island such as this instead of perhaps Phuket or even Pattaya. Maybe they thought the place would be full of single women, who knows, but if they were looking for a party or even a late-night bar then going on the previous night's quiet passing then they might well be disappointed. At one point in the night the generator had run out of diesel so that all was dark and silent until somebody got up and refilled it: hardly a wild party set-up. One particularly big guy with large bulging eyes looked really odd, his fat body squeezed into a tiny pair of speedos, floppy jug ears and big round head stuck onto the lifted shoulders so that he appeared to have no neck; though it may well be argued that we shouldn't judge by appearances alone, it is surely a fact that our vision overrides whatever else our mind or senses might tell us.

Bandana Man was around, lurking amongst the trees, as he so often did, appearing from nowhere at times only to vanish again. We thought he'd most likely stalked us the day before on our walk along the beach, a kind of island lookout. A knife hung from his belt, sheathed but one could imagine it was razor sharp. No doubt he'd seen the big guys too.

When it got dark we headed back to the room to get ready to have dinner, and realised that we'd lost the key. It was the type of lock that had to be locked by key or from inside, so we knew we hadn't locked it in the room. After what had seemed such a good day swimming and snorkelling it felt a pity to end it in such a way, and I felt a twang of annoyance. The trouble with a lost key is that even if the resort people give you another one, not only does it cost money but you lose peace of mind knowing that if someone else finds it then they can get in when you are out, or worse still, when you are asleep. Fortunately we found it down on the beach where we had been sitting, where Amanda had been petting Bozo, the small black dog with curly fur matted from living on the beach. She had taken to him and wanted to treat him for the parasites that were clearly giving him continual aggravation; the trouble was, I saw it as sad but way out of our control, for there was no way we could sort out all the sick animals around Thailand. Though I know Amanda cares much for animals, in a country where people know hardship, poverty, and suffering, their view is different, and they can come across as seeming heartless and cruel when perhaps they are simply resigned to the fact that life can be tough. Besides, having seen clues that in the near past there had been resorts all along the beach that were now closed, washed away, Bozo may well have been left behind when the owners had departed, and may not even belong to our resort at all. It became a sore subject, and unfortunately we ended up arguing over dinner, still hardly speaking when we went to bed. I had a last smoke outside, and locked the door.

There was a strange noise coming from the far end of our block, and neither of us could get to sleep. Eventually I got up, irritated at its persistence, and looked down the row of rooms to see what was going on. Though there was a kind of bamboo cane screen up, outside the end room a small boy and presumably his dad were playing some kind of game with a small plastic ball; the ball bounced on the concrete floor in the same way that a ping pong ball bounces, and echoed around our concrete section. I had another smoke as they continued, and putting it out glanced in their direction in annoyance. Oddly enough, though they were hidden behind the screen so wouldn't have been able to see me, as soon as I glanced at them I heard the father tell the boy that they must stop and go in, and hurried inside their room. It was as if the look had been felt, as if the thought had been shot through space in some kind of astral realm. Back in the room, Amanda asked me what I had done to make them stop so suddenly, and I said all I had done was to look at them.

I must have fallen asleep for I remember waking up and turning over in bed; sometimes my back aches if I lay in the same position for too long, and beds used by who knows how many farang aren't always the most supporting. I assumed it was just my body waking me up to make myself more comfortable until I watched half in surprise and half in horror in the dim light as the door slowly swung open. When Amanda and I spoke about it afterwards we'd both thought as it had happened that it must have been someone from the resort who'd had a key to let themselves in; I'd even thought that perhaps there was some kind of danger on the island, that maybe we were being warned about, like a tsunami, strange as it is when thoughts flash through in an attempt to understand what is happening in the moment.

I was bolt upright instantly, in time to see the fat German walk in through the door. In the moonlight shining in from outside I knew it was him, speedo-man, and worse still he stood there grinning, stark naked, his big fat belly hanging out over a blurry but small, shrivelled dick. What the fuck was he doing in our room? In the heat, I always slept naked too, keeping the arse and all that well aired, but couldn't afford to hold back and confront him. Was he sleepwalking? Was he drunk? Did he think he was in his own room? I shouted out so he'd know we were awake, so he knew he was caught if he was up to no good on a sly prowl, or to wake him up if he was asleep. He moved further into the room, to the end of my bed. I always slept nearest to the door, partly in case anything like this should happen, not that we ever expected it to, so was there to block his way.

'You're in the wrong room! Get the fuck out of our room!' I shouted enough times to have woken him but he continued to stand there, his expression fixed, unchanging, grinning, letting out a low noise that could have been a sinister laugh. As I shouted he shouted something back, which was why, for an instant, I thought perhaps he thought he was in his own room, and that we were the intruders waiting to jump on him. As the scene developed, however, this seemed less and less likely. By now he was in too far, and my only option was to stop him with force. I'm not a big person, I probably weighed about ten stone at the time and I reckon it's no exaggeration to say this guy was nearly twice my size. However, what he didn't know and what may have prevented an even worse scenario, was that I have a vicious temper when trapped and cornered; in younger days I'd had a few scraps, and just prior to this trip I'd practised martial arts intensely for over a year so was well used to sparring. It is true what they say, however, that it is easy to freeze in the moment if fear takes its grip.

So here's the scene: I'm stood there naked, pushing back Fat Naked German, with my left hand on his shoulder and my right fist drawn back level with my right ear ready to launch full into his face; I started by shouting, he shouted back, Amanda was in her bed screaming, and then my shouts became more like some kind of howling animal growl as Fat German and I engaged in some kind of wild stand-off to see who could make the most blood curdling beast-like sound the loudest, and for the longest.

There was enough light for us to see each other's faces and I stared deep into his eyes with a glare, vicious and dangerous. I outlasted him and he went quiet, as if he realised something. I said something in German, trying in the moment to recall vocabulary I'd learnt in school so many years ago, something like, 'Nicht dich zimmer,' which I hoped meant something like 'not your room'. He looked pacified and began to apologise, saying, 'Sorry, sorry, sorry,' too many times without moving. I remained suspicious, senses still heightened and didn't trust him. All it would take would be a drop in guard and he could move back in, gain control of the situation. My stare was fixed, and I tried to balance continued caution with accepting his apology, for what we didn't need now was an argument over whether he had been intending evil or not. Maybe he thought it would be too much effort, too much of a fight, or maybe he was really innocently mistaken, who knows, but he shuffled back out of the door and as soon as he did I shut and locked it.

Needless to say, Amanda and I tried to work out what it had all been about. I had to admit I had forgotten to lock the door the last time I went out, a simple fateful slip, and apologised. We sat there and listened to make sure he'd gone back to his own room but we could still hear him outside. It sounded like he tried the door of the room next door, and we heard him mutter something like, 'Get the fuck out of my room,' as if in mock imitation of something I'd said, or someone else had said elsewhere perhaps, a different intrusion on another night.

After a while all was quiet, though it was impossible to see properly what was going on outside without opening the door, and neither of us felt like doing that. For a start, there were three more of them, all big guys, and if one was up for it then maybe they all were. The mind can start to imagine scenarios like the four of them running around naked all night trying to break into our room in some kind of crazed frenzied orgy of rape and bloodshed, far away from society's rules, remote from any apparent need for morality; but when you start having thoughts like these you have to stop them, if nothing else to stop fear from taking over, but also because in a strange way it seems as if in thinking such things they seem to have more likelihood of happening. 'Perhaps he was just drunk,' I said in an attempt to stop us from thinking the worst, but it was an unconvincing statement, for both of us had noticed he didn't smell of alcohol particularly.

What about the bathroom? Amanda was naturally still panicky, and when I went out the back to check it I felt a few shivers at the thought of fat guy's face pressed up against the window, big ears sticking out, grinning, snarling, making that weird noise; but everything was ok. There was a vent above the shower of opaque fibreglass but it seemed unlikely that anyone would be able to get through it easily, though it would have been just awful to see him come crashing through like in some horror film, unaffected by physical damage like some kind of monster as he just got straight up ready for a grapple, still grinning.

For a while we laid there listening out for any sound in the quiet of the night. Our breath went quiet, frozen as we heard a sound like footsteps outside the door; all went silent for a minute and then the footsteps quietly shuffled off. For sure it wasn't Fat German because it sounded so much different, but we kept the door shut firmly anyway. We continued to listen out but it seemed whoever it was had gone again. It was then, as we were straining to hear anything, that something scrambled across the roof right above us. Amanda was up instantly and over to my bed saying: 'What was that? What was that? There's someone on the roof.' Surely not, it seemed too scrambly, like a lizard might have sounded as it ran off or chased something, or a monkey even, on all fours. Maybe I just didn't want to think there was someone up there. We laid there, hearts beating fast, trying to breathe quietly, trying to stay calm, trying to pass the night as if the morning sun would burn away all the demonic threats of the darkness. I was tired and drifted off once or twice only to wake myself up again with a start, remembering the events still so recent in a vivid replay.

Even before it was fully light Amanda was getting ready to leave. All arguments from the evening before had paled into insignificance as all that mattered now was to get off the island as soon as possible. We'd have to check out early, but since we hadn't paid anything yet we probably wouldn't lose anything, though we'd have to explain to the resort people why we were leaving early. We discussed what would be the best approach, going through the different options: first, we could tell them what happened, at least what we thought had happened, but then we thought there might be some kind of confrontation with the four Germans; this could either turn nasty or might turn into one of those twisted scenes where everything seems sweet right until darkness begins to fall again and we all go back through the twilight zone into some crazy manifestation of thoughts and spirits in another realm. Or, of course, the Thais might take exception to their guests being intimidated away and exact some kind of tribal revenge of their own, them too making the most of the remoteness from any overseeing authorities.

Amanda was convinced that the shuffled footsteps we heard after Fat Guy had gone belonged to Bandana Man, identified by the hushed but audible flap of his flip-flops, whereas Fat Guy had been in bare feet. Woken by all the fuss and noise, it is quite likely that someone came out from the resort house to see what was going on, and it is surely likely enough that if anyone would come out it would be Bandana Man. She even thought it was him scrambling over the roof, perhaps to peek through either the vent or some secret looking point, and who knows, maybe it was. Maybe he'd found Fat Naked German wandering around in the night and had already dealt with him, dealt with all of them, just to be sure. Who would know where these guys had gone once carved up and fed to the sharks; sure no-one on the island was going to let the cat out of the bag. And maybe he deserved it, going round scaring people like that, for if he had a tendency to sleepwalk then he should tie himself down or take some kind of precaution, stay at home even. Or if he really was some kind of crazy rapist who was thwarted from carrying out his full intentions, maybe permanent prevention would do just about everyone a favour. On the other hand, if it really was a one-off innocent mistake then it would be a cruel reaction, excessively merciless and wrong.

As soon as the restaurant and resort reception opened we went over to arrange things, just in case the only boat off the island was first thing in the morning. It seemed all the Thais from the resort were behind the reception, all up ready and waiting for us, as if they were expecting something. In the end we opted for saying as little as possible and gave the line that we just needed to get back to the mainland sooner than we thought. They asked if everything was ok, and we said it was. Was there anything they could do to help? They asked as if they knew something was wrong, as if perhaps they just wanted us to confirm what they already thought, but we said very little. We knew, and I'm sure they knew that something had happened, and maybe sometimes no words are required, for the gut seems to sense things anyway, even if at times it is contrary to any words spoken. Well, all we wanted to do was get off the island and the only way to do that was by long-tail boat, so we asked if they could sort it out. 'You need to leave today?' they continued, surprised, as if the request would be very difficult to meet, and for a few moments we both thought that we would be stuck here for another night.

The guy looked at his watch and said that there was a boat due very soon that could take us back to the mainland, to Trang via the port of Ban Pak Meng, but it didn't dock at the island because the boat was too big for the shallow waters; we would have to be taken out by long-tail boat to meet it on its route. I wondered if he had a brother who had a long-tail boat, and he said that he had a cousin who would take us. It occurred to me that they may have thought it was just Amanda and I having a fight between ourselves, though such an assumption after the extent and nature of the sounds would have needed an acceptance of the excessive as being normal. But neither of us had any injuries, no black eyes or cut lips, and we both wanted to leave as soon as possible, as if the threat was on the island rather than between ourselves. They had always seemed detached, but now it was mingled with concern, though they remained friendly and helpful throughout, even phoning a hotel in Trang for us in case we needed a reservation (which we didn't). We paid for the two nights we'd stayed, bought the boat tickets, and hurried back to finish packing before anything could go wrong.

I don't reckon Amanda has packed up so much stuff and checked out so quickly before or since, for we were out of there in no time. I wasn't sad to leave and as I sat in the sunshine, on the edge of the restaurant, smoking, drinking a coffee that wouldn't cool down quick enough, amongst the small dried flowers and sharp tinder-dry grass, tired from lack of sleep but feeling the need to stay alert, the whole world seemed surreal, three-dimensional in appearance but somehow out of time, dislocated.

A boat turned up and we hurried down to the beach but it wasn't ours. The four big guys still hadn't appeared, and we wanted to be away before they did, to forget the memory and push away the feeling of what might have happened had we been fast asleep when he came in. It was a great relief when our boat appeared not long after, and with our new tarpaulin bag holding all the overflow, we were straight on there, hopefully beyond reach of any danger on the island, mentally urging it to leave before the four

Germans could board.

The Chinese man that we'd seen snorkelling the day before was also on the boat. He didn't seem too happy either, saying very little to anyone, and we couldn't help but wonder if he'd heard the noises in the night and been spooked away. Perhaps it was just that the water visibility had gone, or maybe he was due to leave anyway: we pondered amongst ourselves, always with the feeling that Chinese man knew more than he was letting on. In a silly way I felt an affinity with him, for he had the same sort of hat that I was wearing. After I'd left my cap on the coach, the day on the bike without the helmet, cooled by the breeze but fooled by it too, the increase in temperature and sun strength on this side of the country had caught me out and I'd got sunburned. I'd bought this new one in Koh Lanta, a sort of jungle-style hat, the type with a small rim around that can be folded up or down instead of having a fixed peak: Chinese man had his rim folded up just at the front and I followed suit. It was odd but he seemed somehow safe, and we were glad he was on the boat for it felt that as long as he was on board it would all be ok.

We met the larger boat out to sea – really just a small ferry – beyond all the limestone rocks and islands around Koh Ngai, and did the changeover much like we'd seen the people do on our way to Koh Lanta, fortunately with our newly found kit. It was still a tricky manoeuvre but quite exciting in a way, like escaping on a pirate boat, or even from a pirate boat, and we headed back to the mainland, towards Trang where we hoped to find some safe refuge.

CHAPTER 18
Trang

The boat approached Ban Pak Meng, the mainland port, an area very flat-looking, almost featureless with its modern-looking pier, minimalistic in design, a long straight stretch of concrete that led to a small area for vehicles to deliver and collect passengers. Though our new piece of kit made things easier for Amanda to carry, for me the bags were still just as heavy and I was glad to reach the end of the walkway. I still carried my bag with the shoulder strap, and Amanda's kind of sat half on it and half on my shoulders, balanced so that I was leaning slightly forward gripping it above my head with both hands. Chinese man had already marched off on his way with his little lightweight holdall, and a small gathering of people waited for the connecting transport on to Trang.

When the minibus arrived I could see we wouldn't

all fit on since there were more people than seats even before the bags were loaded. Within minutes I was proved wrong as we all squeezed in somehow, five of us sharing three seats in the back. It was a tight and stuffy drive, feeling tired, slightly in shock still from the night before, and as ever in a sort of dream where the whole world outside was unfamiliar; tropical plants and creatures, strange writing everywhere, different-looking people, different air, different rain, heat and humidity, everything all a long way from home, with a head still rocking from time spent on the water.

It was a relief to get out even though the minibus stopped right in the middle of a busy market full of carts, trucks, people, bikes, and tuk-tuks. According to the book our hotel was round the corner and a couple of hundred yards along the road. In the heat we loaded up and set out to walk it, politely declining any offers from taxis or tuk-tuk drivers who watched us walk by almost in disbelief. Around the corner the road became a very busy street full of side roads, but worst of all turned into a steep incline. By the time we reached our hotel I was sweating in the heat, and when I dropped the load in front of the reception to check in I must have appeared quite bedraggled, T-shirt all wet and wrinkled, pulled half-way round my back, out of breath, asking for a room.

The Trang Hotel had plenty of rooms, the type of Thai hotel that is probably never fully booked, relying perhaps on business travellers as much as tourists, and the room – though basic – was spacious, clean, and bright. What we especially liked was the fact that there were about three locks on the door: one in the handle operated by the key, a slide-across bar, and a bolt. It felt secure to say the least although perhaps it gives reason to wonder why a door might need so many locks: our recent experience answered that for us sufficiently, and after my error Amanda always made a bit of a deal about locking it, sometimes checking it after me as if I was slightly too incompetent to be fully trusted. It all seemed extreme but I suppose it is difficult to describe just how extreme things had felt in the shrieking dark room, and during that time was difficult to forget.

It was a relief to be in the light of day in the safety of Trang, a pretty town with very few farang, reflected in the nature of the shops along the main road all catering for ordinary Thai lives. We were right on the crossroads of two busy streets, opposite a large clock tower, and for a while watched the traffic start and stop at the lights, revving up as soon as the countdown clock got close to zero, mesmerised by the repetitive nature of the sequences. On nearly every street light or road sign was a gold statue or feature of some kind, bird shapes or trees; many buildings were white, also decorated with gold, and most had tall, pointed featured steeples; and there were plenty of elephant shapes and pictures.

We spent a couple of days wandering around the small town drinking the delicious locally ground coffee, trying to forget the 'incident', though we both felt a bit shaken still, uneasy, half expecting to see the four Germans in the street heading for our hotel, Fat Intruder Guy grinning, eyes bulging as if it was some kind of horror game from which there was no escape. Sometimes the feeling changed so that it felt more likely it would be the authorities chasing us looking for four guys reported missing; or even the resort people looking for us to find out exactly what had happened that night. This last imagining was further exaggerated when we considered the possibility that Naked Guy might have repeated his actions but with some less suspecting victim, and all hell may have broken loose. For them, of course, we wouldn't be too difficult to find since they'd phoned the hotel we were staying at to see if we'd needed to book. Whatever dark imaginings haunted us, always there was the feeling that we could be intercepted any moment, always the possibility that something lay in wait around the corner from which we'd have to run.

Fortunately the hotel was the type where so long as you paid for the room first thing in the morning, you could pay for one night at a time, on the same day, allowing more flexibility for planning. It probably looked a bit weird to them, two farang who'd turned up looking in such a state, not knowing what they were really doing or where they were going, and we had the feeling that maybe they too knew by now what had happened. It seems that everyone in Thailand seems to know each other anyway, as if there is a communications network in a subculture tracking unusual movements. Even in the safety of the hotel the first night had been restless, certainly for me, and every time I'd dropped off to sleep I'd woken myself up with a start, as if to rest or relax would allow the danger to reappear. But everyone was friendly enough and the food everywhere was good, and when we'd caught up on some sleep we felt much better.

We needed to make new plans to renew my visa:

although we'd often talked about heading up to little Koh Chang, doing a border run to nearby Burma at the same time, eventually we agreed that maybe Malaysia would be better since we could always visit those islands on the way back up; to return northwards probably would have meant leaving the southern islands for the final time, and I knew Amanda still wanted to go to Koh Phi Phi. So we booked a day trip to the Malaysian border with a lovely lady from the travel agent just inside the hotel lobby; she was very helpful and we felt more at ease again.

The day trip was unusual for we changed vehicle and drivers several times; our final leg to the border was with an older guy who looked like he'd spent plenty of time at sea, dark-skinned and with a kind of leaning forward outlook, as he drove and as he spoke. He took us on a route through dense tropical forests and jungles, listing the animals that roamed wild, like in a world long forgotten in our culture other than in movies or natural history programmes; images and perspectives so different from the real thing. It was once a fairly unknown route, he explained to us, one that he had in a way pioneered to make the journey to the border easier for farang; who knows whether this was true, but it could have been, and it certainly fitted with the demeanour. We stopped off for some refreshments at a small roadside shop/diner where the people who lived had a long-haired cat with cream fur and blue eyes. The cat appeared to be their main focus of attention whatever it did; if it did nothing, they simply indicated how beautiful it was, and with pride a young girl picked it up and brought it out to show us. I drank an unusual energy drink recommended by our driver supposedly with some kind of power content; all ingredients were listed in Thai but I figured if it was for Thais then it would most likely be ok, and he drank one too; without naming brands, drinks designed specifically for farang probably carry more risk.

By the time we reached the border I had been lulled into a relaxed sense of ease at having to do nothing but look out of the window and listen to our driver. He pulled over and pointed to the border gate some thirty yards away. I don't know why but I'd kind of hoped we wouldn't even have to get out of the car, just go round in a loop, showing our passports out of the window. It was ridiculous to think it would be that easy, and I have to say I was a little mentally unprepared. We got out, walked across a line out of Thailand, getting our passports exit stamped on the way, and I found out that the small immigration form I'd got on the plane was actually very important, even though it had not seemed so at the time; I'd forgotten I even had it still when the border guard had asked to see it.

On we went through no-man's land towards the two armed guards that were waiting for us beyond the line that indicated the start of Malaysia, smiling in welcoming anticipation in the same way that a cartoon wolf might smile at an approaching rabbit. There were warning signs about bringing in anything forbidden, and we'd left our small bags in the car – just in case – and thoroughly searched every pocket to make sure there was nothing that could lead to trouble, however innocent it might seem to us. There was a form which required completion, as pointed out by one of the guards: I whispered to Amanda that I had no pen; whether he thought I'd said something about a gun or insulted him in some way, I don't know, but whatever he thought I'd said he didn't like it. Suddenly glaring at me, moving his hand towards his hip as if about to draw and shoot, he told me to repeat what I'd said. There are proverbs warning against whispering, and I can now see why, for rather than a misinterpreted word it may simply have been that I'd said something right in front of him, for his eyes but not his ears, denying him the true understanding of his experience. Fortunately he calmed down just as quickly, though I'd caught his alarmed mood.

There were more forms to fill out on our way round, and after the misunderstanding with the guard I spent the remainder of the time feeling exposed, being watched. The forms aren't designed for farang to cross borders simply to renew visas, although no doubt enough do it to warrant such forms, and include many questions that don't really apply, so the whole thing took longer than we and our driver expected. However, we got through without further mishap and were soon back in the car heading through the trees with another month in Thailand before any further visa renewal was needed. It would have been good to have gone right into Malaysia, but it meant changing money into their currency and digging into a budget already overspent. I was now spending Aussie dollars reserved for later in the trip, and we'd have to spend most of our time working if we were to make it around Australia without going broke; even then we had a week in Bali and a couple of nights in Singapore to cover, although I had a credit card to use for emergencies. I guess our two main obstacles to this plan were that neither of us had a working visa for Australia, being too old to apply, and that Amanda's health was still not good. Even if we could have found enough fruit picking or organic farm work to cover our costs (which I've heard is actually very hard work) I couldn't see Amanda being up to it. And maybe my back wouldn't have lasted either, being a bit of an Achilles heel for me along with the bad knee that actually no longer hurt.

The drive back was pleasant though, and we chatted with our driver who confirmed that his family had been sea people. 'Chao ley,' I said to Amanda, who nudged me to stop saying the words in front of Thais in case they were interpreted as insulting. To me it was more of a compliment, for the sea people certainly appeared to live in a way more harmonious with their surroundings than us westerners, though of course to call them sea gypsies can arouse such connotations in our culture as rough, dirty thieves, not to be trusted but rather feared and avoided, such is the image often so portrayed throughout the media. He told us about an island off of the deep south coast, and said he owned a small guest house, not listed in our guide books, on the mainland close by to the port for boats heading out to it. He did driving jobs during the day, amongst, no doubt, other things including selling trips to these southern islands to farang like us. We tried to find out how hard they had been hit by the tsunami or how much affected they had been, but as with most people we had tried to speak with about this, he just assured us that it was now ok to go and visit; but then he and everyone else weren't going to say anything to the contrary, anything that might put people off. We asked him if he knew of Koh Ngai; he said he knew of it but little else, and we never found out much more because his phone went and he answered it.

He finished talking and pulled the car over to the side of the road. Turning round to us, he explained that there had been some kind of mix-up and that we had to go back to the border. At first, in a moment of fear we thought it was to do with our visas but fortunately not; instead there was a minibus on its way up that had to meet a coach leaving Trang for Bangkok; on board, however, were passengers who had to get to Hat Yai to catch a train. It seemed that there had been delays at the border for them too, and time was extremely tight. They were about sixty kilometres away, and the only way possible was for us to turn around, head back towards the border at top speed whilst they drove towards us; meeting halfway (give or take, depending on who drove the fastest) we'd all reshuffle and assume appropriate direction. It was dead time for us, going backwards and forwards the extra distance over ground already covered, and who knows what would have happened if we'd been insistent on getting straight back ourselves; as it was, we were happy enough to let the ride continue, especially when we knew people had connections to meet. Would he really make it, was it really possible? He thought it might be, though spent the rest of the journey quiet, concentrating solely on his watch and the road. The rendezvous went ahead and we were on our way again, this time crammed into a small minibus full of bags, rucksacks and farang, all tired-looking, already resigned to the fact that the connection would be missed. I suppose where we would be unaffected either way, it was more of a game for us than for them, quite exciting.

The changeover had been so fast that hardly anyone had had time for a quick smoke even, and the new driver let us smoke in the back so long as the windows were open and no-one was looking in. I thought our car driver had driven fast, but this guy was flat out all the way, as fast as possible, overtaking cars even when another was approaching so long as there was space enough to get through the gap in the middle of the road. Once, when a car wouldn't pull over, he went up through on the inside but sight of a police car stopped him from doing this again; they'd noticed his hurry and followed for a while but turned off, and when they did, everyone cheered. He too had a watch, exposed on his wrist to gauge his progress; the road signs told us how far was left in distance, and often I found myself straining to see what his watch said, just to see how we were getting on. It was like a race – tense, fast, with the odd obstacle thrown in. Sometimes the road narrowed, or a car wouldn't move over quick enough, and each time momentum was lost our driver would tap the steering wheel with his fist, utter a sound maybe, then restart with fresh concentration. At one point he must have got a little too close to someone for we had what looked like some road-ragers driving close up behind us, even at our fast speed; to everyone's relief they merged off in another direction on a main bit of road and we continued, everyone urging our man on, willing, as if it helped.

It was all a bit of an anti-climax when we dropped them at the station, for we weren't sure if they made it or not; we were over five minutes late but maybe they had managed to get the coach delayed for enough time, we never found out. We thanked him anyway for all the excitement when he dropped us off, and he smiled, kind of tapped the side of the minibus that now reeked of burning rubber and oil, and confessed that it probably would never perform quite the same again.

There was still no word from home about what was going on, so we opted against heading back out to a remote island so soon after the recent trauma, deciding to go to Koh Phi Phi instead. We knew it had been hit hard by the tsunami for Amanda had friends who'd been there at the time, though had miraculously managed to escape the wave by scrambling up some steps cut into a cliff face; they had tried to help others too but had seen many people swept by, and were obviously around during all the aftermath. I didn't really want to go there, and had said so all along, and one of the reasons for going to Koh Ngai had been as an alternative to Koh Phi Phi. However, after that had gone wrong and been cut short, I knew Amanda really wanted to go there, and since it was her birthday in a couple of days, we agreed on it.

When we approached the hotel travel agent to try and book it up, she didn't think it would be any problem, which was odd because all other sources of information highly recommended checking in advance to see if any resort listed in guide books still existed even; and since so many places had been closed or washed away, there was limited accommodation for the large number of people who visited the island at this time of year. The Aussies I'd met in Koh Pha Ngan had been scheduled for the island somewhere – who knows, the Phi Phi Cabana perhaps – so I knew some of it at least was open, although it was also expensive. The lady phoned maybe a dozen places, each time seeming surprised when there was no answer, or the number diverted to an answering message saying the place was closed; it was as if in all the time since it had happened she hadn't had cause to try and book up anywhere there, even though Koh Phi Phi was listed on all the large signs advertising trips, transport, and excursions around her small glass office. Eventually she phoned somebody she knew who used to live on the island but now lived in Krabi; after a few return exchanges it seemed the person on the other end could book us two nights, and she told us the price. As I say, available places were expensive but we booked it anyway, and perhaps to the relief of the reception staff possibly suspicious of such an odd pair, we checked out and headed back to Krabi: at the port, a guy called Lok would meet us with details of the resort; there was nothing to pay until we got there, which felt slightly uncertain.

CHAPTER 19
Empty Graves

We took a tuk-tuk from the Trang Hotel to the coach station rather than walking the mile or so with the bags in the heat. Amanda had tied her tie-dyed sheet bought from Dan the man back at Lamai around the tarpaulin bag to form a large sack, better-looking than what might have otherwise been construed as a large drugs bag. As we pulled in, a coach was leaving, and in a moment of panic thinking it was ours, our driver stopped it and we very nearly got on board, only to find it was the wrong coach. Off came the bags in a scene of embarrassed apologies with only our misconstrued sense of urgency to blame. When the right coach arrived it was heading all the way to Bangkok, quite spacious compared to any we'd been on so far. Just like us, some people flew around the corner as we were pulling out, so we stopped and waited whilst they sorted out their bags and tickets and found a seat.

It was only a few hours back to Krabi, and by now even the unfamiliar seemed to be becoming familiar; the sounds of Thai voices that had seemed so different were now relaxing, more reassuring somehow, though I hadn't a clue what was being said. It was more like sitting in a garden surrounded by birdsong, where sounds became colours and feelings rather than pictures and meanings. When it's a pretty song sang with a happy smile it doesn't seem to matter so much what it means. Even the written language was pretty to look at, interesting in design, curved instead of upright and formal straight lines. We headed on through small villages, away from the cities, where the culture centred around enjoying and celebrating basic needs instead of futile entertainment, and nothing was neon-lit.

We reached Krabi bus station and were just figuring out how to reach the port when I noticed the tie-dyed sack was missing. Hurrying outside, we waved down the coach that was just pulling out and got him to open up the luggage hold underneath. There it was, fortunately prevented from heading back to Bangkok alone: hearts beating, we just looked at each other and thought, *Phew, that was close*.

We got to the right port eventually, though not without going to the wrong one first, not that it mattered too much for there was plenty of time before the ferry left. The arrangement was to meet this guy, Lok, who would know us by the descriptions we gave over the phone, most notably the sandy-coloured bags. Though he wasn't holding a sign with our names on it, the type of sign promised by pretty much every tout we had met but had never appeared, and that had by now become like some kind of joke, sure enough he turned up before our ferry was due in. His name was actually Loh and not Lok, ending in an unusual vowel sound, a small Thai guy probably in his late twenties. He had a good smile, wore a brightly coloured Hawaiian shirt, and informed us that he would gladly be our guide and accompany us to the island. We thanked him very much, but pointed out that we weren't really looking for a guide, just needed to know how to get to our resort. It would be no trouble, he assured us. In fact it would give him a good reason to go back, suggesting vaguely that maybe he would go over anyway. It didn't seem a bad idea to begin with, for I must say I thought he could perhaps help in carrying the bags; but after lifting each of the bags I carried he opted for one of Amanda's smaller ones instead, typically the bag of valuables, not exactly adding to her peace of mind; it wasn't much of a benefit for me either as we walked the long walk down the pier to meet our boat.

The ferry was a small boat, passengers only, no vehicles, though there were enough people and bags to fill it right up so that out on the deck where you could smoke and sit in the sunshine it was all a bit squashed, no room for the legs if sat down, and with all railings taken nothing to hold onto if stood up. There was much conversation on board about what the island would be like after the tsunami, many people having been there before, some returning as if on some kind of pilgrimage, like they felt they ought to go back. A guy whose middle toe on each foot was extremely long stood chatting to some girls nearby;

the feet kept catching my attention, weird-looking, in what became a bit of an unpleasant journey when the engine started playing up and chucking out all sorts of bad fumes our way, the sort that make your stomach feel a bit sick, made a little worse by the rocking motion of the boat.

After a short breakdown when the engine had cut out, the approach to Koh Phi Phi was truly magnificent as the boat entered the turquoise waters and turned into the bay surrounded by tall limestone cliffs. The large wooden pier jutted out from the water such that from a distance an old tea-cutter would have looked more at home than our modern plastic ferry, and the scene could have looked similar a thousand years ago, like something from Jason and the Argonauts or Sinbad. Up close, of course, the scene revealed something quite different: right at the end of the pier, upon reaching the mainland, an old 7-Eleven store remained standing but closed, washed out and gutted by the tsunami but left un-repaired in a way that a sunken ship holding taken lives is treated as a burial ground and left undisturbed. Conversations confirmed that everyone who was working in the shop on that dreadful day had died, too scared to run when the first warnings came for fear of leaving the shop unattended, no doubt along with any customers as well. Just an empty shell remained, stained now and weathered, like a war monument, an unpleasant reminder.

Eventually someone from our resort turned up with a large trolley for our bags: I would have been happy to walk but Mr Loh wasn't keen, preferring to wait. As we walked behind the trolley, along the walkway, the narrow strip of land between the two chunks of rock that make up the Phi Phi islands – a path lined with shops and bars each side with people sat around, browsing, mingling – it was clear that last-minute escapes from the wave would have been near impossible down at this level. Mr Loh had been on the island when it happened, a fortunate survivor, but had left afterwards, put off by the prospect of another wave perhaps, or having lost the place where he worked, it was never really clear for he was always quite vague about it. What was clear, however, was that many people recognised him, and that he had once lived there but didn't now; he told us it was the first time he had returned since it had happened.

That evening we walked the very steep walk up to a lookout point at the top of one of the islands to watch the sun set. The scenery was beautiful, and the view from high above showed just how vulnerable the small strip of land connecting the islands would have been. Twistedly, this was where most of the accommodation had been situated, especially the cheaper bamboo huts, those most likely to be smashed away. From this distance the small strip looked pretty again with the coloured limestone cliffs as a backdrop, and blue sea, so much so that you would never know by looking what had happened. Mr Loh said that everything had happened so quickly but he'd seen the wave come in, channelled by the rocks either side of the bay so that it gained even more height and thrust; it had simply swept over the isthmus as if it was nothing, a huge mass of water that added insult to injury a few minutes later as the same surge retreated back again, as if to make sure of its job.

Our room was another concrete chalet, clean and neat but almost clinical, without atmosphere or character. Virtually at sea level, though set back a couple of hundred yards from the beach, the interior layout showed that this place would have become a concrete tank from which there would have been no escape; even the roofs weren't high enough to avoid the surge of water carrying whatever debris it had collected on its way. Cheap or expensive places, rich or poor, it seemed the wave wasn't choosy about what or who it took.

Amanda's friend who'd been on the island when it had happened, had confirmed that on Boxing Day morning there had been an all-night beach party the night before; the timing of the wave was such that many people had gone back to bed at a time when normally they would be up and about, as if the recipe had been concocted intentionally for the most effective type of poison. Our dried-out watery grave was not particularly welcoming, and neither of us slept well both nights, very nearly leaving after the first night there, staying partly because we had paid a lot of money and partly since we needed to think of where to go next.

The first morning we were up before dawn to return up the mountain to a sunrise lookout point. We were a bit late leaving, not that it takes long to get up and dressed in Thailand, so the sun had just risen when we reached the top; we saw a herd of wild goats come grazing by – small, pretty things, very timid. It was a slightly hazy view out to sea and we were assured that on a clear day you could see James Bond Island, apparently where they had once filmed a movie. Oddly enough nobody made much of a big deal about The Beach film on the island, and some said that when they filmed that movie all the work was kept from the local Thais; it was said too that much of the beautiful coral had been ruined during its making, and of course as a result of the swarms of farang since who were still heading out there.

We went for a walk to a beach around the headland which was much quieter and looked much better for swimming and snorkelling, being out of the way of all the boats that docked at the small port. The huts here were right on the beach, and we assumed that they would have been hit hard as well. Apparently, though, there was a further twist to the tale of the wave in that this beach was pretty much unaffected; Mr Loh explained that there had been far fewer people staying on this stretch, and that the wave had hit the very beach where most people had been at the time, as if it wanted to do the most amount of damage, have the most impact at a time of year most memorable, as if by intention or through a will of its own. It was an added factor beyond explanation of an already cruel phenomenon that he said made him not want to live here anymore.

Mr Loh continued hanging around as our guide, eating when we ate. He was ok but as time went by it seemed that not everyone on the island was altogether pleased to see him back there, though some were. He had annoyed Amanda the first night when she had overheard him talking with some Thais, referring to us as Mama and Papa, as if we were there to provide for him. It was a strange deal, one that we hadn't requested but didn't know how to end without being rude. Instead of returning to the restaurant for fresh fish like we'd eaten the night before, we invited him to join us in a large plate of fried rice; he accepted but was clearly unimpressed, trying to hide his disappointment, and afterwards wandered off somewhere until the following morning when we were due to leave.

I have to admit that you could see what a beautiful place the island would have been a few years before, and how relaxed, chilled out, and happy the atmosphere all along the isthmus could have been. But there was something missing now, hidden by the smiles of the people who were trying to carry on living there, trying to continue the atmosphere; maybe they were new people, replacements; perhaps it was the soulless concrete resorts that were being built to replace the bamboo huts washed away, huts that fitted with the island and laid-back culture instead of complexes that represented the corporate world of hotel chains, external shareholders, and profit-driven targets, inhuman, such that farang truly are nothing but baht-bringers. It seemed the government had got involved too, putting strict regulations in place that restricted what types of buildings could be built, and where: this simply limited the ability of the survivors to rebuild, for they had no such resources to fund these projects that complied with government legislation, and accordingly their influence over the future of the island was reduced to virtually nothing; consequently the power over their own lives on the island – or even elsewhere – had been significantly diminished.

There was still no news from home so we figured the best course was to leave this island of ghosts and lost souls and take the boat to Phuket. Our last morning in Koh Phi Phi was Amanda's birthday and we had a breakfast of fried chicken, fried garlic, and wild rice, her favourite meal, before setting off for the ferry, this time walking alone laden with the bags back through the narrow drag full of browsing farang. Mr Loh had disappeared after breakfast, perhaps avoiding any involvement with the bags, and we figured that now the meals were over he was probably working on someone else by now. To be fair, he turned up to say cheerio just as we were about to board, and I'm sure if we'd been bound for Krabi, like he'd tried to persuade us, then he would have boarded with us too; Phuket was well out of his way though.

The boat was heaving, rammed with people leaving Koh Phi Phi, and we wondered if it was always like this or if something had happened to make everyone want to leave. Most likely it was just busy, and struggling with all our luggage amongst the bustling crowd, we were one of the last to get on board. All the bag space up on deck was taken, and we had to get down through a hatch and almost vertical ladder into the lower deck to find some stow space, but somehow managed before going back up to stand outside in the fresh air and view the scenery for the journey.

I suppose even beautiful limestone rocks and turquoise seas become commonplace after enough journeys, but still acted as a reminder that we were somewhere far away, so that it was easier to drift off into a dreamlike state. Most people on the boat were just sat around staring at something in the distance, maybe into the waves or the wash of the boat as we chugged along, and in the middle of the sea on a calm, sunny day, not too much seems to matter.

Approaching the mainland was a reminder of the need to think of a plan, a nagging uncertainty that had been ever more difficult to put off the closer we got to Phuket. We knew that it was expensive here too, and had also been hit by the tsunami; in a way we thought it would be similar to where we had just left, and we wanted something different. We'd tried to research on the internet but trawling through so many pages looking for information that is up to date and reliable was something that quickly brought me down; as said before, resort owners are hardly going to say stay away, the party is over. Little Koh Chang near Burma seemed risky now too, for we were sure that it would have been impacted and maybe everything washed away. Amanda was still feeling ill, perhaps even a little worse, though maybe this wasn't helped by recent events.

When we docked, the crowd reversed its actions and piled off, leaving us amongst the tail-enders left with the task of getting the bags out from the lower deck. Getting down was much easier than getting back up; Amanda had to stand on the dockside watching what we had already offloaded, whilst I went back for more; it took about three trips due to the tight squeeze and wobbly gang-plank off the boat, and I only managed it because a stranger offered to take Amanda's bag off me up through the hatch after seeing my two failed attempts. Crowds of people waiting to board began getting on before I'd even finished, adding to the awkwardness. By the time it pulled out and most of those who had got off had gone off in their various directions, it seemed like just the two us stood there amongst a large pile of luggage, still uncertain of where to go next.

The truth is that it was probably then that I realised we couldn't go much further. It's easy to think of good reasons not to go somewhere, or do something; but then life is always about taking chances, even if you're unaware of it at the time, and who knows, maybe things just work out as they do because it was always going to be so. Amanda's health and finances were giving her problems, and I'd well overspent too. Still there was no word from home, and the uncertainty of the trip had added to the problems, an underlying uncertainty that had been stressful on some level probably ever since my gran had died, possibly even before.

So we headed for Phuket Airport to investigate changing our flight dates, where we were told that possibly the Qantas office at Bangkok International could help us. I thought of the couple I'd met in Chaweng way back when I'd first arrived in Koh Samui who had tried to change their dates from the island. They'd been directed back to Bangkok too, for dates could not be altered by phone. Though there is a Qantas office at the airport, they had been told to go to the main office right in the city; it's odd how such conversations become relevant, for there I was, looking at the piece of paper they had given me with the Bangkok office address, also written out in Thai for the benefit of any taxi driver who could not read English.

We flew back to Bangkok as a birthday treat for Amanda to appease the fact that she hadn't been on an internal flight in Thailand but I had. Besides, now that the rest of the trip was off money seemed less of a problem until I tried buying the tickets on the credit card, only for it to be refused. In a way I was relieved to have found it out now rather than when getting off the plane in Sydney, had we carried on.

Though it was very sad to be flying away from the beautiful islands, the view from the air was the most spectacular both of us had ever seen. Rivers met the sea in all sorts of strange S shapes, rocks and islands like smoking volcanoes from a prehistoric age set in the beautiful blues; wild tropical jungles with lush green vegetation. The plane climbed higher, and we left the magnificent views behind for another time.

CHAPTER 20

Samran II

Bangkok Airport was as busy as ever, a world away from the one in which we had woken up that morning. People moved quicker, had an urgency to get somewhere, as if they were in a place that needed to be gotten away from, quickly, as soon as possible. Business suits, briefcases, and shoes replaced the flip-flops, shorts, and rucksacks; brightly lit notice boards and tannoyed voices made announcements; armed police patrolled, making their presence known to remind everyone to behave, and that there could be potential danger.

We found the Qantas office and dealt with a young Thai girl who assured us that it would be simple to change the dates: it seemed too easy and before paying for any changes we asked that she double checked. After several phone calls and conversations in Thai, she then confirmed that the only way to change our particular type of ticket was to go to the office in Bangkok, almost telling us off for even trying at the airport, as if we'd perhaps been deliberately trying to get her into trouble. We wondered what would have happened had we let her go ahead and try to change them, and it all seemed slightly uncertain, unreliable, if even the Qantas people at the airport didn't really know what was what.

One good aspect of Bangkok is that there is a stack of accommodation; I saw a desk with a sign that said 'Hotel Information' so went to enquire about somewhere to stay. 'Where do you want to stay?' she asked, putting me on the spot, for I had expected her to recommend something instantly.

'Maybe the Samran,' I replied.

'Near Siam Square?' she asked, hardly looking up from what she was doing, and I confirmed that was the one. She looked at me like I was a little crazy and said I wouldn't need to book there, just to turn up.

'Do they have rooms?' I wanted to check.

'They will have rooms,' she said, shooing me away impatiently, almost daring me to question or doubt the assertion and waste more of her time.

We took the airport coach back through a route that now seemed slightly familiar now I'd travelled it a few times, chatting to an English guy we'd met in the queue who had exactly the same type of bag that we had. His name was Alistair, a strange guy who admitted to us that he'd burned all of his business books and records to avoid a huge tax bill, declared himself insane so that responsibility for the act was considered to be relinquished, and was heading out to stay here for as long as possible. It turned out he was staying in Bangkok for a few days, somewhere near the Kao San Road, before heading for little Koh Chang, the island we'd thought about so much. That was his plan, at least, and before getting off we exchanged email addresses, for we were still interested in knowing what it was like down there.

We bundled through the Samran restaurant which was fortunately clear of people watching us haul our bags to the reception, and checked they had a room. I recognised the lady who smiled back as if in recognition, though more likely she just always smiled at people like that. My name came up on the records as having stayed there before, and we chatted with her for a while about where we'd been. It was a friendly welcome, and went some way towards making up for the fact that we were back in the city, far from the beaches. Bangkok seemed even hotter now, and even more humid; more smelly too, though it may have just been the sudden contrast with the fresh sea breezes of the islands.

The Qantas office was only a short distance away, and we took a taxi there to avoid getting lost, though when you're looking for one of the tallest tower blocks in the city and you know roughly where it is then it shouldn't be too difficult. The office was on the 21st floor of a building so high that if you stood outside at the entrance it was impossible to see where it ended in the sky. Ground level was full of upmarket stalls selling expensive goods, a few banks and places to eat; above ground level it was all business, as indicated by the suits and briefcases bustling in and out of the six lifts constantly going up and down. I once worked in a three-storey building that had a lift, an old thing that was often breaking down; most people used the stairs, not fully trusting it, but the boss nearly always used it, so when we were sat there working at about half past nine and the little alarm bell started ringing then you could be sure who was stuck in it. These super-fast modern machines were a long way from that little lift, and if you worked there, the chances are walking wasn't an option; in fact these buildings are so high that there are separate lifts for the floors on the top half to avoid stopping at too many floors on the way up, something I'd never even considered before.

The flight rearrangement was not as straightforward as we'd hoped, as if getting to this office hadn't been quite enough effort. It seemed the process was as follows: we picked a date; the lady here would try and reserve the seats and send an email to Qantas in Australia; they would consider our request and, if granted, email their acceptance; then we'd have to return to the office, pay for the changes, and collect the new tickets, hoping the seats were still on hold. Since there was a time difference of about five hours, and because the office only worked business hours from Monday to Friday, there could be some delay. The lady added, when we pushed her for a likely confirmation date, that there was also a backlog due to an unexpectedly large number of people trying to change dates. We picked a date in a couple of weeks, and had no choice but to sit it out and wait for their response.

The reception lady at the hotel was fine for a few

days, allowing us to extend our stay each morning so long as we paid for the night in advance. We ate breakfast there each day to keep everyone happy, and sampled some of the excellent food served at the diners set up along the streets nearby. These are just a few tables and chairs arranged on the pavement around someone cooking over a smoking wok; all the raw vegetables are stored in full view, and people eat as the busy traffic drives by. Some of these street diners were so popular that we had trouble finding a seat, and some places seemed to be for Thais only rather than for farang; this seemed fair enough considering the number of places around that catered solely for farang rather than local Thais.

Days went by without any word, and we spent the time wandering around Siam Square, checking emails, watching Thai life go by like a film, holding us in a different reality, the disbelief of any unlikelihood suspended by the fact that it was all happening right in front of our eyes. It is an old adage that true life is often stranger than fiction, so strange you couldn't make it up.

Then one morning the reception lady caught our attention when we came down for breakfast and told us that the hotel had been fully booked out, and that we would have to find somewhere else to stay, at least for a couple of nights.

CHAPTER 21
The Mouleng Boutique

Everywhere around Siam Square was fully booked out; apparently there was a large conference happening somewhere nearby, so with the weekend shoppers every bed was taken. By chance as well, the Siam Beverley where I'd first stayed had been fully booked too, where a Chinese wedding party had taken over the entire hotel; in the end we booked somewhere several miles away. It was a bit of an obscure place, unknown even to the travel agent lady in reception who'd found it in a listing after rummaging through a drawer when she'd tried all the places that she'd known.

We stored our luggage for the day, leisurely wandered around some of the many Thai markets, and took a taxi to the Mouleng Boutique through the Friday evening rush hour. In a metered taxi the clock ticks along even when sat in traffic, much like ours do here, except that when it's only going up in increments of two baht each time, it doesn't matter too much. The journey ended up taking nearly half an hour, and our driver had trouble finding the place at first, tucked away through some narrow one way streets, but it still only cost just over the equivalent of a pound.

The building itself looked ok, sort of Roman in appearance, with pillars, black railings around a courtyard, set amongst a few shrubs indicating that life could at least survive, but it was located right beneath a main highway interchange. As soon as you walked down the road, all you could see were road structures, dull concrete supports, metal fences and railings – an industrial nightmare. It seemed to rub off on the hotel: up the stairs, the walkway around that overlooked the courtyard below had more of a prison atmosphere about it; instead of being in a Bangkok hotel we felt like we were on B wing, serving time, and we had about thirty-six hours left to do.

The first evening we ate in the restaurant downstairs, not wanting to venture out to explore the local vicinity in the dark, and had the worst meal we'd eaten for some time in a somewhat frosty atmosphere. We were the only ones eating, the waiter was over-attentive, appeared new to the job, and the chef could be heard fuming in the kitchen, as if either rushed off his feet or feeling absolutely wasted in a place with no customers; who knows? Perhaps he didn't like cooking what we ordered.

The room was clean and comfortable, and certainly looked good enough at first glance. But things become noticeable only after a while, upon closer inspection, like the bullet holes in the door that had been patched over, and the scars of where the door had been forced open sometime in the past. What sort of place was this? Some kind of meeting place for drug runners? Pimps? Who knows, but when we found that the door wouldn't lock properly we were a bit concerned. Actually the lock worked fine, you just couldn't lock it so that it would stop someone outside who happened to have a key that fitted. There was no bolt, and the door opened outwards so it was no good just putting all the bags or some furniture in front of it. In the end I rigged something up with my long cable and padlock, the cable tied around the door handle and fed around a heavy wooden table; it had to be tight enough so that if the door was prized open slightly there would be insufficient room to reach in and slip the cable off of the handle. It wasn't fixed immovably, for the table slid along the tiled floor but with the bags stacked in front of it movement would be difficult, and noisy enough to wake us up (so long as we hadn't been drugged by the chef downstairs).

It was an uneventful night, fairly quiet considering where we were, and we went downstairs for breakfast. There were a few people sat around eating, including the owner, some guy from Cyprus married to a Thai. There'd been some kind of argument and a family were moving out for some reason, something we'd missed and never found out what it was. We ordered a couple of American breakfasts, as always, and when they arrived the fried eggs were still raw, the white hardly cooked. I'd eaten barely fried eggs enough times to try and make sure beforehand with the waiter that they were well cooked; there is a phrase that

Thais use, something like 'zug-zug', to mean fried both sides. They never seemed to understand when I said it, but always said it themselves when I made the unmistakeable miming action with my hand of turning it over and frying both sides. So we'd asked our waiter, who had assured us he knew what we meant; when he put them down in front of us I think he noticed and scurried off quickly. Eventually, after clearly avoiding eye contact for several minutes, he returned so we asked him if the chef could put them back in the pan for a while. He took them back as if knowing there would be trouble, like perhaps Manuel would have taken something back, bowing his head in anticipation of some kind of vicious retaliation from the monster hidden in the kitchen. The eggs returned after a few minutes, not much more cooked than before, and the owner called the waiter over to find out what had happened. A few minutes later, in a bizarre scene that mirrored what had happened to us, the owner stood up, called the waiter over and declared loudly that his eggs weren't cooked enough. He looked like he was going to swipe at the waiter, and sent him off with a few plates. It would have all been quite tense had it not been so surreal, and in a way it was interesting to see what might happen next.

Back at the room, the chambermaids wanted to come in and clean. In most places, these ladies give you the option, knocking on the door and leaving if you say you don't need anything, perhaps just taking the rubbish away, replacing the toilet roll if you use it, saving everyone unnecessary bother. Not here: though we explained we only had one night left so didn't need anything, they insisted not just on cleaning the room but doing it whilst we went out.

We packed pretty much everything away, locked the bags, and went out to explore the local urban vicinity in daylight.

Under the concrete structures and beyond were some main roads down at ground level, a few shops, not much, so we went back to the hotel and drank some coffee. It was expensive after the cheap but delicious coffee on the islands; some things are cheaper in Bangkok, and some things are dearer, it is odd. When we got back to the room one or two things were missing, and we never knew whether the maids had taken them or just thrown them away thinking it was rubbish.

That night we took a taxi to the Siam Beverley and had a meal in the restaurant. The big chef who had got me the chicken satays and ice cream was still there, smiling. I knew a few more Thai words now, though we were hardly going to be having a conversation; still, it reminded me that much time had passed, much had happened. After fully indulging in the superb buffet, eating a little too much, the foods now familiar, identifiable, and difficult to resist, we went outside and saw Sawat waiting with his taxi. I guess many people had come and gone since we'd last met, and for a while we chatted without me letting on that we'd met before. After a while though he remembered the Koh Samui trip and his eyes screwed up, his face broke into a big smile, and he made his happy Thai sounds, pleased to meet again.

He gave us a lift back to our hotel, getting lost himself in the maze of roads and tunnels that led underneath the concrete monster above, unimpressed and concerned at the area in which we were staying;

we explained about all the hotels being booked up. He gave us his new business card, a black and white print of a brand new Mercedes along with his name and number, so if ever we needed a taxi or a tour somewhere we could find him; he listed all the different Buddhas, temples, and markets for Amanda's benefit, encouraged by her interest.

We checked out the next morning, skipped breakfast, and took a taxi back to the Samran to try and sort things out with Qantas the following day. Even the journey leaving the place was unpleasant after an argument with our driver over the fare. Refusing to turn the meter on and fixing his price at 150 baht, I argued that it had been half that to get here through rush hour. He argued that it was a Sunday, and more expensive. Anywhere else and we could have simply waited for another to turn up, but this guy had blocked the way and, knowing where we were going and that we needed a taxi sooner or later, wouldn't move. Before it turned too sour we agreed, after all the difference would mean very little back home. In a way I knew this was the point he was making; on the other hand, who wants to be ripped off especially when both parties know it's a rip-off? It got worse when he then began to mock how much I'd paid for a beach mat, telling me that if he'd bought it he would have paid a quarter of the price. His phone went and he began a conversation where he seemed to be taking great delight in telling someone what had just happened, and then we very nearly crashed into the car in front that had stopped suddenly. To be fair he reacted quickly and screeched to a halt, stopping with only inches to spare. Everyone went quiet for the rest of the journey; I know my heart had jumped and was beating hard. When we got there we gave him his fare; if he'd agreed on the first price I probably would have tipped him too, so he would have got almost as much, but then looking back, as is so often the case with hindsight, I could have handled it much better too. Never mind, no harm was done, and perhaps it was fitting for the time and place.

CHAPTER 22
Samran III

Back at the Samran the lady checked us back in, though not quite as friendly as before, as if a couple of farang staying for a few nights was fine, but to keep returning not knowing for how long or where they were going next perhaps aroused some kind of suspicion. It didn't matter too much for the next morning we called the Qantas office in Bangkok for any news and they confirmed that our changes were ok, so long as we came in and paid that day. The emails from Qantas never actually came, and if we hadn't phoned, who knows? If we'd booked tickets ourselves online, apparently none of this would have happened, but that's the way it goes, in the end you spend your time and efforts doing something, even if it's not what you planned or expected.

Outside the tower they were giving away free

bottles of lemon tea, some kind of promotion. We had one on the way in and another on the way out though, of course, as is always the case with drinking and travelling, you are never far away in time from needing another pee, something the Thais know very well and fully utilise; but then, who wants someone else's waste brought into their own garden?

The news from home had suggested that the scattering of Gran's ashes was unlikely to take place just then due to various reasons. Some had said there was no need to rush back, not to cut the trip short unless I really wanted to; everyone said how cold it was. It was difficult to imagine in the Bangkok heat, still seeming so far away, but by now I suppose in our own minds we knew we'd be going back, and after all the uncertainty it felt more settled when the date was fixed, at least as sure as anything in Thailand feels fixed.

The office tower was on the same street as the TAT office where I'd first met Noppi, and we walked there to see if he knew the best way for us to get down to little Koh Chang for our last week. On the way a strange man accompanied us, friendly, chatting and guiding us across the crazy junctions that produce traffic from unseen directions like rabbits from a hat. Just before our TAT office he tried to divert us to a market, the cheapest in Bangkok, owned by his brother – he was on his way there now anyway, it would be no trouble for him to take us – and we should go just to take a look. We politely declined, told him we'd spent our money and were off home, and he went off on his way.

Noppi had a good memory, and remembered I'd been to Koh Samui. I laughed and said how much better it would have been had it not been in a monsoon; he fidgeted slightly, smiled, and managed to laugh it away, saying that was how he'd managed to get such good places for such good prices. There had been times when I'd thought, *If I see Noppi again I'll tell him he ripped me and he knew it*, but after time had passed it really didn't matter, certainly wasn't worth making a fuss over. He couldn't help us with our plan for it was beyond the TAT trail to which they were restricted, and didn't even know too much about it himself. He noted all the bus times to get down there though, telling us where we could pick them up from in the city; then wished us luck on our adventure, and we went off to investigate further, time now of the essence.

Back at the Samran we had a strange experience when we got out of the lift on the wrong floor, stepping out into a large room full of Buddhist-type statues and all kinds of strange carvings. It turned out to be the storeroom for goods shipped down from up north somewhere, though for a while it felt like wandering into yet another different world, a strange land within a strange world. When the lift door opened to take us to our floor, Frederick the Norwegian was stood there. He looked as surprised as we were, and it seemed a neatly timed meeting, beyond coincidence or mere chance. He was in Bangkok to sort out some visas, just a fleeting visit, and was only there because he'd had to wait for the consulates to open. We only saw him the once for the next day we were out of there ourselves.

Little Koh Chang proved too difficult to get to with such little time left: I didn't trust internet bookings, and waiting for confirmations was too frustrating, too time consuming; by then I'd spent too much time searching through travel sites and forums looking for information that could be trusted. Alistair hadn't emailed so we never knew if he made it out of Bangkok or not; he'd admitted that sometimes it can hold a person there for longer than planned.

On our last night in the Samran we went out to eat at a street-side diner just down the road. We found a place that looked busy, smelt good, and a waiter approached us and asked if we'd like to eat. He led us to a table and when he returned with our drinks whilst we chose what to eat, it became evident that he was from the not nearly so busy diner next door. We were somewhat committed to eating now, with the waiter, the chef, the owner, and the Thai wife who took the money all stood over us, watching, waiting for us to make any attempt to escape. The traffic roared by along the main road just the other side of the metal railings where we sat, hemming us in. An elephant appeared amongst the traffic, at first like a mirage, but then too real. Led by its owner through the busy Bangkok streets, who sells bananas to farang so they can feed the beast, it had a very sad look in its eye as it trudged along, even as it ate, and was a sad sight to see. Though maybe it's not for us to judge, one cannot help but wonder what the world has become when this is a means for someone's living, perhaps even the elephant's.

The chef showed us a tray of fresh fish, which to be fair was delicious-looking, and I enquired about one of them. We changed our mind and ordered king prawns instead, huge, barbecued in garlic sauce, superb. As we were eating the waiter asked if we would like rice with our fish. What fish? The fish I'd ordered, it seemed, by pointing. When I began to question it the chef, the owner, and the Thai wife all stood up again to back up the waiter, keen to know if there was a problem. No, there was no problem, we assured them, but no thanks on the rice. We ate the fish which turned out to be excellent even if not strictly what we ordered, and not that cheap, and whilst we were still eating the police turned up. After a few heated words with the owner, they then sat down and joined the people already there watching us. We ate, paid, and left before anything could go wrong.

In the end we booked a flight back down to Koh Samui. At least we knew Bophut beach was safe and we could relax; besides, there was a dress Amanda had seen in Bophut village that she'd seen and not bought first time around, continually regretting the decision as soon as it had been too late. I promised to buy it for her, partly as a birthday present, and partly because we both knew I wanted to spend one more week swinging in a hammock, relaxed and peaceful, hot and sunny, before facing the realities back home. I called Mr Tong the morning we were due to fly and checked he had a room; he would find somewhere for us, he assured me.

Just to make sure we had plenty of time to get back from the islands to catch our flight home, we booked one night back in the Siam Beverley to give us a final day in Bangkok; if anything went wrong with flights we should then still have time to get back some other way.

CHAPTER 23
Back to Chao Ley

It was a relief to be leaving the humidity and fast bustle of Bangkok. Even now when I look back all I see is multi-coloured traffic amidst noise and fumes, everyone moving around fast, as if here, for some reason, heat increases speed, and tall neon-lit buildings, overbearing, representing an alien world. Some people love it, and millions of people live there, but it's not for me.

We checked in and went through the formality of having our hand luggage scanned. It was the first time for me that I'd flown out of Bangkok, each flight before being back into the city, and was much more formal and guarded even than Phuket. When the lady at the end of the x-ray machine conveyor belt checked if it was my bag before asking me to step to one side, I thought it was either a mistake or just a formality. She pointed to an object shown on the scanning screen and asked me what it was. Thinking I'd been thorough with my checking I was sure it was just a black marker pen looking like something else. I put my hand in and even before I'd pulled the thing out I knew it was actually my multi-bladed tool, exactly like those that are shown on all the posters as being disallowed, though a cheap replica rather than anything authentic. A wave of instant regret washed over me that I hadn't noticed it right down the bottom of the bag, laying along the seam. I showed the seam of the bag to the lady who began to speak quite loudly in Thai, and I began to apologise, trying to explain that it had been a mistake. Did she think I intended stabbing the pilot on the way to Koh Samui? I really hoped she didn't. In the end she confiscated it and said I would be able to collect it at the other end, warning me that if it had been an international flight then things would have been different. I had to stand to one side for a while and wait, as if told off.

Koh Samui Airport was a totally different world, hazy when we landed though very hot. We collected our bags, and after everyone had wandered off I approached the airline desk to try and retrieve the confiscated piece that had only been allowed to board the plane if carried in the cockpit of the aircraft. It was only a cheap imitation, not worth getting into trouble over, and I wondered if anything else would be said. I prepared myself for more scolding but unnecessarily for it never came; I had to sign a form to say I'd retrieved it safely and that was that, as if the journey to the land of the relaxed had affected both reactions and events.

To be honest there are parts of Koh Samui that are far from relaxed, and even though we'd been in Thailand for several months we were just more farang on their way to spending some more money. Touts at the airport tried to tell us that Chalee Villa had closed now, just a few days ago, but they knew somewhere even better; after a brief discussion I said I'd spoken to Mr Tong only that morning; they feigned slight confusion, smiled, and said that they had meant a different Chalee something. But Bophut was far enough away from the crammed bars not to notice the full on thrust of the rush for free paradise, whatever it costs, especially at our end of the bay; yet at the same time it was not too far out, not dangerously isolated. A minibus ride from the airport to Bophut, via the northern end of Chaweng with a few drops off on the way, showed that the tourist season was still in full swing; maybe it just seemed busier because it was hotter and everyone was outside, but it sure seemed busy; dusty too, more so than ever, a light brown scattering everywhere. Everyone wore sunglasses, flip-flops, and looked thirsty if they weren't drinking, hot and weighed down with the effort of moving. Heat hazes hovered over everything, shimmering, as if life was seen through water, or the air had substance that vibrated.

It was a warm welcome when we arrived at Chalee Villa. The reception lady and Mr Tong had some kind of discussion in Thai before he explained that he hadn't been sure if it was me he had spoken to on the phone that morning, though he'd said he'd recognised the voice; now I'd arrived, he remembered. The lady said she had told him it was us, as if she had won some kind of bet that we would return. We told them we'd come from Bangkok where we'd met Frederick by chance; Mr Tong was less surprised than we were at the coincidence, and said that Frederick was coming back to Chalee Villa soon. I asked if he had heard from him. No, but Mr Tong was sure of it anyway, in a mysterious sort of way.

Our hut was up near the top of the avenue this time, with only one other between ours and Mr Tong's brother's at the very top. Over the way from us was the hut where a few of the staff slept, including Mr Lee who that evening came across with a small amount of weed; it was all he had for now but would bring the rest over later. I smoked a small joint, the first in a while, stronger-tasting than before, sticky on the fingers. Before long the effects began, and I wasn't sure where to sit, inside or outside. Mr Tong's brother was shooting more than ever these days it seemed, even from the cover of his own hut, so that if you ventured out into the avenue, all you heard was the *pa-choo* firing out from the shadows; it was unnerving enough to move me back inside, though of course then who knows what could be going on outside, unseen.

I was ok until my ears went all blocked up and a strange tone began to hum inside my head, dulling out the sounds of the outside so that Amanda's voice was in slow motion, like cotton wool. She kept asking me what the weed was like. Was it trippy? Was it good? I had trouble gauging the speed in which to move my mouth so that it would sound sort of normal, and even more trouble making any sound come out when I tried. The more I thought about it the more intense the effect became; I began to see lights flashing in the dark, eyes open and shut, still the lights. If I stayed like this I was in real trouble for communication had become impossible. It seemed the world only existed in a small space around me, as if each direction was merely a picture projected, made to appear real. The walls began to wobble, and the ceiling started breathing, moving away then towards me. I found all I could do was lay on the bed; knowing that the effects of marijuana often intensify as time passes, I wondered where this trip could be going. Amanda gave up questioning, making little sense of my random words that flitted about trying to describe something I had no idea about, and a knock at the door pulled me out of it.

Mr Lee had brought over some more weed; judging by what I had just smoked I wasn't going to need much more of it. I tried explaining that I didn't need anywhere near as much as he wanted to sell me, and he said he had very little money, hardly anyone had been here smoking. I paid him and wished I hadn't even quibbled, feeling a little awkward after that.

The following morning we walked into the restaurant for breakfast to see Noppi sat drinking coffee and chatting with Mr Tong. 'Aah, you come back to Koh Samui after all,' he said, smiling. 'It's a small world.' We were surprised to see him there, and he explained he was just sorting out some business matters.

A few days later Mr Tong disappeared, apparently sorting out some business matters in Bangkok. Mr Tong, Noppi, Tong Chai Tours, the Cabanas... what else? All connected, who knows? Who could tell? Except everyone seemed to know each other everywhere we went. I studied Noppi and Mr Tong to see if there was a family resemblance; perhaps there was, though partially hidden by the city clothes and demeanour of a younger generation. Mr Tong was barely dressed, dark-skinned and tattooed, had a few teeth missing, living a life on the beach facing the seas and islands beyond. He looked a true pirate, a sea person who'd had to make the most of a world where the land people had pushed him back to where the two domains met; his brother too, dragged in by war maybe and then pushed back to the edge of a world no longer free. Sea people captured and forced to conform, chao ley... the name of the resort began to make sense for it could well have been called Chao Ley Villa instead.

Our hut happened not to have a hammock, one of the few without, and though we could have tied our own ones up it didn't seem too safe out there, though we both pretended it was for other reasons. Next door, between us and Mr Tong's brother, was a young couple, probably only about eighteen, gap year students, girlfriend and boyfriend. One of Mr Tong's brother's jobs, in fact I think his only job, was to get rid of the rubbish when people had checked out. As the season had progressed, perhaps the effort increased with the heat, and he'd taken to burning the rubbish bags in an area between his and their hut. The wind always seemed to blow the smoke all down the avenue, flooding it as if recreating the scene of a war zone, smogging the way for safe under cover passage; we wondered if the bonfire was lit only when the wind direction was such by intention. It stank, mostly being plastic bags full of used toilet roll, and I couldn't help but wonder if in some way it was his way of showing what happens when you bring western ways to an unspoilt land. There is no need to use the stuff anyway, especially to stow it afterwards in a plastic bag for someone else to deal with when you leave. When we swam in the bay that week we could feel a smooth sludge beneath our feet, and could see the tiny flecks of paper yet to dissolve fully, effects of several months of visiting farang putting paper down the toilet, into the sewers and out of sight, without the rough seas needed to flush it all away. The young couple checked out after just one or two nights, constantly smoked and fired at, complaining to Mr Tong before they left, and the hut remained empty until the night before we left.

The day after we'd arrived I found out that the scattering had gone ahead already. I suppose in the end it didn't matter, we'd had our own ceremony at the time, had even seen the figure in white walking through the sea, which was more than anyone had seen back at home.

We spent most of that week taking a songthaew to Chaweng beach each day, where the water was cleaner, the waves and currents strong enough to wash away the waste, and where Amanda preferred to swim. It seems there is a common theme across Thailand, a game that's played everywhere: that is, see how many farang will squeeze onto any given mode of transport. On one journey there were even about six of us stood on the tailgate of a crammed songthaew, just enough room to reach through and hold a bar with one hand. In the evenings we returned to Chalee Villa at sunset for dinner and banana pancakes. Back at the hut, Amanda and I had a bit of a game going on where I had to go outside to smoke cigarettes, and she would follow me, sniffing the fumes. I'd made the mistake in Lamai once of blowing smoke on her and she'd spent the night coughing, as if the tiny bit of smoke could have caused so much damage, so after that I made sure I wafted it well clear. The trouble was it wasn't cool to be sat outside smoking weed; not even Mr Tong's brother smoked in view, nor did hardly anyone, so I had to smoke in the hut. Amanda would sit outside for a while until she had been shot too many times for comfort, and then have to come back in. It was weird weed, for when I smoked it she happened to look just as stoned as me without her even touching it, as if feeling the effects just through the atmosphere, the vibrations. It sure was strong weed, and staring down the avenue some nights at the small rectangle of sea visible, with the lights of boats moving around, the moon reflected in the water, beach walking shadows that passed by like on a cinema screen, projected, I could see how Mr Tong's brother could easily get lost in a world of memories hazed with Thai weed and whiskey, wanting to take pot-shots at the farang who have turned up like consuming invaders, leaving their waste behind.

In the hut on the other side to us was a Greek guy obsessed with small coloured flags that hung everywhere from his hut, and a German guy with him. They were keen on going to the Green Mango, the busy night-life in Chaweng, and probably would have stayed somewhere nearer had they not enjoyed smoking too. They were on a two-week holiday, happy to spend money and enjoy the sunny beach life for a short while. One day I saw the Greek had a beaten-up face, stitches, and a bad black eye. He told us the story: they'd hired out jet-skis and apparently had collided into each other; whether it was a genuine accident or a joke gone wrong, who knows, but the Greek guy had come off with an injured face and a broken jet-ski.

According to his account there had been a lot of blood involved, running down his face and body when he'd got out of the water, looking all carved up. There had been much concern from the Thais on the beach, though he admitted that it had looked much worse than it was. They took him to the hospital, got him cleaned up, made sure he was alright and then told him he'd have to pay for the jet-ski. He thought they just meant pay for the damage, and he expected a bill; instead they wanted him to pay for a brand new machine, arguing that there was unseen damage that would only materialise after he'd gone. Maybe they were right, maybe they were just trying it on, but the Greek was having none of it. They wanted compensation for loss of earnings too whilst one of the machines was down. An argument developed and the police were called, who arrested the Greek guy and held him until he agreed to pay.

He called his Consulate but there wasn't much they could do except tell him his rights, for what they were worth, which he already knew anyway from working in the tourist industry himself. He managed to track down a solicitor on the island who came and tried to persuade him just to pay the money and have done with it. He said the policeman and the solicitor both took turns at interviewing him, putting their pressure on in different ways. On principle the Greek refused, though when he found out that the policeman was related to the family who owned the jet-skis, and the solicitor was married to one of them, he knew he was fighting a tough cause. In the end he made them an offer good enough to end the otherwise stalemate situation, though they held him for about six hours. As soon as he had paid up the family returned to being sweet; they invited him round for a meal, spent the evening filling him with food and drink, and let him take their daughter out, who was there the following day tenderly placing fresh dressings on his wounds as he lay there, indulging, almost wallowing in the attention. He was ok though and gave us a small flag each.

Personally I dislike jet-skis intensely; they are like laying in the garden listening to a lawn mower, and would have preferred it had there been none of them in Bophut Bay. On the other hand I wouldn't wish harm or injury to people that use them, just that I wish they didn't, but never mind.

But I guess that even quiet little Bophut will keep getting busier as time passes; along with more people, the new replaces the old, and things are never the same as they were. Developers were just starting to build a brand new luxury hotel next door to Chalee Villa when we left, the last remaining space at the far end of the bay, and maybe the faraway charm will be forever lost, swallowed by the shadows overbearing and consuming. I dread to think what Mr Tong's brother made of it all when it was built and in full swing, the movie at the end of the avenue developing with the futuristic special effects brought by the new world landing. What can you say but mai pen rai, and carry on, adapt perhaps. Pa-choo!

We said our goodbyes for the final time, all sure we would meet again; Mr Lee, Mr Tong, the cook who may have been Mrs Tong, the reception lady who may have been Mr Tong's daughter; the waiter and waitress, girlfriend and boyfriend who spoke very little English; the fisherman who seemed to live there; even Mr Tong's brother was around. Everyone returns to Chalee Villa, they said, and I thought of the number of times they had played Hotel California whilst we'd sat in the restaurant, or swung in the hammock.

Mr Tong gave us a lift back to the airport, passing by the Big Buddha looking out across the bay. In the twenty-odd years that he'd lived on Koh Samui he'd witnessed many changes. Not all were for the good, he admitted, yet he spoke with an accepting voice as if that was just the way things were, that was that. People wanted air-conditioned rooms, concreted and tiled, sterile and clean; what could he do about it? After all, it was them bringing their world to his, not the other way around. We said we hoped his huts would always remain simple as they were, and he admitted that being so far from the main road there was insufficient power supply for air-con units to work in his huts, he'd already tried. I asked what would happen when the big hotel opened, and he seemed to think that they might have a power problem too. 'Of course,' he smiled, 'if they manage to run a cable down to it maybe I could tap in for free, no-one would know.' I guess the old pirate spirit was still inside, still alive, taken from the sea maybe, but on the land waiting for opportunity to take a share in whatever happens to be going.

CHAPTER 24

So Long Sawat

Our taxi from the airport to the Siam Beverley retraced the journey that had first brought me into Bangkok, except that this was a metered taxi and cost only half as much. But then I've paid more to get back from town on a Saturday night just because I couldn't be bothered to walk. It's easy to lose perspective, especially if caught inside a world of budget travel guides and forums all telling you how you're getting ripped off. Does it even matter? After all, we only have to get back home and start working again to make these small payments seem as insignificant as they really are. Time is only once, but money can always be replaced, more can be earned. This fact was something very much on my mind since I knew I would soon have to return to working in some mind-numbing meaningless job made up seemingly for the purpose only of occupying someone's time, perhaps to make someone's life a little less comfortable, less free, more restricted and enslaved. I felt a bit like a sea person myself, caught in a net, trapped and forced into a life at the mercy of other people's actions and decisions. The thought of tight shoes instead of flip-flops; shirts and trousers instead of just shorts; cold grey days instead of hot sunshine; withdrawn faces grimacing from both the weather and the mundane lifestyle of the working week awaited, Monday mornings and rush hours, road rage, ambulances, and bollards; a bullshit culture decorated with plastic crap. I put the thoughts away for another time, still a long way from home, as if the geographical distance was enough to override the fact that in terms of time we weren't that far away. It was still Bangkok after all, so different, still just as crazy.

Back at the Siam Beverley we sorted out the bags, making sure nothing that could be classed as dangerous was in the hand luggage, and nothing classed as illegal anywhere at all. The final night seemed quiet, no monkey bird, no cockerel, perhaps both now morphed into mirages in the shadows on Bophut beach, who knows? Sawat took us back to Siam Square for some last-minute shopping, and we took a trip to the Kao San Road, the market street where everything is for sale and costs whatever you can agree with the seller, according to your needs and means and his minimum price, which may or may not be dependent on your first offer, still far away from the world where values are fixed by the barcode ready to be scanned, immovable and beyond human negotiations, though who knows for how long. But then would you trust a scanning machine down the

Kao San Road any more than a tuk-tuk driver? And even if the price is fixed, open, declared, and the same for everybody, it won't make the scarf that somehow shone two-coloured under the lights of the shop but wasn't nearly so shimmering when you got it outside any better, nor any different. All it will do is take away a bit more human interaction and let the machines of big businesses move in.

We bought some padlocks to go on the suitcases we'd got for any overflow: they were cheap but are still effective as locks even now. It was a strange feeling, for Bangkok was far from my favourite place in Thailand, yet I knew leaving it would mean leaving it all behind; no more beaches, no more hammocks, no more chirping sounds of Thai words that meant nothing to me but sounded like a pleasant song. Thailand is known as the land of smiles: England's image is a bulldog.

Our flight was around midnight so we had to get to the airport before ten o'clock. We had one last buffet meal in the restaurant back at the hotel where we'd stored our bags, fully making the most of our last Thai food before a long flight home, and eating just a little too much again. As we sat in reception passing the remaining time, repacking bags with presents to take home, several coachloads of Chinese people turned up and flooded the hotel lobby. We decided it was time to leave before our bags got mixed up with theirs, as if it was a fitting cue for action. Sawat wasn't around to take us to the airport, hopefully off on another job somewhere with some real tourists who were happy to make the most of his services and local knowledge. Maybe another time.

We flagged down a taxi and went on our way, through tall neon-lit skyscrapers advertising the latest names in hi-tech goods, and that it was 21:30 and still 35°C outside. We were still in shorts when we arrived at the airport and had to change into warmer clothes ready for landing; I put on pretty much everything I had to wear though mentally, in the humid heat that now didn't feel too bad, quite comfortable even, it was impossible to imagine how cold it was going to feel getting off the plane at the other end.

With all the signs advertising the death penalty for drug trafficking, Bangkok Airport made us feel quite paranoid; every possible opening and pocket had been locked, and every bag searched before we checked the bags in and I found out how much weight I must have been carrying. I was relieved that part of it was over now, though as tough as it had seemed at the time, looking back it was without doubt worth the effort just to have been there, and right then sad that the trip was over.

CHAPTER 25
Trip's End

I spent the night watching the map, listening to the radio as it looped round and replayed the same two hours over and over again. The flight takes longer going west than east, perhaps due to the wind, or maybe the turning of the earth. It was about six thirty in the morning, just getting light when we landed: the temperature outside was hovering just above zero. I felt numb anyway, tired from no sleep, my mind still back in Thailand even though my body was back in England. It is a shock for the mind, everything is different again straightaway: the signs are different, the colours, the language – even the fonts used; the air feels different, smells different; sounds and conversations were mostly English, either reserved or aggressive perhaps, stern, official, as if everything was serious, less tuneful.

We stopped off at the toilets before collecting our luggage, and I noticed just how cold the water was when I washed my hands – freezing cold, almost painful. I shivered and the glow from the adrenaline rush of getting off the plane cooled so that I felt cold all over, the sort of cold that no amount of clothes will warm, only a hot steaming bath. I still had to find somewhere to stay and amidst the shock of landing I couldn't help but wonder where I'd be that night. Then there was a job, what to do? Would I need a car? How was I going to find somewhere to live without a phone even? Thoughts that I'd deliberately put out of my mind began to creep in. In Thailand I'd simply decided that everything would work out ok in the end, it always does, something happens even if it's not what you expected, what does it matter? I thought the same then, *Not to worry, it will all work out*.

We got the bags and headed for the coach terminal way over on the other side of the airport, getting the tube that connected the terminals. There was a bit of waiting around for a train, some confusion about where to go, and when we reached the point where the trolley could go no further we had to resume duties, this time with two suitcases wheeling along as well. After all that carrying in Thailand free from mishap or injury, I managed to twist my knee getting off an escalator, and I thought of the doctor in Bangkok, all her good work undone.

We reached the coach station and watched our first chance leave whilst we were queuing up for tickets. It meant waiting another hour and a half in the freezing cold, drinking coffee that seemed ridiculously expensive. Just before our next coach was due we went off in turns to the toilets. We had over five minutes to spare still when we saw our coach pulling out. I left Amanda with the bags and ran out towards the reversing coach, waving him down to stop. He saw me, snarled and waved me back like there was no way he was stopping. I ran out further as he pulled back far enough to swing back round and drive away, his big fat arms turning the wheel, determined to ignore my shouts and gestures. A few people around had seen what had happened, and someone with a uniform appeared. We made a complaint, and at first it seemed that there was a chance that the coach would be called back if it could be proven to have left early.

We waited and a supervisor appeared, introducing herself as the supervisor, wondering what our problem was. The tide had turned, and suddenly it was our fault for not being out on the bay ten minutes before departure time. She had a go at me for running out onto the bay, accusing me of breaking the law, risking my life unnecessarily, as if I was too irresponsible to know danger from safety. I told her I was a grown man and knew where I was safe to stand, and wanted to know why a coach was allowed to leave before its stated departure time. She insisted it was clearly written on the ticket to be at the bay ten minutes before departure time, somewhat altering the definition of the term. I asked her to show me where. It is in fact written in very small letters on the cover of the ticket wallet, and took her five minutes to find, even knowing it was there somewhere. I wanted recourse, wanted her name, the driver's name, but really just wanted to have been on that coach out of the cold, but that was too late. For a few moments I had thoughts of writing to complain but in the end what does it matter? We got the next one an hour later, which, we noted gladly, actually did stop as it was pulling out to let more people on at the last minute. When I finally arrived at a bed and breakfast back in the town where I'd grown up, the room was only just ready for me anyway.

When the coach pulled into our stop, Amanda went off back to stay with a friend of hers. It was an odd feeling, an awkward situation. It had been stressful at times to say the least, and there were moments in the final week where it seemed the only thing stopping us from walking away from each other for good was that circumstances didn't allow it. The moment we had loaded her bags into the taxi I felt the responsibility lift, and when the taxi drove off it was like she was back in a world in which she was more at home, puzzling perhaps but familiar. She had things to sort out, just as I did. Amazingly we stayed good friends.

My dad had his operation and made a successful recovery. I found a job just before I maxed out on the credit card which had been refused in Phuket. The family divisions got slightly worse but were finally fully resolved. Sawat's business card shed its ink over the contents of my wallet in the heat one day, leaving a reversed imprint of a Mercedes as a reminder. I ended up moving away and working for a couple of years, managing to save enough money to take some more time off and write down what happened before we forgot, not that that was ever likely to happen.

Printed in Great Britain
by Amazon